My sincere thanks to Tyne
East Lothian Library Services an
I am eternally grateful to Tom, Norman, Michael and
Brenda for their constant support and encouragement.
I dedicate this book to Anne

To Peter and Margaret.

Jake xx

Tyne & Esk Publications

Printed by Clydeside Press

GLASGOW GREEN
Jake Walker Curley

Chapter One

'Let them shut the door.'

'Is this advice?' the young guy asked.

'Don't take it to heart - they're only doing their job,' the older prisoner said.

The younger man was taking it to heart. He was going through his nightly ritual of getting stressed out at lock up. 'You're starting to sound like a bit of a guru, mate,' he said.

'Point taken,' Joe chuckled. 'It only took me twelve years to heed that suggestion.'

'Fuck, I'm hoping to be out in twelve.'

'Hopefully you'll be quicker on the uptake than me.'

The bunk shook as the young guy underneath growled a huffy cough in reply.

"Guru," Joe thought, fighting the urge to laugh out loud. This prison was full of gurus, all legends in their own heads. At least his guru was a good one. His guru was the best.

Joe pulled out a piece of paper from his back pocket, delicately unfolded it and held it up to the light.

This is Joe's amends list, but the names on the list have no relevance to this story. However number one has. Number one is simply that, a number. It is circled twice and underlined three times. Adjacent to this number is a faded, brown, oversized question mark. The question mark is eleven years old and is written in Joe's blood.

Joe began his own ritual, quietly saying his prayers inside his head and in his heart. He thanked Harry Lawson for enriching his life and he thanked God for placing them in the same prison cell for twelve years. Tonight Joe added a postscript to his usual prayer. He asked: 'God, could you help me fall in love?' He looked at the faded brown question mark and asked: 'Please tell Owny, if I could square things here on earth, I truly would. Amen.' He folded the paper, placed it in his back pocket and lay back on his bunk, contented. It still astonished Joe how content he'd felt that first time, that night, when he'd taken Harry's advice and simply let the screws close that door on him.

*　　　*　　　*

There was a before and there was a now. Comparing the two conjured an edgy confusion. Was release slower last time? Progress, eh? Bureaucracy had slowed in twenty years. But Joe was in no hurry to get out. While the desk officer itemised the baggage of his past, he took his chance and approached the tall grey-faced guard.

'I'll no mind if you say no – but can I see him?'

The OK that followed irked the two men who made up the desk personnel. The old guard shot them a look that made them happy to hit the pause button. The prisoner was quickly led through an old, solid, black oak door out onto the back of D Hall. It didn't look like a graveyard. It looked like a place you'd go for a sneaky cigarette. It was totally covered in tarmac. There were no plaques, zero information and nothing indicating what lay beneath.

This was where the big, bad, scary stories from the past did the big stretch. Here the badly-wired decomposed and waited until their soiled souls passed through heaven's sieve. This was where executed prisoners were interred. Property of the state - allocated a pitch and then pitched over. As they walked along the grey sunlit path, the old guard pointed to a piece of cracked tarmac.

'Peter Manuel is there.'

'He's no' making a break for it, then,' Joe muttered but the old guard kept walking. 'How can you be sure that it's Manuel?' Joe asked.

'Cause I helped put him there.'

Joe looked around him trying to figure out how many bodies were under his feet. When he looked up, he saw the guard had walked off and was now standing at a small garden area. As Joe approached, the guard pointed to a small apple tree sprouting out of a circle of soil. Tied to the thin trunk of the tree was a small plaque. The words were frugal:

"Harold Lawson   1942 - 2003   Missed"

A little basket of flowers hung underneath the plaque; they looked fresh. 'They're from me,' the guard answered the quizzical look.

Joe leaned over and began to fuss over the flowers. 'Are all his ashes here?'

'Aye, he's made a pretty good fertiliser.'

Joe laughed; the laugh brought out tears and the guard had the decency to turn away.

'He never wanted out, did he?'

'No,' the guard sighed. 'C'mon, time you were on your way.'

Both men approached the wee door, snugly positioned inside those great, big double doors, and as the prisoner stepped through that small aperture, he voiced this niggling thought. 'Is it bad karma being reborn into a world you don't know anymore?'

'Take good care of yourself, Joe Ray.'

'Thank you, Jim.'

Jim Cassidy nodded and pulled the door closed.

*　　*　　*

Joe was heading for home, although he wasn't quite sure where exactly home was. He felt like he was leaving home. He decided he'd walk to Bridgeton, opting not to use the Day Saver bus ticket the prison had generously supplied. He started walking downhill, knowing he'd eventually find his bearings when he hit Duke Street. Familiar surroundings disturbed him more than the new buildings that had sprung up over this part of the city. The cars at first seemed startlingly space age; then quickly began to look very "samey". It was hard to tell a Ford from a Vauxhall or a Peugeot from a Nissan.

Freedom's edgy - that's the thought that sustained Joe's apprehensive swagger towards his mother's house. A different house to the one he'd known. It was just her there, for a start. This was her "wee pensioner's house". That's the way she'd described it in the letter. What gripped at Joe's empty stomach was the realisation that all the previous household memories, good and bad, now dwelt there. His recent "training for freedom" sessions did nothing to ease his anxiety, as emotions got the better of him. Guilt pangs began gnawing at every nerve-ending he possessed. The image of his dead father came into Joe's head. The face looked beaten and withered, pensively expecting more dreaded news. Joe tried to shake the image from his head. But it remained there, static and unforgiving. 'Hello, Pops,' Joe whispered and sat down on the pavement and began to cry. The tears were acute and long overdue.

For the first time in twenty years Joe Public communicated with Joe Ray. Two concerned passers-by came to his assistance. Joe told them his father had died and tried to explain the image in his head. 'He won't go away, he won't leave me, my father won't leave me...'

The two strangers looked at each before performing their civic duty. It was a Glasgow thing. They helped Joe onto his feet, straightened him up, and steered him into the doorway of a derelict shop and went about their day.

*　　*　　*

He knew where Iona Street used to be, but couldn't quite remember what it looked like. Joe asked somebody for directions. There was something familiar about the man. Then Joe twigged, he was speaking to BP.

5

Twenty years ago, the guy was always drunk. By the looks of it, nothing much had changed - BP was still drunk. They called him BP, because his tanks were always full. Joe saw the man's face struggle for recognition. Joe gleaned what he could from the slurred instructions and left BP scratching his head, trying to put a name to a face from the past.

*   *   *

She had not said it was a sheltered housing complex. He didn't like the sound of that.

Approaching the "complex", he saw it looked similar to those wee Lego Land starter houses that were all the rage two decades ago. An old associate, Big Yogi, had wrecked one at a party one night. The young owners of the house had insisted that you could swing a cat in their tiny living room. Big Yogi attempted a cartwheel and the result meant the remains of their G Plan furniture could have been posted through their mock-Tudor letterbox. Joe steadied himself, aware his mind's recent detour was only putting off the inevitable, and he walked up the wheelchair ramp towards his mother's door.

'Is that you, Joseph?'

'Aye,' he said and entered the house.

She came out from the kitchen, looking frailer than he had imagined, and put her arms around him. He stooped and received a kiss on each cheek, and one on his wet lips. She briefly ran her hand over his yellowing red hair, momentarily retracing a boyhood parting. Awkwardly, she made her way back to the kitchen. He stood, towering over a highly polished coffee table, conscious that he might fall over it. His body racked, trussed by invisible tethers, his stomach and neck muscles tied in old sea dog's knots. One word came slowly and repeatedly.

'Sorry, sorry, sorry.'

'You've been sorry all your life son,' his mother's words resonated from the kitchen.

'Ah'm sorry for everything, Ma.'

'I know you are. Just be sorry for your stuff, Joseph.'

As Joe struggled to force some air into his lean frame, his mother spoke again. 'I forgive you, son.' He fell to his knees crying as his mother shut the kitchen door on him.

She lowered the basket of chips into the deep fat fryer and stared at the two brown speckled eggs that had sat on the worktop all afternoon, waiting to be cracked.

*   *   *

JJ McGuire sat alone at the small, crescent-moon counter in the lounge of the Straw House public bar. The day could best be described as a lazy Thursday afternoon. Money came in at a slow steady pace. That pleased him and added flavour to the single malt he sipped. It would be late into the evening before his mind would get niggled about non-payments or ventures that had not quite gone as planned.

Big Yogi, acting bar manager and trusted servant, delivered another whisky, niftily spun around on one leg and back-handed his boss the remote.

'Are you needing the toilet?' McGuire asked, sparking up BBC2. He liked watching the antiques shows on TV. They'd proved useful a few times; especially when toe-rags offered up pieces of plunder as payment in kind.

'What are you going to do about him?' Yogi asked.

'Him?'

'Him,' Yogi stressed.

'He's only been out two hours.'

Yogi leaned across the bar, whispering, 'Remember, it was him that fucked up.'

'Everybody fucks up some time, so you fuck up and let me watch my programme.'

The big barman quietly wiped the bar counter.

McGuire stared up at the huge TV screen, but today the programme held no interest. His thoughts were focused solely on Joe. This was something they had been doing with regular consistency recently. He wasn't sure why, but knew it wasn't just down to Joe's release date. He wondered what his former "best pal in the whole world" looked like these days. Naturally he'd be changed, but how drastic would the change be? Would Joe have that wounded look he had seen many times on the faces of those released from the big stretches? Would Joe be brandishing hurt, vulnerable eyes, still interred inside a menacing facade? Eyes like that scared McGuire, giving his soul a jolt and reminding him that one of nature's gifts could be taken from him. He thought back to Joe's father's funeral. The memory brought a rueful smile to McGuire's face. They'd only exchanged glances as Joe was shackled to two prison officers. He'd looked good though. He wouldn't have looked out of place in the pop magazines of that time, festooned with photos of Spandau Ballet or Duran Duran. The pose at the graveside had made all the papers. Female columnists were vocal in warning their young female readership against the dangerous allure of the bad boy. The bad boy went back to prison with his grief, only to be inundated with letters from girls unwilling to follow journalistic advice.

The same photo resurfaced every time they did an exposé of McGuire's criminal empire. The last time he'd seen that photo, he realised it had crossed a threshold and had become quaint. It was like getting a nostalgia hit from an old school photo. The image warmed the heart, but reminded the ego that we can all go astray in our choice of clobber.

McGuire's eyes remained fixed on the screen, masking the fact that his heart yearned for Joe Ray to walk into his bar. But there was no chance of that. Joe had rejected him long ago. He understood his reasoning. He pressed the off button on the remote control and turned around in his bar stool. This was the cue for six members of his team to make a beeline to their boss and await instruction or ridicule.

* * *

Joe composed himself on his mother's sofa, comforted by the fact the volume on the chip-pan had gone down a notch and grub would be served soon. Looking round the room, his eyes settled on the fireside wall. There were many new additions to the array of old family photos. He'd seen some of these photographs before during visits from his mother, but he decided to wait and let her explain who's who.

He felt like the furniture and ornaments in this modern little house - a remnant from another time deposited among familiar pieces, but still stranded in a different world. He was heartened and ashamed to see the old Waverley photograph holding pride of place above her armchair. It was taken in the mid-sixties on a trip "Doon the Water" on the old sea-going paddle steamer. He re-sensed that feeling of hurt, remembering the over-fussy photographer calling his parents "Granny and Granda". Joe was a late baby, very late. His siblings used to love calling him "the Mistake". His parents countered by saying he was their "wonderful wee surprise".

Joe's childhood was different from his school friends. Jesus Christ, he had nephews older than him. At family gatherings, the mistake topic would often crop up. His father would say, 'you're my last and best hoorah, son!'

'Huh, I don't remember much hoorahing,' was always his Mother's reply.

These comments brought raucous laughter, but underneath the laughter there was always a hint of animosity emanating from Joe's siblings. It was the usual family shite. All about "whys" and "how

8

comes". How come it's different for him? Why is he allowed to do that and why weren't we? Maybe resentment blinded his brothers and sisters to the obvious. They were too close to see how their parents had changed and how circumstances had improved. There was no financial pressure in a less crowded and uncompetitive house-hold. It was their mum and dad's second chance at parenthood and Joe was raised in a mellow, nurturing environment. Both parents were conscious that their advanced age might embarrass the boy. They compensated for this by spoiling him something rotten. Young Joseph brought joy. Sadly, he also brought grief - lots of grief.

*   *   *

On the drive home, Prison Officer James Cassidy's thoughts settled on Joe Ray's release. He'd known Joe for all of two decades. At their first meeting, he'd placed Joe firmly in the Mad and Bad camp. Cassidy had seen the madness on a couple of occasions. He'd spotted that slight pause in the eyes and knew no one could be certain what was going to happen next - especially Joe.

Somehow Cassidy could communicate with him. He'd tried to analyse why, but could never come up with a reason. A siege situation in June '87 meant he was called on to mediate. Joe had teamed up with a nut job from Inverness in staging a rooftop protest. It was a spur of the moment thing, as they hadn't even the foresight to compile a list of grievances. The situation was made all the more delicate by the fact they had taken a young officer hostage.

The novice warder had just returned from honeymoon. In Scotland, it was front-page news. The hostage was extremely vociferous in his pleas for help. He had every reason to be. They were threatening to cut off equipment the recently married man was at last confident of using on a regular basis. In total, Cassidy spent over ten hours trying to talk some sense into them. It was easier when the Mad Highlander was absent from the discussions. He'd be on the roof playing up to the cameras, looking like the big villain in the Charlie Chaplin movies, continually re-enacting a mock decapitation scene with his hostage.

Joe Ray brought the situation to a peaceful conclusion in the wee hours of the morning when he knocked out his deranged accomplice with a two-foot length of water pipe.

The Mad Highlander was offloaded to Peterhead, where a year later he had killed himself in a segregation cell. Dramatic right to the very last, he'd managed to almost hack his own head off.

Cassidy had made Joe aware that there would be repercussions. He made sure that he was a member of the repercussions squads and, as promised, successfully tempered the beatings. After the Highlander's suicide, Joe had done the Grand Tour of the Scottish prison service. It was three and a half years later when Joe returned to "Cassidy's Hoose". He came back mad, but teachable. The problem is that prison is full of teachers and anybody who has done a couple of stretches is suddenly an authority on all sorts of crimes.

It was only when Cassidy got Harry Lawson to enter the frame that a solution for Joseph Ray began to manifest itself. Jim Cassidy considered Harry a close friend. He was reliable, and someone you could truly communicate with. Harry hadn't been around eighteen months ago when Freda went, when he had needed a friend most. There was a poignant similarity about both their deaths. It just felt so cruel. As he approached his new apartment, he relived a moment that never strayed far from his thoughts. It was the night they were watching the box in their wee suburban palace and he turned around to find Freda sitting dead in her armchair.

*   *   *

On the face of it, Margaret Logan seemed pleased. Thanks to a new supported accommodation programme, she'd just acquired a brand-spanking-new two bedroom flat, slap-bang in the city centre. It was a good start - something so unusual, she felt a strong urge to discuss these feelings with her caseworker, Heather. Hopefully, all being well, Nicola and Emma would be making their way back to her. Heather had dropped hints to that effect. She'd also hinted that her circumstances were about to improve as well. Caroline was not with her now. She'd been placed in a safe house somewhere in Scotland - Margaret hadn't a clue where. She'd been told that Caroline's wee girl Cheryl had been taken into care while Caroline got her life back on track. Margaret couldn't understand why they all had to be separated. Why were people putting up obstacles? Why were they stopping them being together? Why could they not all live in the same house? They were family.

Margaret scrutinised her surroundings, all supplied by social services. It was more than she'd ever had in her life and not quite as much as she'd anticipated. The television and the radio both remained switched off as she sat there, yearning for the voices and the touch of her children. She wanted to feel their hearts beating, she wanted soiled clothes piled high against her brand new washing machine, ready for a quick reload, and she longed to hear the rhythmic drone from a shiny new tumble drier

10

that stood doing nothing. She wanted tiny food-stained hand prints decorating those perfectly painted walls. The apartment smelled like the toiletries aisle in Tesco's when it should have been filled with the smell of her children's mishaps. She imagined cleaning her girls and getting them ready for bed, and hearing their contented voices. She closed her eyes and felt Nicola's sticky hands clasping her hand, and she could taste Emma's sweet, sticky lips kissing her own.

When she eventually dried her eyes, she could see from her living room window the old prison officer entering the building. He owned his flat and was entitled to a parking space. The building had been described as an exciting new social experiment. Half the flats were privately owned and the other half allocated to the social needs of the inner city's manageable misfits.

He'd seemed friendly enough when he'd introduced himself the other day. She'd thought she'd performed adequately during her little stab at social chit-chat. It wasn't easy with her case worker, Heather, hovering above her shoulder.

Heather was the latest in an extensive catalogue of support. Margaret's and her sister Caroline's case files were reaching encyclopaedic proportions. In another pile sat an equally extensive collection of excuses why this help had failed to reach a satisfactory outcome.

Margaret was determined to keep Heather sweet. Experience had taught her this much. She'd become expert at reliving their tragic childhood. She spoon-fed information to her inquisitors and carefully manoeuvred them towards the answers they yearned for. Heather was proving to be slower on the uptake than most of her predecessors. Still, she had to persevere with her, because it was too late in the game for a change of manager. Margaret considered the old prison officer living above her a bonus. It would be good to be near someone who looked like the law - might make certain people think twice before starting any shite. He seemed genuine enough. 'If you need anything, just ask,' he had said.

What Margaret needed above everything else was to be with her wee sister. Sadly, her wee sister, Caroline, knew better than that. Caroline was being held, head down, in a bath of cold water. She was swallowing hard, letting the water flood her lungs and, as her neck expanded and her eyes popped, she prayed for Margaret to look after wee Cheryl.

*   *   *

Joe was having difficulty digesting the food his mother had served up, even though the food had been excellent. He was thinking about how to actually live in the now and do things a whole lot differently than he had in the past. He'd left prison with a plan. Truth is, the plan was a pledge Joe had made minutes after hearing of Harry's death.

There were many times on the inside when Joe was either in the pits of despair or in full rage mode. These situations could go on for days, even weeks. Harry's solution was the same in either case and he intuitively knew the right time to speak.

'Think about the stuff you got away with,' he'd say.

'I never got away with anything,' Joe had snarled.

'If you think hard enough, something will crop up.'

That was all Harry said that first time. It was all that was needed. It always worked, but it had taken all of twelve years for Joe to truly understand what Harry had meant. Joe remembered back to that morning, when Jim Cassidy got word to him from the hospital that Harry was gone. Joe had fallen to his knees, clutching a photograph of Harry to his face. Out loud, he thanked God for Harry's friendship, publicly thanked Harry for enriching his life. As those words left his mouth, Joe Ray was aware something significant had happened to him. He knew that he had changed. He felt it in his soul, understood it more fully than anything he had ever known before. A power surged through him. Electric grief, that's what he ended up calling it. There was part of Harry inside him; he felt it was biblical. He didn't normally use words like "biblical", but the word "biblical" somehow helped him make sense of what was happening. He felt his former cellmate had navigated his way inside his head and was in the early process of reprogramming a head full of shite. Joe stayed on his knees and quietly attempted this mantra: 'Make up for the stuff you got away with, make up for the stuff you got away with.'

Joe's cellmate, who'd been observing quietly and a little apprehensively from the top bunk, now felt duty bound to make some ill-informed comments about what he'd just witnessed. Questioning Joe's state of mind was understandable and would have brought an explanation. However the prisoner started making degrading references to Harry's sexuality.

Joe rose from his knees and slowly approached his antagonist, and placed his forefinger on the trembling man's lips and said softly, 'To know him was to love him.'

With that, Joe slipped into his lower bunk and tried to adjust to the charge flowing through him. After a short while, he stared up at the top bunk - *ten minutes ago I would have bitten that prick's nose clean off and swallowed it.*

The days that followed were filled with fruitful reflection. He wasn't bothered that there was no chance of going to the funeral. They were only burying the dead bits of the man. There was plenty left, and he felt he had the best of it. Pennies dropped, chains linked, gears meshed and when he could, Joe lay there and just let it happen, almost orgasmic at his lack of control. As much as it was strange, it was beautiful. He slowly gleaned the simplicity of what he had to do. He had to wait. Wait until they gave him a release date.

Wee Harry chose to be the longest serving prisoner in Scotland. He'd served thirty seven years at the time of his death. He never ever put his faith in God, hinting God might let him out. So the wee man was rightly considered an expert at doing time.

The judge had stated that Joe would serve eighteen years minimum. He passed that milestone a year after Harry's death. It hadn't bothered him when he wasn't released. He'd been prepared for that possibility. They'd let him out when they let him out. It was their problem, not his. He'd accepted he had no control over it. If he had to do another ten years, then that would be recompense for the crimes he'd got away with. Every added day in prison was another slate cleaned.

Joe's crime was triple murder, two intended and one accidental. The accident was some poor wee soul who'd lost his way trying to find the M8. The man had approached, friendly and apologetic, making light of his poor navigational skills. He was the type of guy you wouldn't mind as a neighbour, who, unfortunately, walked in on a gangland hit and his own murder. Joe had been speeding out of his tits that night, downing a couple of double vodkas to balance any discrepancy between mind and body. Joe knew as soon as he'd confronted the two men that this job was going badly wrong. He'd left the Uzi he was meant to use, in the car. JJ McGuire had acquired it from some paranoid paramilitary, high up in the Dennistoun Orange Order, who'd panicked when he'd felt Special Branch was getting a bit close to him.

Joe chose to ignore McGuire's advice and went with the handgun. He wanted the two men to be in no doubt about who was ending them. Cowboy stuff really. Three desperate men standing on the pavement in Duke Street with weapons concealed on their person. Joe was only half sure his targets were holding blades. Then the wee lost soul made his fatal approach and it kicked off. The two men thought the wee guy was Joe's accomplice and as they made their move, Joe shot them both in the chest.

It was the bemused look on the face of the man asking directions that haunted Joe. The wee man timidly knelt down and tried to stem the blood flowing from one of the men writhing on the pavement. He looked up at Joe, seeking confirmation that the unthinkable was happening. Joe fired point blank at his temple and the little man jack-knifed on himself and died with a bewildered expression that scanned far beyond the sparkling street lamps. Joe unleashed a flurry of blows at his intended victims. This only helped curious witnesses pinpoint the source of the commotion from their tenement windows. Three people had clearly seen Joe fire two bullets each into the heads of the men moaning and screaming on the pavement.

When it got to the court case, there was a touch of irony about the proceedings. Two of the three eye witnesses turned out to be opticians. The young couple's rented flat looked right onto the scene of the crime.

'Pray the third witness is Mr Magoo,' Joe's lawyer had joked.

During that time, Joe's head was filled with one all-consuming thought. How could it go so wrong? Half a lifetime later, that thought had taken a monumental shift. "It was wrong!"

Joe looked at the collection of photographs above his mother's fireplace and began to realise just how much he had missed out on.

Chapter Two

Margaret Logan went through the motions of cleaning a spotlessly clean flat. Heather's phone call had disturbed her. She'd told her to remain indoors and finished with, 'We'll be round soon.' It took considerable effort to keep in check the hope that she was getting her children back. Between tracks on the radio, she made her way to their bedroom and just stood looking at the emptiness of the room. It had been a constant struggle to stop herself from blagging toys, or stealing anything that would remind her of the children. She'd come too far to muck up now. Her mind raced. *She wouldn't bring the kids back before the beds arrived.*

Walking back into her living room, she caught sight of Heather through the lounge window. Heather was walking in front of the police, lots of police. Margaret went into shock. Unable to move or even to think, her eyes started reeling, looking for God knows what. Intermittently, she caught glimpses of her own frozen limbs in the mirror above the fire. This was meant to be her "different future", the chance she was going to grab with both hands and never ever let go.

Heather's manic pleas on the intercom were not registering with Margaret. A consensus was forming among the police at the entrance of the building *Maybe we could have done things differently.*

Jim Cassidy looked down on the activity at the building entrance. His heart jumped, optimistically, hoping he might be needed for some situation at the prison. When his bell failed to ring, his heart sank a little. He recognised some of the policemen and was on speaking terms with one of them. He could hear a woman screaming into the intercom. 'Margaret, don't be silly, let us in, Margaret don't b...................'

Jim Cassidy decided against activating his door entry system and quickly made his way downstairs and let them in. 'Is there anything I can do?' he asked as the crowd brushed past him.

'Margaret, please let us in,' Heather said, as she pounded on Margaret's door.

Cassidy looked around and spotted a face he knew.

DCI Mark Henderson gave Cassidy a look of acknowledgement and disdain as he barged past his colleagues. He wrapped his arms around Heather and her pink duffle coat, and carried her out the building, telling uniform, 'Force the door.' Henderson placed the poor woman on the garden path, growling, 'Stay, stay.'

'Is she all right?' Cassidy asked as the policeman re-entered the building.

'Hard to tell,' DCI Henderson said, adjusting his jacket. 'Didn't realise you stayed here. I'll need a word and maybe a favour, Jim?'

'What about her?' Cassidy shot a glance in Heather's direction.

'See if you can teach her to roll over,' Henderson smiled.

* * *

Margaret sat there numb, bewildered, not knowing who to answer, or who to ask. The room was crowded with people who were all very understanding. It was a room full of concerned looks, but that was just a façade. The reality was they were like a pack of wild dogs, tentatively coming in from obscure angles, having a little nip or bite at her. DCI Henderson was the Alpha male, keeping constant eye contact with her and carefully orchestrating his officers' questions.

'Any idea who would want to harm Caroline?'

'Been involved with anybody recently?'

'Has anyone threatened her?'

'Does she owe money to anybody?'

DCI Henderson coughed, cleared his throat, and asked, 'Has Caroline made any allegations concerning her past?'

There was the slightest look of hesitation in Margaret's eyes.

Henderson continued, 'Could she have been blackmailing somebody?'

Margaret never said yes and she never said no.

This was as good an answer as Mark Henderson was going to get on this day. He decided to calm proceedings for the moment. Right now, he wanted a word with Jim Cassidy. He wanted to know if Cassidy had seen anything and he wanted Jim Cassidy to keep an eye on Margaret Logan.

* * *

'AND,' Henderson said, exaggerating the word.

'And what,' Corrie Strachan asked, looking a little bemused.

'I need more than "she suffered a sustained assault".' I know she suffered a sustained assault. I want you, Miss recently-qualified Forensic Pathologist, to tell me what I don't know.'

'Oh,' Corrie flinched.

'I need more than "Oh".'

'She did not put up as much resistance as you would expect, Mr Policeman.'

'That's better – that's saying something I don't know. Keep going. Keep going – more.'

'DCI Henderson, I'm not sure I like the way you're speaking to me.'

'That's good. We might make you into something more than MacLeod's answer machine.'

'I'm not Professor Macleod's answer machine,' Corrie answered a touch too quickly.

Henderson rolled his eyes for effect. 'I do know how he likes his titles and the letters after his name - MFI, B&Q, KFC.'

Corrie Strachan stifled a laugh, but her complexion had definitely mellowed.

'So tell more of what I don't know, please.' Henderson smiled half-heartedly.

'You don't know much about anything. That's my opinion.'

'Good – your opinion, that's what I'm after. What do you think happened, Miss Strachan?'

'I would have expected more defensive wounds.'

'AND,' Henderson asked in a friendlier manner.

'The scratches and bruising on her head should've been more pronounced. It appears she just let herself be drowned.'

'Was she drugged?'

'No. No sign of drugs or alcohol in her body. She had taken two paracetamol around about three hours before her death. I found bruising on her fingertips and thumbs that suggest she might actually have assisted her own death.' Corrie Strachan stopped speaking, looked round and picked the chair closest to her and dragged it towards a huge stainless steel sink. She placed the back of the chair against the sink, knelt on it and lowered her head into the sink. Her voice resonated as she spoke. 'You would expect bruising on the palms of her hands if she was pushing away. She placed her hands onto the lip of the sink and pushed hard.

'Can you see? Can you see?' she asked.

Henderson approached the sink, trying hard to ignore Miss Strachan's posterior, playing peek-a-boo from the slit in her draping white coat, and looked along the edge of the sink.

As the pressure on her palms mounted, Strachan's gripping fingers spread out irregularly and spasmodically. She lessened the pressure on her hands and took in a deep audible breath. Then she clamped the sink's lip with fingers and thumbs shaped like eagles' talons. 'Look now, can you see?'

Henderson's eye looked along the sink's edge once more.

'I think she assisted her own death.' Strachan gripped the sink tighter and pulled herself down. 'Can you see? There's hardly any pressure on the palms of my hands.'

'Now you're talking,' Henderson said, impressed.

'Why she would want to speed up her own death is your job, Mr Fast-approaching- retirement Policeman,' Strachan said, as she raised her head up and stepped down from the chair.

'What about sex?' Henderson said and then grimaced immediately.

Corrie Strachan ignored the faux pas. 'There was no sexual assault. Nothing that would suggest recent sexual activity, and according to the SET people, no signs of drugs at her home and nothing indicating that she brought punters back to her house. The killer or killers were scrupulously clean, clinically clean, if you want my opinion,' Corrie Strachan said, as an icy draft entered the room.

'Miss Strachan, be careful what you say. DCI Henderson has a predisposition to misconstrue.' Professor Alexander MacLeod stood rigid and frozen with formality, holding the lab door ajar.

Henderson's face fell, but he smiled warmly, 'Miss Strachan, thank you for your help and assistance.' He walked to the door, stopped, looked MacLeod straight in the eye and quietly said, 'Fuck you, Miss Construe.'

*   *   *

Caroline Logan's death did not come as a shock. It was always going to be a case of when, rather than if, concerning both sisters. His gut instinct told him that this was no mad moment from a disgruntled punter or the latest lap of a Psycho's killing spree. Corrie Strachan's assessment of Caroline's final minutes only confirmed his thinking. Somebody wanted information from Caroline; information she was not prepared to divulge, even if it meant giving up her life to safeguard that information. There were only two people Caroline Logan would give her life up for: her own daughter and her big sister, Margaret. Henderson had been told that there was no boyfriend sniffing around, so that meant it was someone from the murky past. There was a lot of murky past to trawl through. He knew for a fact that there was a profusion of case files on both sisters. An abundance of follies from every institution concerned with social care. Henderson had personally been involved in one of those follies. Margaret must have been on the verge of fifteen and turning tricks in a garret in Partick. As usual, she was supporting Caroline and, on this occasion, some wee schemie from Easterhouse, in his first sustained effort at pimping. Margaret never claimed to be the sharpest tool in the box, but, she was always smart enough to take Caroline with her when absconding

18

from their current institution. They'd been away for four weeks, on this occasion, before they were captured. There was no real way of calculating just how many men had abused them. According to the medical people, the girls were showing the same symptoms - gonorrhoea, chlamydia and some other affliction he couldn't quite remember, and they were about to undergo serious counselling.

Recent events had shown that the counselling, however serious, did not really have much benefit. The two girls had been placed in separate care homes, seemingly for their own good. They both created so much havoc, it was decided they be reunited for the common good.

The schemie eventually got two hundred and forty hours community service. Seventy two hours into his community service, he was dead. The result of the worse drugs scam in the West of Scotland's history. He was found on Possilpark's Stronend Street. He'd suffered a horrific beating and his throat had been cut. Stuffed into his shirt were two twenty notes wrapped around cut-up newspaper that failed to pass itself off as a substantial wedge.

Henderson put an end to his trip down memory lane. At least the wee schemie is out of the equation.

The CID man looked around until he found his sergeant. 'Get things sorted at the morgue.' He cast a backward glance at Margaret Logan. 'I want her to ID the body, soon as.'

The sergeant nodded, pleased to be doing something.

Margaret's case-worker Heather had managed to make her way into the flat, remaining implausibly quiet during DCI Henderson's brief interview with her client. Hearing Henderson's instructions to his sergeant, she decided it was now time to make her presence felt.

'What clothes are appropriate for this sad occasion?' she asked.

'Possibly something that buttons up the back.'

Heather's wounded expression hinted at a lack of cross agency co-operation.

*   *   *

Caroline Logan's corpse was laid out for identification. Henderson had made it clear he did not want the video link used. He wanted to be close, wanted to be near, hoping he might decipher something. It might be sobbed, screamed, or even a name, spoken in a low vengeful curse. He knew it would be traumatic. "Volatile" was a word strongly associated with Margaret Logan. Two female constables were in attendance because it could get physical. It would be better for the Force's male ego if two female officers got decked. He was glad they were using the Saltmarket

19

morgue. He hated these places, but at least this place was near some decent pubs, men's pubs where people minded their own business. That's where he'd be heading. He'd plump for the Old Ship Bank. There was bound to be someone he knew in there, probably a few he'd jailed. My God, that would take the edge off this horrible day.

*   *   *

Mark Henderson quietly ushered Margaret towards the trolley and they both looked down on the dead girl who lay beneath them. Caroline looked young, really young, and Henderson struggled for a word that would describe the family resemblance between the two sisters.

Then the word came. "Withered", that was it, but there was still a wee bit of bounce left.

The female officers took up their shielding position. They were not needed. Margaret just bent over and kissed her kid sister tenderly on the lips. She held that position for what seemed a long while. It was one of those moments where nobody quite knew what they were supposed to do.

Margaret Logan knew what to do. She just let warm tears fall on her sister's cold face. The constables and Henderson exchanged awkward glances and then backed off.

The coldness of the surroundings seemed to sharpen Henderson's senses. He knew Margaret had not just lost a sister. She had lost a daughter.

Margaret Logan had adopted her baby sister on the day the authorities had taken them away from the family home. She made the decision when they took their seats in the back seat of the social worker's Ford Cortina. She knew even at that tender age that she was all that Caroline really had. Now Caroline was dead, lying beneath her with lips cold and unresponsive. Another child taken from her and one that would never come back.

Henderson played the impassive onlooker well, but he'd come to a decision. He was definitely going to get those responsible for this crime. Margaret hadn't let on she'd recognised him, but he'd remembered her. Henderson saw the Logan girls as Mother Nature's disenfranchised. They would keep hooking up with Mr Wrong until the day Mr Wrong destroyed them. Now Caroline Logan was lying dead in the morgue at the age of twenty three and Margaret, the sister who'd become her mother at such a tender age, was crying over her.

Chapter Three

Night-time brought darkness, anonymity and the freedom Joe preferred. With less chance of recognition, he could roam old haunts, find new ones and try planning a future. Fuck, he'd maybe get to the stage where he'd let the future happen all by its little old self. He was glad of the windproof jacket his mother had given him, though he still fought the temptation to pull the hood up. He pulled the zipper up just under his chin and tucked his neck in. The wind wasn't strong, but it was cold. As he walked along London Road towards Bridgeton Cross, he was surprised to find pleasant memories cropping up with unnerving regularity. Childhood memories, and not entirely innocent either.

The stroll ended and was replaced with furtive trepidation as he turned the corner into Forrest Street and he made his way into the close where his cousin lived. He'd last seen him about five years ago, but Joe had always been able to get information on his cousin while inside from fellow junkies or from his own mother. All the information painted an accurate and very predictable picture of young Terry's lifestyle. 'He's back on it.' 'He's off it. He's going into rehab.' 'He never made rehab.' 'He's good.' 'He's bad.' 'He's worse than ever.' 'He's beyond human aid.'

Funnily enough, they had never met up in prison and Joe saw that as luck on his part. Still, Terry had managed to keep a tenancy for seven and a half years and even managed to pay the rent for a six-week period in the year 2000.

Joe had good reason to remember Forrest Street. There used to be a carpet factory at one end of it. Now a huge corrugated warehouse stood in its place. Joe gave the new building a cursory glance and he remembered his first attempt at smoking. With his side-kick John Joseph McGuire in tow, they'd taken 10 Embassy Regal and a penny book of matches around the back of the old carpet factory. It was the day after Joe's tenth birthday and he was made up. He'd successfully mastered the inhalation technique a lot quicker than his buddy. Young McGuire had spewed his ring. Joe wondered if kids still said, "spewed your ring up."

They put the penny book to another use and lit a small fire. The fire was more for a heat than anything else. Unfortunately, their little bonfire was next to a chemical storeroom. A big sheet of plywood, boarding up a broken window, took hold and half a minute later the place went up like a Roman Candle.

The resulting blaze was so spectacular that many of the local pubs emptied for a good ten minutes on a very cold Saturday afternoon. Impressive when you consider the pubs closed at half two in those days. Joe had never told a living soul about the fire. Momentarily, he wondered if his friend had either.

As Joe reached the first floor landing he saw four doors and instantly recognised his cousin's. It was a cheap panelled door with a piss-thin coat of white undercoat that barely covered 90% of the surface area. There was ample evidence of previous Yale locks. The door was covered in graffiti, mostly scratched and filled with different coloured pens. There were numerals next to names indicating the year that they were carved. With a smirk on his face Joe kicked at the bottom of the door.

Young Terry answered quickly. He was wearing a blue, quilted body-warmer over a grey Puma T-shirt. The emaciated arms on show advertised the fact that he was clean. They stood there facing each other, not quite knowing what to do.

'I suppose you want a cuddle?'

'A hug,' Joe said. 'It's a hug you give me.'

Joe put his arms around Terry and actually felt good showing the silly fucker some affection. They hastily made their way into the living room. The place was reasonably clean, although there was a stale odour permeating from what Joe assumed was the bedroom. Joe looked down at cables and what looked like a gear-stick strewn across the floor and decided it was better not to ask. Sadness emanated from his cousin, the energy required to show "I'm doing OK" just wasn't there. It looked like it had been missing for quite a while. He'd always been called young Terry, strange really, because there wasn't an old Terry in the family.

'How come you never come round earlier? It's been four days.'

'I'm not too sure about – meeting – people,' Joe mumbled apologetically.

'That's a pity because...' Terry did not need to finish the sentence as JJ McGuire walked into the cramped living room.

'Do I get a cuddle?' McGuire asked.

Joe stood speechless, dumbfounded and frightened.

'You'll want tea, eh?' Terry asked, giving himself a neat exit.

'Of course', McGuire smiled cheesily.

Terry side-stepped the taller of McGuire's two side-kicks as he made a beeline for the kitchen.

'Are we OK?' McGuire asked.

'Of course we're OK,' Joe replied.

The handshake that followed was firm but fleeting. This was their first real contact in half a life-time. Both men sat down slowly and faced each other.

'Do I get an introduction?' Joe enquired.

'Sorry, Joe,' McGuire seemed genuinely apologetic. 'Get in here.'

Two young men, in their late teens or early twenties, confidently walked into the living room and McGuire performed the niceties.

'This is Whitey, my star pupil.'

The blonde-haired man, well used to the compliment, remained aloof, affording Joe the briefest eye contact.

'And this is Alex Scott's boy, Robert. We call him Scooby because he's not got a fucking clue,' McGuire said almost as an afterthought.

Scooby looked slightly miffed by the introduction.

'You're the spit of your auld man,' Joe mused.

The young man looked to McGuire and duly received a nod of approval before offering Joe his hand.

'My dad talked about you a lot,' Scooby said softly.

'Break out your best china, Terence,' McGuire hollered through to the kitchen.

Terry came running through from the kitchen, looking like Norman Wisdom after his Horlick's was spiked with LSD. 'Somebody's got a loan of my good stuff. I can't, I can't remember who,' Terry said, frantically clawing at his face.

'Just bring what you've got. Make sure it's fucking clean.' McGuire shot a look of shock horror towards Joe and they sniggered in unison.

Terry ran to the kitchen again and McGuire leaned forward, whispering. 'Do you think he'd go toes up if I asked for doilies?'

'Let's take the chance,' Joe replied.

McGuire smiled before screaming, 'Bring doilies or coasters if you've got them.'

Sounds of panic emanated from the kitchen as Terry failed to muffle cries of exasperation. McGuire turned to Scooby. 'Give him a hand or we'll be here all night.'

Joe felt slightly safer as he sat back in his chair. The wee stab at frivolity had dulled his nerves slightly. However, Joe was very aware of the guy called Whitey. There was something about those eyes. They had that Donald Sutherland look, that "I know something you don't know" look about them. Joe knew that look all too well; JJ McGuire was a past master at it.

Joe now felt confident enough to converse, asking. 'Is this the cream of the "Young Team"?'

'Sure is, Joseph. The boys are progressing, though Scooby's still got his cherry.'

Joe clicked straight away. There were never innocent remarks with McGuire. Everything said or implied was a double-edged sword. He was being told that Whitey, young as he was, had killed for McGuire. Scooby had not. Maybe he was supposed to be Scooby's first hit. Joe mulled that thought over in his head as Terry brought mugs of tea in, two at a time, and placed them on the small, shabby coffee table, saying apologetically, 'Scooby's bringing the milk and sugar.'

Joe stood up and offered to help out, but McGuire motioned that he remain seated.

'They're the cream of the young team all right. People say educational standards are slipping, but I disagree. They're still churning out the likes of you and me with unnerving regularity.' He then winked at Joe. 'The two of them went to our old school.'

'Is Al Capone still the patron saint?' Joe cracked the old joke.

'No, I am,' McGuire said, nonchalantly.

McGuire's gag had a ring of truth to it. JJ was seen as something of a God in Glasgow. During Joe's long absence, McGuire had risen to the top of the underworld in Scotland. He was a major player in Manchester and Liverpool and heavily involved with respected London outfits.

Terry finally sat on the far end of the sofa, with his knees up under his chin, hurriedly taking sips of tea.

'Been a stressful day, eh Terry?' McGuire commiserated.

Terry nodded and sipped some more.

'I told him to keep shtoom, didn't want him ruining the surprise.' McGuire smiled at Joe.

'It was a surprise?'

Joe nodded, feeling very uncomfortable because McGuire was staring intently into his eyes like an optician performing an examination.

'I was surprised you never came into the Straw House. People were expecting you,' McGuire said, finally allowing himself to blink.

Joe was puzzled and not sure how to respond. 'I was going to ask Terry how things were going with you, first.'

'You not read the papers when you were banged up? I'm opulent!'

'The papers always exaggerate, make it seem more.'

'They're not exaggerating, not in my case. I'm a multi-millionaire, and I'm very, very - rich.'

'I'm happy for you, JJ; I don't know what you want me to say. I didn't want to come around in case you thought I was after something.'

'Something like money, is that what you mean?'

'I don't want anything, JJ.'

'You're entitled to something. We were a partnership, quite successful, until...'

'Until Ah fucked up,' Joe answered.

'That was a long time ago, eh?' McGuire smiled and then looked to his men, 'Go down to the Treble Two and get a wee cargo in.'

'I've got a dozen Becks,' Terry chirped.

McGuire looked across the room and said, 'Take him with you.' McGuire nipped Whitey's arm as he passed. 'Tell Wullie to give the wee cunt a couple of quarters.'

Terry's ears pricked up like a sleeping dog hearing "walkies" mentioned.

As soon as they left, McGuire reached into his jacket, took out an envelope and placed it on the coffee table.

'I've put two grand in there. Get yourself some new clobber.' The image of Joe chained to two prison officers briefly entered McGuire's head.

'I don't want your money, JJ.'

'It's not a request.'

Joe picked up the money and stuck it in his back pocket as his old friend went on a bit of a tirade, espousing the benefits and drawbacks concerning current designer gear. Some of the names bamboozled. 'Prada's good, Dolce's not bad and Versace's best for suits.' Joe stated his preference would be Marks and Sparks.

'You'll not go wrong in there,' McGuire said. 'Good off-the-peg suits.'

McGuire was dressed impeccably, although he didn't look flash. He was sporting an electric blue-grey casual suit and an immaculate, tailored, black shirt. He removed the jacket, revealing the Versace label, then smartly turned the jacket in on itself before placing it on Terry's sofa.

'Did you think because you'd been tucked up for twelve years that no cunt had a beef with you?'

'It wasn't like that,' Joe said, startled

'Was it not'?'

'No,' Joe shouted.

McGuire's impassive face demanded explanation.

'I was giving a message to the inside,' Joe said.

'Oh, that's what you were doing?' McGuire deliberated.

'JJ, I was just wanting a different life - telling the world and its uncle I wasn't a player any more.'

McGuire stood up, undid the second button on his shirt, saying, 'Different life, different life. You should be thanking me for having a fucking life.'

'Look, I know you were watching over me, even if I did tell you to.' He struggled to find the correct words: 'to, to, to go fuck yourself.'

McGuire allowed himself the flicker of a smile as he cast a critical glance at Joe's hair. 'Is it natural?'

'Is what natural?'

'Your hair, it used to be ginger.'

'Course it's fucking natural,' Joe countered. 'You think we spent all our time doing each other's hair in there.'

'I thought it might have been a mid-life crisis.' McGuire pawed at his own locks, now greying all over, but more prominent at the temples. 'Ah thought of maybe getting a wee rinse myself.'

'We're nearly middle-aged,' Joe said. 'You're nearly as white-headed as your old man.'

'Scares me shitless that.'

'You do look like him.'

'I know.' McGuire winced, and then leant forward and said, 'I need a safe ear – private stuff Joe, personal stuff, you know.'

Joe edged forward, intrigued, as the door opened and he heard Terry castigating the Glasgow Cleansing Department's stair cleaning programme.

'It'll keep.' McGuire winked.

The three men entered the room, carrying with them a substantial amount of alcohol.

Whitey informed his boss that he had brought clean glasses with them.

'Good boy. Pour us a Becks.'

McGuire then turned to Joe, saying, 'I don't like this fashion for drinking out of bottles. You can never be sure where the bottle has been, eh Joe?'

Joe shuddered because, for one brief moment, he was back inside that condemned building watching poor Owny MacNee pull himself along the floor with broken hands and broken fingers and blood seeping from his back passage.......

'What's your poison, Joe?'

The question startled and brought Joe back to the present; he was not quite sure what to say. The truth was this. He was shit scared because his last drink was fifteen years ago.

McGuire sensed why Joe was nervous. 'It's not that old chestnut, the truth comes out in drink?'

'I'm not used to it, a wee bit wary of making an arse of myself.' Joe admitted.

'The truth doesn't come out in drink. A fucked up version of the truth emerges, and then things take their natural course, usually a violent one.' McGuire smiled, impressed by his revelation.

Joe's head was scrambled. He was sure JJ was pulling his chain, but that was the thing, you couldn't be entirely certain. One thing was certain. McGuire still knew how to get inside your head and get you agitated, so that you do say something unfortunate and then things travel the violent course. 'I've got to be back at the halfway house by ten. It's the rules.' Joe seemed pleased with the factual excuse.

'Don't worry, I'll make it OK.'

'You can do that?' Joe pondered aloud.

'I can do anything I like. Don't you read the papers? I'm beyond reproach.'

McGuire's sidekicks cheered, giving the impression they'd heard the speech before.

Joe sat there, fucked, not knowing what to do next; reluctantly he relented saying, 'I'll have a lager.'

McGuire spoke to Scooby, 'Give him a Becks and clear that shite away.'

Scooby handed Joe a beer and started clearing up the cups.

Here we fucking go, Joe thought as he took a sip of lager.

Joe's dilemma was twofold because he was just as worried by what his cousin might say. If it came to the bit, Terry was the only person he fancied his chances with in a fight and even that was not a foregone conclusion. Joe felt really uneasy. What made it worse was he knew that was exactly how McGuire wanted him to feel.

McGuire leaned forward and whispered, 'Is your Father still in your head?'

How the fuck can he know that? I never even tell't Harry that.

'I can thoroughly recommend following my example when it comes to parental control. There can only be one alpha male, no second favourites at the dog track.'

Joe stopped internalising, realising McGuire was now talking about his own father.

'I like to think of my father looking down on me,' McGuire chuckled.

'Boss, is this us seeing your soppy side?' Whitey asked.

'Always do right by your auld man, son,' McGuire said to Whitey

Joe thought, they don't know, they don't know the story. One cold December night, when JJ was just thirteen, he followed his father home from the "Marquis" free house and hung him from a tree opposite Arcadia Street on Glasgow Green. McGuire had come round to Joe's house straight afterwards, telling him it would be their secret. Joe was the only person he could tell. He had to tell somebody and he'd chosen Joe for the role of Father Confessor. He couldn't tell a priest, because they were meant to keep their mouths shut. Thinking back, Joe was impressed how succinct young McGuire's explanation had been. This secret meant they'd always be friends. Joe would always have something on him. It was meant to put them on an equal footing, make them partners.

Joe struggled to relax as the conversation turned into a "who's who" of who'd been topped in the last few years in the city of Glasgow and surrounding areas. He recognised some of the killers and some of those killed. Even if you stop being a player, you can't ignore the rumours that circulated inside prison. Now, he was sitting listening to information that Strathclyde's finest would pay a small fortune for. Billy Davis and William Tonner kept cropping up in the conversation.

'I'll kill that cunt Hutchinson, for fuck all, boss,' Scooby volunteered as McGuire sat smiling.

'I'd love to do a number on any of them Bar G bastards,' Whitey said, forcing himself into the conversation.

McGuire coughed and cleared his throat, bringing instant hush to the room. 'They Bar G bastards have got long memories, Joseph.'

Joe sat bolt upright in his chair. He hadn't seen this coming.

McGuire continued. 'You think, just because you did the big stint, everything's hunky dory? Well, you're wrong pal. We are still pals?'

'Of course we're still friends,' Joe stated a little too hurriedly.

'They still want to kill you. I stopped them. They wanted to kill your brothers. I stopped them. They were about to drown that dippy cunt through there.' McGuire referred to Terry. 'I stopped them.' McGuire lowered his voice. 'He's a fucking disaster; no, that's not right. Disasters eventually clear themselves up, but no' him. Fuck, my boys have dropped him off at the Royal three times with ODs. The only thing he's got going for him is the fact he thinks I don't like him,' McGuire said, looking in the direction of the drink, and Whitey replenished his glass. 'Can you imagine the bother he'd cause if he thought I might back him up? The fucker's not bright enough to have a death wish. He's just careless, or couldn't care less, to be precise.'

Joe inched forward saying, 'I've not even had a chance to talk to him yet. I've not seen him in five years.'

'Lucky you,' McGuire retorted.

Joe hesitated before gingerly asking, 'What's the score with the Bar G mob. Do they know I'm out?'

'They know you walked to your mother's.'

It felt like a blender had started up in Joe's bowels.

'They know you're tucked up at night in Abercrombie Street and they know I'm paying you a visit.'

'How?' Joe asked open-mouthed.

'I told them,' McGuire smiled. 'Try not to fret, Joe - boy.'

Chapter Four

Cornel Wagner was taking ten minutes to himself after just completing his rounds of the seven saunas and four houses he managed. He was deeply involved in the world's second oldest profession, collecting the money the girls had earned. He'd barely sat down when the "I ain't seen an elephant fly" ring tone made him stand bolt upright.

'How's the situation?' The voice was brisk but polite.

'I've got people looking but ve are having no joy,' Wagner explained in his strange accent, a hybrid of posh Kelvinside and an Eastern European dialect.

'I want resolution immediately.'

Wagner asked more in hope than expectation, 'Vould it be possible for you to instigate enquiries from your end?'

'Don't be absurd.'

The phone went dead.

Two of the girls who'd got shot of their clients early, made moves towards the office, looking for a natter and some tea. Wagner waved them away as he sat back down tiredly in his comfy chair, and cried as he pondered murder. It had to be done. He kept repeating that to himself. He'd loved her but he had loved Margaret more. He remembered the look of helplessness in her soulful eyes that had eaten into him. They needed someone and somewhere to hide, and he provided both. He needed somebody and something, and Margaret provided both. Then Caroline came into the picture more and more. She brought a kind of normality to the situation. Watching Margaret as a mother child was enchanting, but "enchanting" doesn't last. The time at the cottage had been beautiful, but that doesn't last either. Now he would have to find Margaret and he would have to kill her. She might come looking for him again in her hour of need. He smiled to himself. This was becoming a bit too Shakespearian.

*   *   *

Snowed under was the norm for Mark Henderson or, as the Assistant Chief Constable neatly put it, 'he'd a lot on his plate.'

Henderson suggested visiting a Tupperware party and purchasing some side dishes. His superior said he wasn't in the mood for vague references to a lack of manpower. Henderson was too quick with a correction.

'It's girl power I want, boss.'

'Just make a request and I'll see what I can do.'

The result of that request was the two female officers who waited pensively outside his office.

He ushered them in, quickly shook hands and made the introductions. He passed them two identical looking dossiers on the Logan sisters. He gave them a minute or two to look through the reading material. He was about to discuss his own thoughts on the murder of Caroline Logan. This was something he'd neglected to do with any other CID colleagues.

Both officers had been recommended by Tank Williams, the duty sergeant at Stewart Street nick. Henderson and Williams went way back. They'd walked a beat together in Maryhill in the early seventies. Although their careers had taken different paths, they'd remained close.

Henderson had previous for using Williams as a talent scout. He'd told Tank his requirements over a couple a pints. Stating age preference and stressing the need for shrewd, rather than looks. Things had gone better than expected and Tank supplied two novices from CID: Helen (Nell) Hannah educated at Edinburgh University and Marian MacCallum, a Parkhead girl, who'd excelled in every aspect of police work.

DC Hannah's superiors thought she'd the credentials for a rapid rise through the ranks. She was modern thinking, upper class, terrific at functions, and she was a looker. The best accolade both girls had was that Tank Williams rated them. DC Hannah, despite the posh accent, could handle herself. Williams had been impressed when she'd lost her temper and put a few senior officers straight on how they should conduct themselves in her presence.

So Henderson had got what he wanted, two young officers around the same age as Margaret Logan. They'd be "multi-tasking". Henderson grimaced, disturbed at using these words in his thinking process. He wanted those young officers to sift through the records and unearth something. They'd be keeping an eye on Margaret Logan. He felt she was in danger but, until that danger materialised, it would remain just that - a feeling. He hoped their style of clothing would rub off on Margaret whose dress sense still hinted at "working girl". His main hope, however, was that companionships could be struck up and Margaret might feel inclined to open up to DC Hannah and DC MacCallum. Tell them things she would never disclose to an auld, battle-hardened inquisitor like him.

Luck was on his side at the moment. The papers had reported the murder, but it had been low key. There was so much reality or celebrity nonsense going on that murders and serious assaults were relegated to small headlines and the bare bones of a story.

Henderson knew the papers would come sniffing sooner rather than later. His feeling that this case would get mucky and downright nasty was down to pure logic. He knew something of their history and that meant a few dark secrets would be raked up. He might not be able to pin a murder on someone but a few people might get done for putting their peckers where their peckers were not allowed to go. Soon some hack would get a sniff of something and then every paper in the country would be on his back wanting answers.

Mark Henderson knew he was playing at "My Fair Lady" or "Pygmalion" by placing Margaret in the company of young women who had something going for them. She'd be a world away from junkies, assorted prostitutes and their controllers, who normally polluted her environment. For Christ's sake, the lassie deserved something from life. And the big question at the forefront of Henderson's mind was - could he stop Margaret meeting the same end as her sister?

Henderson steadied himself as he rose from his desk. His eyes settled on Marian MacCallum as he spoke. 'I don't want you discussing this case with anyone but me. Is that understood?'

Both detectives nodded.

'I want you to go home now, pack a small bag and be at Roselea Gardens by six o'clock.'

DC MacCallum smiled nervously. 'Should I bring my laptop?'

'That'd be great; make sure you bring reading glasses, even if you don't wear glasses. You'll need them - you will - believe me.' Henderson sighed.

'Are you implying there's plenty reading material - sir,' DC Hannah asked.

'Yes, DC Hannah, I am.'

*   *   *

Everything seemed a struggle these days for Jim Cassidy; retirement easily topped that list. Of course he'd thought about it, but he should have given it a lot more thought. Retirement was something you were supposed to do once. If you messed it up, you had the consolation of knowing you didn't have to make that mistake again. His pension was sorted and the money from his house sale safely tucked away. He wasn't wealthy, but he'd a lot more than he needed. What frightened him most was the probability he'd spend his money on shite.

The job had always been seen as exactly that, a job. He knew, and others knew, he was good at it. Job satisfaction was never that important. He worked simply to earn money for Freda. Then it was for Freda and the kid. That's what he'd called it, even though it wasn't born. It had been "we'll get this for the kid. Or we'll do this for the kid". The kid died in the eighth month of Freda's pregnancy. The kid was a boy and there were never any more.

When Freda died, Cassidy found he was snookered, not knowing what to do. Work meant nothing apart from taking up a huge chunk of the day and helping him sleep away the rest. He didn't want another woman and he was content to play the spoilt child. If he couldn't have her, he wasn't playing.

Freda's old record collection was too precious to give away. They were at least forty years old, from their courting days and their early married life and, like him, they'd seen better days. So he started trying to update the collection onto CD. It was a definite attempt at restarting his heart. Thoughts of Joe Ray had accompanied his daily excursions into the old music store on Sauchiehall Street. He'd been toying with the idea of contacting him and asking him to decorate his flat. The truth was he wanted company, pure and simple. He just wanted to go about it in a way that suited both parties.

Joe had excelled in the painting and decorating course he'd overseen at the prison, and Cassidy had always been impressed with Joe's artwork. He placed Matt Munro in the CD tray, sat in his armchair, and fiddled with the remote and pressed play. His mind was made up; tomorrow he'd contact Abercrombie Street and offer Joe some casual employment. However, Cassidy had a nagging doubt; ten days into his retirement, he was beginning to turn into a nuisance.

Chapter Five

Joe had been sitting for an hour and a half staring at the list, taking Harry's advice a stage further and making amends to people he'd wronged before he went inside.

'Focus on the stuff you got away with,' Harry would say. Harry knew all about doing time. He was Britain's longest-serving lifer. He'd served thirty eight years and was determined to do more when bowel cancer curtailed that aspiration. Harry had killed his wife, their two children and his homosexual lover. Harry failed to kill himself, although he'd taken enough drugs to kill a horse.

The ambulance driver assumed, just like the doctor, that all five occupants of the house at Burgher Street were dead, but when he placed Harry's body on a stretcher, he realised his body temperature was not as cold as the others. Then the faintest hint of a pulse was detected and, seven weeks later, Harry came out of the coma.

Harry was pragmatic about his escape from death. It was a sign from God that he would pay for his sins on earth. The witty ones in the house, and Bar L's full of them, were just as pragmatic, naming him the Wee Murdering Poof. Reason being, that there was a Big Murdering Poof on the same wing. Harry took a lot of beatings in his first year inside because he was considered a Ba' and Harry did nothing to dispel the myth.

The skin on the porridge saved him from serious burns, when a huge pot of porridge was tipped over him. Ironically, the Wee Murdering Poof was raped on several occasions. Rumours that he was riddled with gonorrhoea stopped those assaults.

Harry was sparse with his vocabulary during the first two decades of his incarceration. 'Yes sir, no sir,' to the screws, 'Guilty,' to the cons, 'Innocent,' to the authorities, 'Sane,' to the psychiatrists. And the last thing he said every night was, 'Fuck you, God.'

When twenty years had passed, they foisted shrinks on him, hell-bent on getting him to take responsibility, admit his guilt, show something approaching remorse, and he'd walk on parole.

'You gave me life. That's what I'm going to do,' he'd say.

Harry's failed suicide attempt was the only reason he hadn't visited the Hanging Shed at Barlinnie. He hadn't even blinked when Lord Blakely put the black tricorn cap on and passed the death penalty. Others, some influential, successfully petitioned the Scottish Secretary to recommend the royal prerogative. Harry remarked, 'I take the hint, God.'

A quack once asked. 'Do you still intend to take your own life?'

'I will, when I've completed forty five years.'

'Is that fifteen years each, for your wife and children?' the shrink calculated.

'How do you know that the forty five years aren't for Gavin?'

Joe thought back to their first meeting, the night Jim Cassidy escorted him from the Wendy House back onto B wing and into Harry's peter.

Cassidy's introduction was economical. 'Joe, Harry. Harry, Joe.'

'Hello,' Harry said, pointing at the bunks, 'I'll move if you want'

'No, I'm fine up there.'

*   *   *

Sometime in the middle of the night Harry spoke, 'I am in here because on the twenty eighth of April, 1964 I killed my wee boy. His name was Peter, he was three years old. I killed my baby, Morag. She was one year and one day old. I killed their mother, she was my wife. Jean was just three days short of celebrating her twenty first birthday. That same day I murdered Gavin Goodwin. He was what you would call my boyfriend. We both ended up in the Glasshouse at Shepton Mallet during our National Service, for similar offences. And I have been in Bar L since the fourth of July, 1964.'

Ten minutes later, Joe spoke.

'I'm in here because I shot three men dead. Two of them might have deserved it - the other definitely did not.' Joe was silent for a long while until he added, 'There's a strong possibility that certain people in this prison will come into this cell and kill me.'

'I know,' Harry said.

*   *   *

Joe jumped from his bed in the cramped, self-contained unit on the second floor of the 'Sore Thumb'. That's what the locals called the "halfway house" on Abercrombie Street. Today the house was quiet for a change. Joe looked at his face in the small mirror above the hand basin and wiped tears from his eyes. Thinking of Harry always made him emotional. He wasn't ashamed of this - well; he was to a certain extent. He felt guilty because he'd felt more grief at Harry's passing than he had for his own father.

Jim Cassidy's phone call had given him the opportunity to put the amends list on hold. At least he'd looked at it. He chuckled, thinking

35

about the old Chairman Mao saying, "A journey of a thousand miles starts with one step". Well, he had put his socks on in his journey of atonement. *'Harry, the trek's no' postponed, merely delayed.'*

He would take Jim Cassidy's job offer. In fact he looked forward to it. He didn't need the money. What he needed was a reason for having money. As well as the two grand he'd got from McGuire, his mother had also chipped in with five hundred. He had to carry the money with him everywhere. He wasn't fretting about the arrival of the Giro, but he had to pretend to fret about the arrival of the Giro.

Everything in this shithole was about keeping up appearances; he felt scrutinised on all sides, constantly facing a barrage of questions from inhabitants and staff:

'Are you OK? Do you need any assistance in going to the Benefits Agency? Willie will chum you, won't you Willie?'

Willie was something of an institution in this place and only too glad to be of assistance. Joe just wanted to keep himself to himself. He knew someone in this house was keeping tabs on him for McGuire. That was obvious from their conversation at Terry's house. It could be a resident or a member of staff. Knowing McGuire, it was probably both.

Jim Cassidy's company was something beneficial to mind, body and soul. He liked Cassidy. The prison siege, all those years ago, had started it. Joe became aware then that he'd taken advice from someone he did not fear. The norm was prisoners hated screws. Some they hated less than others. Time and familiarity had conquered contempt and in some cases bred alliances. The dividing line still remained in place, but Jim Cassidy had crossed that line on a couple of occasions for him and Joe was grateful for that. Joe wanted to see him and catch up with things. It was simple really, when you weighed it up against conversations he'd engaged in with the residents of this shithole.

Chapter Six

Henderson had dressed down for the occasion, playing the part of the distant relative. Thankfully, he'd opted for the navy blue, quilted anorak, because it was a cold sun that shone on Glasgow this day. He looked around, thinking people just don't know how to dress for a funeral these days. His mind travelled back to his own father's funeral forty years ago, a staged event, where people intuitively dressed wisely and adopted a sombre attitude - but had the decency to leave the crying to the family of the deceased. Perhaps, forty years from now, somebody would be pacing these church gardens, longing for the days when football club colours and pop posters polluted the funeral march.

The service was still half an hour away, and Henderson had a couple of lookouts milling around the huge red-brick Sacred Heart chapel opposite the Parkhead Forge cinema complex. They were looking for known faces or faces that did not quite fit in. Henderson wasn't sure what he was looking for exactly. He'd pushed for Caroline's funeral to be brought forward, hoping it might bring something or someone to light. Information received yesterday could prove fruitful. He'd shown an old photograph of Margaret Logan around the station. It was taken when she was fifteen. Eventually, the photo brought recognition from Old Topper, an elder statesman from the Vice Squad. He remembered the girl hanging around the Palms Sauna, opposite Anderston Bus Station. If she was hanging around there, she'd be working for Cornel Wagner. Wagner ran the sex trade for JJ McGuire. Of course that did not mean McGuire was involved in Caroline Logan's murder. Any villain you turned over in Scotland had a link to McGuire. Fuck, it would be like winning a double rollover if he could bang those two up for this.

He'd given his DCs carte-blanche to arrange the funeral how they saw fit. Marian MacCallum had said Margaret's initial hostility was gradually subsiding and being replaced with civility, and sometimes even a touch of courtesy. Henderson hoped his young detectives were bright enough to realise they were not just "babysitting the maladjusted" here; they were involved in something a bit special, something major.

He looked west along the Gallowgate and caught sight of the small cortège at the mini-roundabout that enabled traffic to access the busy retail park. His view of Janefield Cemetery was blocked. He was glad of that. The old bone yard had suffered a lot of vandalism in recent years.

Most of the headstones were toppled and desecrated by arseholes spraying their monikers on them.

Funny, this sad day would be tinged with delight for Margaret Logan. She would get to see her daughters and her sister's child. Henderson knew from the feedback that Margaret had plumped for little red coats for the kids, just like the one the little girl wore in the Polish ghetto in Spielberg's "Schindler's List". It couldn't get any more poignant, he thought. Henderson was wrong.

The cortège consisted of a hearse and three funeral cars. The immediate Logan family could easily fit into one car, but Social Services had vetoed that idea. Margaret Logan sat in the front car with DCs MacCallum and Hannah holding her hands. The second car contained Margaret's daughters, who sat with three staff from their care home. Three year old Cheryl sat quietly in the third, flanked by two social workers getting to know the fluffy Dalmatian toy she met an hour ago. Facing them was a friendly-faced plain clothes policeman with size thirteen feet.

Henderson was impressed by how hard his DCs had battled to ensure that Margaret would get to see her daughters today. And it would be MacCallum and Hannah who'd perform the handover. Hopefully, Margaret would appreciate their hard work. Social Services had accepted playing the role of the bad cop today and, later on this afternoon, they'd be taking the children back.

The approach of the hearse gave the detective full view of the floral tribute resting against Caroline's coffin. Two words, "MY LOVE", were simply constructed with white roses. 'It does not get more apt', Henderson muttered, feeling a little embarrassed that he'd spoken out loud. He was heartened to see that Social Services had not scrimped. The floral tribute looked expensive. Behind the funeral cars, five private vehicles made up the cortège.

Jim Cassidy sat at the rear of the funeral procession. He was there simply because it was the neighbourly thing to do. Inside his pocket, he carried a small ornamental "Essence of Violets" perfume bottle. Every week he sprinkled some scent where he had released Freda's ashes.

DCs Nell Hannah and Marian MacCallum had more than earned their crust in the last few days. Now their heart-strings were being stretched to breaking point as they watched Margaret's tear-stained face move from one window to another window in order to catch glimpses of her children in the other car. They could see her children screaming recognition when they caught sight of their mother.

Henderson met the funeral cortège and helped Margaret from the car, while the DCs went to gather the children. The haunted look on his face was genuine and his eyes implored her to be patient a while longer.

As the coffin was carried into the chapel, Henderson saw MacCallum and Hannah huddle the three children together. The scene, with the children in their red coats and their matching berets, could have graced the cover of Cosmopolitan.

Gently, Margaret slipped from Henderson's hand and slowly walked over to Nicola and Emma. She was heartened and saddened by how much they'd grown. She dropped to her feet and pulled them into her. The wails and cries shrilled from them like a harem in mourning. Then Caroline's kid, Cheryl, joined in.

'Thanks for being so patient, Father,' Henderson said to the priest standing in the doorway of the chapel. Henderson felt the bile rise in his stomach as he watched the children with their mother. He could see the same stacked deck being reshuffled. The children had inherited their mother's beauty and by the looks of things were about to be brought up the same way.

The priest conducting the ceremony hadn't a lot to work with, but he was long enough in the tooth to make a little go a long way. He touched on Caroline's happy times with two sets of foster parents. These happy times, in actuality, added up to about eighteen months in a life span of twenty three years. The priest soldiered on as two foster parents put consoling heads together. Margaret sat with her arms wrapped around the children, memorising every spoken word, seemingly content that her instructions were being carried out.

The priest paused, nodded twice, and Heather from Social Services took this as the cue to come forward and read an extract from "The Adornment".

'What's an adornment, Mummy?' Emma asked.

Margaret's low voice stunned the chapel. 'Something that makes things better; your Aunty Caroline made me be a better person.'

As the pall-bearers slowly exited the chapel, Margaret's agitation transmitted to the children. Instinctively, they knew there would be more goodbyes this sad day. The shrill wailing began again.

This was a critical moment. DCs MacCallum and Hannah flanked Margaret on either side and ushered the children down the aisle, both officers fearful that Margaret might try and make some crazy run for it with the kids.

People attending the funeral ceremony probably thought Caroline would be buried in Janefield Cemetery on the Gallowgate, a stone's throw from the chapel. But she was heading for St Peter's Cemetery at Auchenshoogle and, pretty soon, the cortège would be snaking along the London Road.

Auchenshoogle used to be the end of the line for Glasgow's old tram system. Henderson remembered getting off a tram there in his early twenties. Paralytic drunk, he decided on taking a short cut through the graveyard. He still remembered squeezing through those huge wrought-iron gates. Then, it turned into a Hammer House of Horror picture. Suddenly, the weather became horrendous and torrential rain pummelled the paths between the graves. Henderson was never quite sure how long he had spent in the cemetery that night. It seemed like a lifetime, slipping and sliding from one muddy path to another and tripping over countless fallen gravestones. Eventually, he emerged from the same gates he'd entered. Mark Henderson knew better than most just how big St Peter's Cemetery was. That's why he'd persuaded Tank Williams to have a day away from the desk at Stewart Street and hover around the Logan family plot.

*   *   *

Old Father Michael stood by the open grave and smiled benignly at Margaret, who was taking the opportunity to show the children their ancestors. 'That's your Nan and that's your Granda, and there's my Uncle Owen and that's my wee brother, baby James.' The children looked as if they were thinking over the information, but not sure if a reply was necessary.

Henderson knew the family history. Nan and Granda (Katherine MacNee and James Logan) had died of drug overdoses, barely making it into their thirties. Uncle Owen had topped himself at the tender age of twenty three. Baby James had died on the on the sixth of October, 1987. So that's why Margaret wanted Caroline buried today. Henderson did the calculations and asked himself if Baby James' death was the start of this family's drastic decline - when things started to go badly wrong for Margaret and Caroline Logan. Henderson had agreed to the burial today because it could be months before he got someone for this. Caroline would be better here with her kin than stuck in the cold morgue.

Manic wailing startled Henderson. Caroline was being lowered into the grave. Father Michael spoke his final words and then Margaret, Nicola, Emma and little Cheryl crumbled fresh earth onto the coffin. The children never wiped the dirt from their soiled hands.

The gravediggers, a man in his mid-fifties and a boy of about seventeen, lingered in the background. Beyond them, a gardener sat alone behind a huge ornate monument, toying with his mobile. He had one final check of the photograph he'd taken of Margaret standing at the graveside, and then his grubby thumb pressed "send".

Chapter Seven

Joe had spent most of the day in the city centre. Some of the shops he used to frequent were still there; only the names had changed. He messed about for about an hour and a half, musing, deliberating and finally rejecting everything. Walking the streets proved more fruitful, scrutinising the apparel of anyone he considered to be in his age group. The fact that it was a Friday afternoon meant that it was mostly business suits or boiler suits on view. A Saturday would show better how these same people dressed casually. Joe was struck by the number of beggars on the street. It was Biblical in a way. Some of them had dogs with them, the animals covered in blankets. A shrewd move, Joe thought. Thing was, the beggars weren't too shabby dress-wise.

He walked into Marks and Spencer, wilfully ignoring McGuire's advice about trying out Princes Square. He wouldn't be turning into a McGuire clone again. Walking that walk had cost him twenty years.

He located a female assistant in her mid-thirties. Blonde and a touch overweight, she was pushing all the right buttons until he clocked the wedding ring. He opened up a touch, informing her that he'd been away for quite a while.

'How long is a while?'

'A long, long while,' he answered

'That is a while. Best behaviour today, eh?'

She was quick on the uptake and Joe was instantly smitten. The hour and a bit that followed became the best time Joe had had since leaving prison. Her name was Delia and she knew her stuff. All right, she was on commission, but there was an instant trust. And it was nice the way she took an interest in the selections he made. He took her suggestions on board and ended up spending close on £750. As he was leaving, he asked her what nightclub she would recommend.

'When I get the chance to get out, we head for Plaza Exchange.'

'Who's we?' Joe asked boldly.

'Me and my pals,' she said smiling.

'I'll check it out, eh?'

'Please do.' She smiled once more.

Leaving the shop, he hailed a taxi and immediately asked the driver to let him have a cursory glance at Plaza Exchange before taking him to his mother's house. He settled back in the seat, glowing. My God, I might actually bump into a female I know in a Glasgow nightspot. He wasn't aware he'd just participated in what they called retail therapy, but whatever it was had put him a mind to hit the town tonight. He'd leave most of the clothes at his mother's. Hopefully, she wouldn't have any family visiting.

*   *   *

He started in a familiar place, The Drum, a busy wee pub in the heart of the Barras. There were faces he knew, but he decided against approaching them and he was grateful they returned the compliment. Then he made his way to the Old Tollbooth Bar. He did not want to get too bagged up, but still plumped for another pint of lager, his third. The place was packed with many, just like him, starting their night off, and a few who should have called it a night this afternoon. They had that angry, defiant look on their faces, almost begging for someone silly enough to tell them it was time to go.

Joe knew he was on dangerous ground. He might be out, but he was out on licence. That meant he had to be constantly aware of his own behaviour and be even more aware of the behaviour of those surrounding him. It just took one arsehole to do something and he could be back inside for who knows how long.

Just as he was about to leave, a face from his past entered the pub - Rab Greene, a former cell-mate. They exchanged shocked expressions of greeting. The guy had been OK when they were inside but this was outside - and there was a difference. Still, Joe bought the guy a drink and they got chatting. Turned out Rab's last stretch had been 1993 and now life was idling along nicely. He was actually making a not bad living, selling supposedly hooky gear in the Barras. The reason he wasn't pulled regularly was that his merchandise was totally legitimate. His adeptness at persuading Joe Public they were purchasing a dodgy bargain had brought him a steady income and he was discerning enough, now, to ignore most iffy opportunities coming his way.

So they talked about faces they knew and recalled well-worn stories from the past. Rab offered to tag along and ease Joe's passage into Glasgow's current nightlife. Joe politely declined.

As he made his way to the exit, Rab placed a hand on his shoulder and imparted some friendly advice. 'Take it easy with yourself the night. If you don't like a place, if you feel uncomfortable, leave.'

Joe nodded agreement and made his goodbyes. As he walked from Glasgow Cross, he realised he'd already taken Rab's advice on board.

Joe never made it to Plaza Exchange. He'd sampled a few "posey" minimalist bars and then settled on downgrading.

*   *   *

McGuire woke up in his own time. He knew it was early, as he could hear his young sons arguing. As he made his way downstairs he heard his wife stress, 'Boys!' He guessed Eileen was getting beyond bothered.

She rose from the sofa on seeing him. 'What do you want to eat?'

'You're all right. Go back to your bed. I'll make you something.'

'What about them?'

'They'll be good.' McGuire smiled.

His two boys simultaneously removed their heads from the front of the huge Plasma screen, guiltily watching their mother make her way upstairs. McGuire frowned at Robbie and Wee Jack.

'If you two can't be good, be bad quietly.'

The first thing he did on entering the kitchen was to make some decent coffee and put a healthy dent into a fresh pack of cigarettes. It was going to be a busy day. Some serious business was going to be concluded today. However, McGuire was determined to spend quality time with his family. Outside, Old Freddie badgered three of JJ's men into weeding the garden.

'Do it properly,' Freddie snapped at them.

McGuire could hear muffled grunts in reply.

Eileen hated his men coming in and out of the house all the time, so at least Freddie had them do something constructive when they were on duty.

Freddie was the exception to that rule. Eileen had insisted that Freddie move into the Granny flat at the bottom of their garden. Freddie was sixty three years old and he'd been involved in Glasgow's underworld for almost fifty years. Now he was considered the closest thing to a grandfather that McGuire's sons had. Tonight, Freddie would be overseeing one of the young team during his first stint at real work. Johnny V would also be in attendance. 'Learn from the best, son,' McGuire said to himself.

Before making breakfast, McGuire crept silently towards the living-room door and had a sneaky listen to his sons arguing quietly. They sounded reassuringly pathetic and he was so glad of that. They were not like him. Since infancy, he'd constantly observed them, scanning for any similarities to him, searching for that touch of malice in their genetic make-up. If they hadn't looked like him, he would not have believed they were his. They'd inherited his looks and their mother's nature, and he was more than content with that.

Fifteen minutes later, he told his sons their breakfast was in the kitchen.

Aye,' he answered their wide-eyed pleas, 'you can eat it in front of the telly.'

He made his way upstairs, entered the bedroom and looked at his wife, who was pulling a brush through her wet hair. Placing the breakfast tray on the dresser he said, 'Eileen let's eat it cold.'

'I thought something was afoot,' she said, continuing to brush her hair.

'C'mon hen, it's not that big.'

'I wish,' she said and gently giggled at her own joke.

McGuire wrapped his arms around her towelled bathrobe and pulled her into him, tenderly kissing the back of her neck.

'What about them two?'

'They're fine; they're eating and arguing in whispers.'

'Thank God for that.' She swivelled around in his arms, coyly grinning.

McGuire's hands gently cupped her hair and pressed it back to expose the whole of her face. He kissed her once, and her thin lips opened to reveal their softness as he gently sank his face into them. Her saliva was a quicker fix than any narcotic he'd ever tried. They made their way to the bed, undressed and lazily positioned themselves in their favoured side-on position. The foreplay was mostly verbal as social intercourse took precedence over its sexual counterpart.

Eileen wasn't sure who needed this most, and at the moment she didn't really care. All she knew was this: the feelings were mutual. For the next wee while at least, they had entered their world, where only they mattered.

She lay there, watching her husband breathing, content to let him have another snooze. She was under no illusions about how he operated on the outside world. In their world, he was always gentle. She looked at him again, watched his chest rise and fall rhythmically. Her throat suddenly felt dry. She would have to broach the subject today, he'd have to listen - he would just have to. She fought hard, trying to stop tears filling her eyes.

*   *   *

He paid his money, got a drink and took a seat near the dance-floor. There were four small groups of women dancing together in close proximity and one "over-imbiber" failing to connect with any of them. Two bouncers skilfully manoeuvred the man from the floor and planted him in a seat. Obviously the club wasn't busy enough to throw him out now. The drunk served as a good icebreaker. Joe sparked up a conversation with a couple of females in their mid-thirties who drank straight from the bottle, their fingers toying with the removed straws as if they were musical instruments. The music was noisy and the girls mimed criticism of the drunk on the other side of the floor. So the evening was starting off well. The girls looked good, sober. Odds on, they'd look better as the night progressed.

*   *   *

Twenty years ago, when Joe and his associates went dancing, liaisons with the opposite sex weren't the number one priority of the night. Back then, it was more a parade of power - a bit like prison, only with seductive sexual ornaments in tow. The bouncers and owners of the nightclubs were primed as to where you stood in Glasgow's pecking order, and catered accordingly. Teams nodded salutations to each other, and the females who accompanied them worked well together, keeping rogue lionesses at bay. Every now and then, one of these beautiful strays would be cornered into the ladies' toilets and given a vicious beating - her only crime, catching the eye of a villain they ran with.

Each team usually took a couple of chaperones with them. These guys would be clued up, sober and straight. Diligently, they would travel back and forth between adversaries, passing on apologies from one of their own or pointing out that one of their opposing numbers was in danger of crossing a line. Basically the night consisted of standing around posing, getting high, drunk and sniggering at the plebs dancing. Although not a lot of dancing took place, the end of the evening would see most gang members scramble to the floor, propped up by their lady attachments as they smooched "Through the Barricades" with Spandau.

*   *   *

Joe had no difficulty accepting that he was just one of the plebs now, and then felt as if he'd just blinked and the place had become mobbed, and this mob was as unsightly as any mob could be. It could be best described as an orgy where you kept your clothes on. Everything was extreme as he watched his own age group indulge in the mating ritual. Getting to know someone on a verbal level wasn't on the agenda. There were skirts on parade that should have had Public Order Notices served on them. There were men on show who should have had a restraining orders stapled to their foreheads. It made any teenager's first drunken party seem classy. The wise move would have been to leave there and then, but he stayed, tried his hand at "anthropology" and suffered the consequences.

The next hour saw a succession of arseholes make approaches. The second of these approaches proved the most troublesome. The joker had made his way over to the two women Joe had talked to earlier. Abruptly, the joker was making a departure and, before too long, he was offloading his concerns onto Joe.

'She told me to fuck off,' he said.

'Who told you to fuck off?' Joe asked, amazed that he was interested.

'Your two pals over there, tell't me to fuck off'.

'I don't know them, pal,' Joe shrugged.

'You were with them.'

Joe looked at the man. He was skinny, balding and the worse for drink. He didn't look handy but that theory goes out the window when the singing ginger is in the belly.

'Look mate,' Joe said cautiously, 'they said wrong, honestly. I don't know them. I tried to chat them up earlier and got the same result as you.'

The man took this as his cue to sit down and attempt to chill. Then he erupted, 'Fucking slappers - I mean we're all here for our hole, but we can at least be civil, eh?'

His name was John and they conversed for a short time. The reason it wasn't longer was John's resentment was stewing and he was getting in the mood to quibble. John was about to instigate an assault. It was 60/40 whether he'd be victim or assailant. Joe was not hanging around to find out which. He went to the toilet and then sat somewhere else.

He decided to try his hand at dancing and asked a wee, round-faced lady up for a dance. This was another bad move. He'd been watching people dancing all night and he thought he had the right amount of lager in him to make a half-decent attempt. He was thinking he was doing not too bad when, eight or nine bars into the track, she looked him up and down and sneered, 'You've got a tendency to love yourself, eh?'

Joe wasn't just lost for words. He was lost, cast adrift amongst a sea of human shite. Apologetically, he mumbled in her ear that he just liked dancing. Her cherubic snarl disagreed with that statement. Joe left the dance floor at the earliest opportunity and made his way to the bar for some respite, where he was accosted by someone best described as a midget who accused him of bumping his glass. Joe left the dancehall with one of Harry's wise pearls reverberating in his ears. "You can go the rest of your life without sex, and believe me, Joe, you might have to."

Joe pulled the blanket over his face, closed his eyes tight. However, he failed to blot out the image of the wee, round-faced lady and the "Tendency to love yourself" remark. What does that mean, really, what the fuck does that mean? He kept asking himself the same question.

Chapter Eight

It was on the edge of darkness when the manky white Transit drove along the Hamilton Road, heading east. Reluctantly, the driver switched on the headlights. Johnny V, one of the three occupants, was gibbering about maybe slowing the van down and getting a better look at the pristine cars in the glass-cubed showrooms in this part of the city.

Old Freddie said, 'I'll tell you what, John, I'll make a point of stopping on the way back.'

'Is that a promise?' Johnny V bit back.

Both men glared past the much younger man sitting between them. Nobody spoke again until the van slowed and pulled into a little dirt road that nestled between two large houses. Freddie spun the van around in four jerky movements. He switched off the lights just as the younger man tried to glimpse himself in the rear view mirror.

'You're beautiful,' Johnny V assured Whitey, the youngest member of this three-man team.

'Let him out, John,' Freddie said as he slipped his seatbelt off.

Johnny V did as requested and the men made their way to the back of the van. Freddie cast an eye to the distance. 'You see the flats, son?'

Whitey looked up at the four high-rise tower blocks silhouetted against a darkening sky. The towers looked like sentinels peering over Sandyhills Golf Course.

'Hard not to,' he responded.

Freddie thrust a Yale key into Whitey's hands. 'Take this, and if things fuck up, you make your way along the golf course to this path.'

Whitey broke in, 'What do you mean, things fuck up?'

Johnny V suddenly got serious and Whitey instantly became attentive. 'Listen, son, things can always fuck up.'

Freddie resumed his instructions. 'Make your way up that path - it'll bring you out near the flats. Make your way to the first building - on the right - head for the seventh floor, flat three, OK. Use the fire escape stairs, no fucking lifts, mind - and let yourself in.'

Before Whitey could nod agreement, Johnny V had grabbed hold of him and started pushing him, aiming little slaps at his head and asking, 'What he say, what he fucking say?'

Whitey neatly sidestepped the next attack and calmly repeated his instructions verbatim.

'Good boy,' Freddie said.

Johnny V placed an arm on Whitey's shoulder and led him to the back of the van. He quietly pulled the back doors of the van open and peeled back some oil-stained blankets, revealing a small arsenal of weaponry. Whitey picked up the smallest weapon on display, neatly tucking it inside his jacket.

Johnny V patted Whitey's cheek. 'Brilliant; let's go kill this cunt.'

The cunt in question was Pedro Wilson, who intermittently worked for various teams in the city of Glasgow (when at liberty). This in itself did not make him dangerous. The shite that spouted from his mouth placed him high in the "At Risk" category. Pedro had contacted some of the city's younger criminal fraternity, alluding to knowledge of the working practices of certain powerful people. A friendly warning had been issued and ignored. People like Pedro find anonymity difficult.

Tonight Pedro was making a personal appearance at his niece's twenty first birthday party being held in The Woodend Inn. His nature would, as usual, come to his enemy's assistance. The "do", as such things are called, was taking place in the upstairs lounge. The crowd was mostly youngsters, but there were plenty adult relatives eager to cause embarrassment. There were twelve locals and two passing trade, who were staying at the nearby B&B, drinking in the downstairs bar.

Whitey sat quietly at a corner table with his back to the bar. His eyes were focussed on the fruit machine and the bar staff didn't take too much notice of him. To them, he looked like a "wee ned" waiting to score blow from somebody. As long as they didn't see him in the act, then he was the least of their worries. Their major concern was the ruckus coming from upstairs.

The locals were a different matter. They'd clocked the threat from the stranger straight away. The way he just sat there staring at the puggy, diligently calculating how much money it was being fed. They'd been seeing to the machine's nutrition all day and they were adamant to a man that one of them would benefit when the fucker finally vomited cash and tokens. They were taking it in turns, guarding against the stranger using the machine. As soon as one player's money looked like running out, he'd look to the bar and a replacement would take over.

Whitey sat, biding his time, tickled that he was a source of so much agitation. He was just waiting for the moment when his target upstairs would come down and grace the bar with his presence. That would happen long before any of these arseholes collected their jackpot. V and Freddie were positive Pedro would visit the bar. They were as sure as the fruit machine was that it would never go hungry. It was Pedro's way.

After he'd done his cabaret stint of introducing himself upstairs, he would have to entertain the public bar and let them know a face was in the building.

Pedro made his way downstairs, followed by two young guys, obviously delighted to accompany him.

'Three large Southern Comforts and Diet Coke,' Pedro barked at the bar staff.

Whitey stood up and downed the remnants of his drink and slipped the slim half pint glass into one of the Parka's side pockets. He pulled the gun out from under his coat as he approached Wilson and shot him through the neck. The big man spun around with pained disbelief on his face.

'It's happening,' Whitey said, making eye contact.

Wilson clamped his hands around his throat and Whitey shot him twice in the head. One of the locals pulled the fruit machine on top of himself as everyone else scrambled to find that elusive back seat. Shrill screams could be heard on the stairs to the lounge, amidst the sounds of tables crashing into each other, as Whitey swiftly made his exit.

In the car park, Johnny V blasted the pub windows with a pump action shotgun. Freddie held the driver's door open with his foot, aiming a sawn-off at the pub's entrance. When Whitey and V scrambled into the back of the van, Freddie blasted the doorway, and the fancy lighting surrounding it, to pieces. He threw the shotgun onto the passenger's foot well and floored the accelerator.

Johnny V asked 'Did he say anything?'

Whitey removed the baseball cap with the sewn-in ginger locks and placed his hand over his neck. 'Yes. He said "Aghya".'

'What a fucking pussy,' Freddie roared, and slid the gear stick into fifth as they cruised away from Mount Vernon.

*   *   *

Freddie stood inside the scrap yard, looking at the mangled cube that was once a Ford Transit. He held his mobile tight to his ear. 'It's done,' he said, sounding extremely satisfied with his night's work.

'What's done?' McGuire asked.

Freddie could not answer, his head was gone. He was not sure if JJ was at the wind-up or that he'd forgotten. *I'm getting too long in the tooth for this game*, he thought.

Chapter Nine

Mark Henderson got into work at seven o'clock, far earlier than required. He'd flaked out during an argument yesterday, and woke up intent on getting out of the house before it resumed. He'd made his way to the canteen and had managed to keep down a couple of coffees before Tank Williams turned up.

Henderson's old friend, and clairvoyant, had bought him a sweet black tea and a bacon roll.

'Get something solid inside your stomach,' Tank pleaded

'Ah will. Just give us a minute,' Henderson said.

'It must have been a good session, if you've not heard about Pedro.'

Henderson's hung-over brain scrambled to attention.

'Come again.'

Tank Williams used his best court voice. 'Peter (Pedro) Wilson was shot dead in the Woodend pub on Saturday night.'

'Thank fuck for that. Ah thought it was never going to happen,' Henderson said.

Tank expanded on the carnage at the scene of crime. 'It's a miracle nobody else was killed – thirty six casualties, that's a quiet Auld Firm match,' Tank stressed as Henderson struggled to take in the information. 'Quite a few skirmishes broke out - most injuries were down to flying glass. Two separate shotguns were fired at the pub's windows, so we know there were at least three shooters in attendance.'

Henderson stretched his eyes and his gaping mouth. 'Is anybody in the frame?'

'No, but a seventeen year old lassie suffocated under the weight of three tables during the mayhem ..... Luckily they resuscitated her.'

Henderson mulled over the information. Pedro Wilson was a miracle. He should have been done in so many times, it defied odds.

'So who have you been slumming it with?' Tank asked cheerily. 'Anybody I know?'

'I slummed alone – and I slummed at home.'

Tank's dramatic sigh showed his misgivings.

'I thought she was away for the weekend', Henderson wearily rolled his eyes, 'Ah don't know if it's somebody serious she's seeing, but she came back early --- and --- .'

'So you made a mistake, Mark.'

51

Henderson expanded. 'I made a mistake - it's a mistake I'll have to listen to for the foreseeable future'

Further explanation was unnecessary. Tank Williams was well aware of Henderson's tendency for the occasional bender. 'Try and eat the roll at least, and I'll order you more coffee,' Tank said, and headed upstairs.

Henderson took half the advice and left half a bacon roll. He decided to have a snooze, as it would be an hour and a half before his girl detectives were due to brief him. Some of the smart arses in Stewart Street had already named them Mr Henderson's Girls. He fell asleep thinking of Marian MacCallum again.

*   *   *

Joe Ray was about to start his first ever real job today, approaching the age of forty one. The work wasn't technically legal, but Jim Cassidy had managed to OK it with Joe's Supervision Officer.

Joe felt a bit overdressed for the task ahead. Everything he was wearing was brand new. He'd get Jim Cassidy to stump up for a pair of overalls before he did a brush stroke. He liked his little pun. It gave him a good feeling for today. He felt hungry. Maybe that was down to the thought of hard graft. He kept scanning around, looking for a takeaway café or roll shop. He'd eaten earlier, so food wasn't a necessity. He quickened his pace and reported for duty two minutes late.

Cassidy seemed a touch nervy when he welcomed Joe into his house, but Joe was shrewd enough to realise that might be put down to his own paranoia. A lifer consorting with a retired prison officer - it just wasn't right.

Cassidy calmed Joe's mind, explaining, 'I'm a bit ring-rusty at entertaining. I've not had many visitors lately.'

'Entertaining? What are you going to do Jim, juggle?' Joe joked nervously.

Cassidy laughed, louder than necessary, but the laugh did the trick. The ice was broken.

'I might do the juggling act after I've rustled up breakfast.' Cassidy motioned Joe into the living room and shouted information from the kitchen. 'There's a paper next to the telly.'

Joe picked up the Record and sat back, taking a cool, slow look at his surroundings. The flat looked beautiful. It certainly didn't look in need of an overhaul. Maybe other parts of the flat were shabby or had a garish colour scheme. Maybe the old guy was just lonely, or maybe Joe was being teed up for some dodgy proposal. Fuck sake, relax, he remonstrated with himself. He hadn't even started working yet and already his mind was off on some iffy diversion.

When Jim Cassidy brought the food in, Joe was standing by the huge, triple window casting an admiring gaze at the approach of DC Nell Hannah into Jim Cassidy's building

'Who's she?' Joe asked.

'She's one of the students down below,' Cassidy answered. 'Wait till you see the other two.'

'Well, I'm not sure how much painting you want me to do, Jim, but rest assured, I will stretch it out.'

Cassidy placed the tray of food on the table and said, 'C'mon, get this down your neck'.

*   *   *

Margaret Logan wrung the dishcloth, and neatly folded it in half and hung it over the plate rack. She raised her voice as she passed the bathroom, 'Marian, we're out of coffee. I'll not be long.'

DC MacCallum never heard a word because she had her face pressed close to the shower head and was relishing every moment of a long-overdue hot shower.

Margaret ignored the small grocer's shop at the end of her road and headed further afield to Gregg's the bakers. She purchased an assortment of cakes for her house guests; they weren't police, they were her guests.

On the way back to the flat, Margaret's head was filled with the dilemma of which of the cakes she should choose for herself. She could make a start on her favourite right now and end the debate there and then. On the verge of calling herself a selfish cow, she spotted a homeless guy walking towards her.

He had the mandatory shabby white blanket, rolled up roughly, protruding from under his left arm. His hood was up, giving him the appearance of a leper. She decided he was due a cake and some of the loose change crowding her purse. Christ, she thought, I might know him. As the man got closer, Margaret stooped slightly, trying to see under the hood.

The jar of coffee fell from her hands and smashed on the ground, scattering granules everywhere, as Margaret was felled by a blanket.

The homeless man bent over his prostrate victim, frantically trying to wrap the blanket back around the small length of scaffolding pole it was meant to conceal. He knelt on Margaret's chest and felt her neck for a pulse.

Across the street, an old man, walking his West Highland White Terrier, screamed weakly, 'No, no —stop.' His pleas were ignored, so he desperately tried to tether the dog to a bollard barring a private parking space. The old boy shouted 'Help' like a stuck record. Abruptly, he changed tack. Remembering people take more notice of the word "fire", he combined the two, 'Help – Fire,' his low voice hoarse but constant.

The assailant's response was to calmly make sure his hood and baseball cap covered his face. He wedged the blanket under his right arm and began dragging the girl by her left trouser leg towards the Escort van with its motor running.

DC Marian MacCallum was adjusting her dressing gown when she spotted the incident in the street. She grabbed for her mobile and rushed out the door. In the hallway, she stopped momentarily and quickly called for help. If she had been a split second earlier, she would have seen Joe Ray pull the door of 39 Roselea Gardens closed behind him.

As soon as Joe reached the pavement, he had walked slap bang into the middle of an altercation. Joe never even thought about the consequences. Instinctively he grabbed at the man's arm and tried to free the woman from its grasp. This action gave Margaret's assailant added momentum and he spun round and thrust the scaffolding pipe hard against Joe's Adam's apple. Joe lost consciousness as he fell on top of Margaret Logan.

*   *   *

With consciousness, came an awareness that Joe's first stab at real work had not gone particularly well. As soon as the paramedics got him to stand up unaided, he was placed under arrest.

DCI Henderson, rudely awoken from his slumber, hollered explicit instructions at the duty desk: 'Get DC Hannah on her mobile and tell her to get her arse back to the flat pronto.'

'What's her number?' was the droll response from the desk.

'Check your list, dickhead,' Henderson growled.

As Henderson approached the scene, he gave an extremely irate Jim Cassidy an assurance that he would see him shortly and put him in the picture. He entered the flat and saw DC MacCallum sitting on the sofa with a protective arm around Margaret.

Luckily, Margaret Logan's face wasn't badly marked. Her main concern seemed to be the state of her hair. However, the ambulance crew wanted to get her to hospital straight away.

'I don't know who he was,' Margaret said, shaking her head rhythmically.

'It's alright, I believe you,' Henderson said, as he leaned over and whispered into DC MacCallum's ear. 'You go with her in the ambulance, keep a couple of uniform near and keep your mobile nearer.' As they left, he nodded to Margaret, 'We'll talk later.'

DCI Henderson turned to the officers left standing in the living room. 'Start asking questions, I'll take care of Mr Cassidy up above.'

The old detective stood alone, checking himself in the living room mirror to make sure he wasn't smiling. He was a happy man. Somebody had shown a hand. He had his suspicions, but for the moment, they didn't really matter. He knew for definite now, that Caroline's murder was no random event, and NOW he had justification for the manpower this enquiry required.

*   *   *

Jim Cassidy opened his front door to be confronted by 'What the fuck's Joe Ray doing here?'

Henderson barged his way in.

'Because I invited him,' Cassidy screamed. 'He's a guest in my house. You, Detective Chief Inspector Henderson, are not.'

There followed what could be best described as a Mexican stand-off as both men huffed and puffed. The impasse was resolved when they decided to huff and puff sitting down. Cassidy grumpily offered to make some tea and Henderson grumpily admitted he might drink some.

*   *   *

Mark Henderson's head was full of too many questions. He told his driver to stop for a moment. He needed a breather, time to think. Circumstances meant he hadn't found out how the weekend had gone. He'd instructed his DCs to bring up the topic of Cornel Wagner with Margaret. How they broached the subject was left to their discretion.

Cornel Wagner ran the saunas for JJ McGuire. Every hooker, pimp and regular John in Glasgow knew that. Now Henderson was making his way to interview Joe Ray, McGuire's former partner in crime. Suddenly, the murder investigation was starting to fit together too easily. The biggest name on Glasgow's crime scene was on the lid of the jigsaw puzzle. Fuck, he didn't even need to nibble any ends to get the pieces to fit. It was frightening how quickly things change. While he was trying to nap the edge off a hangover, a static case had taken off like a rocket.

*   *   *

Joe sat still, praying that the girl he'd tried to help might return the compliment. He'd known just over three weeks of freedom in twenty years and now it looked like he was going back inside for who knows

55

how long. "Indeterminate." Fuck, he hated that word. He knew he was innocent, but what did that matter?

Henderson entered the room and immediately helped himself to one of the ciggies on the table. The detective's failure to turn the tape recorder on and the fact that he was alone gave Joe optimism.

'Why were you at Jim Cassidy's house?'

'I've told your mates, I've lost count how many times.......'

'Listen if you want to walk out of here today, you'd better start telling me.'

The tension eased a little and Joe's brain regained its capacity for logical thought. 'How's the lassie doing?' he asked.

'We're not sure yet. Are you going to answer my question?'

'Look, Jim Cassidy phoned me last Friday and asked me if I fancied some work - painting his house.' Confronted only by silence, Joe carried on, 'So I started this morning, I was going to B&Q, when I saw this maniac dragging the lassie along the ground'

'And?'

'Fuck sake, I tried to do the right thing. No, correction, I did do the right thing here. Look at my neck.' Joe stretched the collar of his top down, revealing evidence of injury.

'We might let the doctor have a wee look at that later.'

The bruising to Joe's neck was extensive but he was feeling no pain. Fear of incarceration was an excellent painkiller.

'So do you know the lassie?'

'No.'

'You sure about that?'

'I don't know any lassies. They were a bit scarce, where I've been.'

'Aye, but you might know this one. Her name's Margaret Logan. Ring any bells?'

'No, like I told you, I don't know her.'

'Her sister was murdered a couple of weeks ago, just about the same time you got out of prison, so we've been keeping a wee eye on Margaret, just in case somebody tries to murder her.'

Joe stared at the detective in disbelief, blotting out thoughts that he was being fitted up.

'We're good that way,' Henderson continued. 'Were you impressed by our fantastic response time, Mr Ray?'

'I don't know, I don't know, I can't remember.'

'We're quicker than the US Ca – val –ree. If Big John Wayne was alive today he'd be one big jealous bastard, eh Joe?'

56

Joe clammed up, as every documented miscarriage of justice sought houseroom inside his head.

'You don't know the sister either? Her name was Caroline?'

'No,' Joe screamed.

Henderson sat down, adopting a quieter approach. 'You see, Joe – it's not that I don't believe you. It's the nature of my job not to believe people like you. I believe Jim Cassidy, Ah've known him a long time. He tells me you're a baddie who's trying to be a goodie.'

'That's true,' Joe said.

'But other bad names from the past are cropping up,' Henderson whispered.

'What do you mean?'

'Let me explain. Margaret Logan has been under strict police surveillance since her wee sister was murdered. This morning Margaret is attacked in the street and a bad name from the past, YOURS, foils "her abduction". This city always surprises me, Joe. It's not often a triple murderer comes to a damsel's rescue.'

Joe's eyes couldn't disagree with Henderson's assessment.

'Then, there's another even bigger surprise. Margaret Logan is the niece of the late Owen MacNee. You remember Owny don't you, Joe? He was a bad name, just like you. You remember what you did to Owny, don't you Joe?'

Joe's head dropped onto the interview table, pole-axed by a memory.

Henderson carried on, 'Joe, do you think if big Owny was alive that some low-order piece of shite would snuff the life out of his niece?'

Joe wished he was back in prison, back in solitary, back somewhere, anywhere, just not here.

DCI Henderson spoke precisely for maximum effect. 'Big, bad name number three, the biggest, baddest name in the fucking business, John Joseph Mc – fucking - Guire, your auld buddy, partner in crime. I mean the result you and McGuire got with Big Owny was absolutely outrageous.'

'That was over twenty years ago,' Joe protested.

'It doesn't matter how long ago it was, it's fucking fresh in my mind.'

Joe pulled at his hair saying, 'I don't know what to say, I don't know what you want to hear, I just don't know. I've not seen JJ in half a lifetime....'

'Yes, you have, Joe, yes you have.' Henderson stood up and shushed Joe quiet saying, 'I'm off for a good shite and maybe a bite to eat. I suggest that you use that time to become super-plausible.'

* * *

The Shettleston Health Centre waiting room seemed normal for a Monday afternoon. Behind the reception counters, some clerical staff had remained long after their shift had finished; they were hoping to catch a glimpse of notoriety.

At 2:47pm, three men entered the waiting room. Dr Donovan was standing in front of the reception desk. 'Could you come this way, Mr McGuire?' he asked quietly

Big Yogi and Johnny V sat down on the comfy seats in the waiting room and stared benignly at the reception staff. Johnny V leaned forward, reaching towards the magazines and asked casually, 'Are you OK with an OK, Yogi or would you prefer a Closer?'

The big man's eyes glazed over the magazine covers.

'I've already read them.'

V reached over and pulled out an issue of Heat, sandwiched inside another magazine. Big Yogi's demeanour brightened.

McGuire took a seat and stared up for a moment at the tall, gaunt looking doctor with the tangible Belfast accent. 'The wife says I might be able to talk to you - says I might get on OK with you.' Dr Donovan remained silent, with his pen hovering over McGuire's medical records. McGuire carried on. 'She speaks very highly of you, to me that is. Ah hope for your sake its no' a wee crush she's got, eh Dr Donovan?'

The doctor decided not to respond, and lifted the thin folder containing McGuire's medical records and took a quick glance through them.

Stunned, he turned to his patient, asking, 'You were last here in April 1979? Sorry, you couldn't have been - we weren't built then.'

'It was the auld surgery on Old Shettleston Road,' McGuire cut in.

'So how is the verucca? Cleared up all right?' the doctor asked.

'Wonderful, Doctor - I hope you don't think I'm a hypochondriac, but it's something else.'

The Doctor leaned forward in his chair, apparently more at ease after his lame attempt at humour. 'It's remarkable really, and extremely refreshing to find someone who hasn't visited a doctor's surgery in twenty five years.' He lowered his tone. 'There are faces in that waiting room I see more than my wife's.'

McGuire pulled his seat closer. 'Ah take it you know who I am.'

'I am well aware.'

'Everything's true, even the lies,' McGuire smiled, then sat bolt upright and asked, 'I tell you what's wrong with me doctor, is the drill still the same?'

Dr Donovan simply smiled in reply.

'The wife has been on my case a lot at the moment. She thinks I'm going gaga.'

Dr Donovan remained muted, forcing McGuire to reluctantly carry on, 'Says I'm forgetting a lot of things, says I'm different, and says I'm....'

'What do you say, Mr McGuire?'

'I say I'm frustrated, niggled, narked with myself.' McGuire opened his eyes wide, relieved to be talking. 'I'm embarrassed - I couldn't do my wee boy's sum the other day. My head's jumping about all over the place. The past keeps interrupting me.'

'What was the sum?' the doctor interrupted.

'Twelve divided by four. I knew the answer, but I just did not know how to work it out.'

'What is the answer?'

'Three, the answer's three.'

'I'll have to ask you certain other questions, Mr McGuire?'

McGuire raised an eyebrow.

'How's your alcohol intake?'

'Extremely moderate and, as we're going down that path, my drug intake is non-existent. Apart from the stuff you read about in the papers, I lead a bit of a boring existence.'

'Have you suffered any head trauma?'

'Not that I'm aware of, doctor. I don't, personally, get physical these days.' McGuire pointed to his forehead.

'Have you had a heavy drink or drug dependency in your past?'

McGuire took his time responding. 'How can I put this, doctor? In my line of work, it's imperative you be in control. Drugs impede control. I have a few select experts willing to try them out for me. Did you know they used to call me Mr Switzerland? That was Glasgow's sardonic reference to the amount of pharmaceuticals I supplied the city with.'

'Mr McGuire, please don't tell me anymore than I necessarily need to know.'

'Sorry, doctor, I did not mean to bring back bad memories.'

The doctor looked troubled momentarily, but said nothing.

'I know all about the difficulties you had in West Belfast.'

Dr Donovan stood up and made a piss-poor attempt at showing McGuire the door.

McGuire did not bother to look up. 'Please sit down, Doctor. We know this consultation's over when I say it is.'

Dr Donovan complied.

'I've been reliably informed that my wife has discussed my situation with you three times.'

'True,' Dr Donovan said.

*   *   *

"Licence revoked". Those two words kept barging to the front of Joe Ray's tortured mind. Occasionally, they'd be replaced with "Owny's payback". Twenty one years after the event, Owen MacNee had his revenge.

There was no way Joe could possibly have seen this coming, even though he'd been praying for it, every night asking for a way of making amends, asking for the chance. Joe racked his brains trying to remember Henderson's exact words.

'If you want the chance of walking out of here, today, you'd better start talking, and 'you'd better be super-plausible.' That was it. But why believe Henderson, why believe a copper?

Joe's predicament was absurd. He couldn't even lie. He couldn't be plausible, far less super-plausible. He'd absolutely nothing to bargain with because he hadn't really seen anything. All he'd seen was a pair of blue eyes. *Police are looking for a man with "blue eyes".* He sniggered painfully.

Twenty years ago, Joe could have thrown Henderson a name, put some poor bastard in the frame for this and be plausible enough to get the law off his back. Now, his mind was blank, he had no names, no hand to play. He'd forced himself to forget about the street, shun the rumour mill in prison. That was where the super-grasses and the super-grassed bleated noisily about honour and told each other Jackanory stories. Joe purposely stood back from hearing other people's truths, because one day it dawned on him that the most lies told in prison were the ones prisoners told themselves.

Now Joe thought about his own truth and making amends for a crime he'd gotten away with. JJ McGuire had gotten away with it too, but then again, he got away with everything. "No Strings" Owny MacNee endured four days of torture before the ambulance men found him crawling half-naked from a derelict, third floor two-apartment in Lilybank. The ambulance reached him at around chucking out time on a

60

cold wet Thursday night. When they got to him, blood was leaking profusely from horrendous anal injuries. JJ McGuire had enjoyed keeping his promise.

Sometimes you get what you pray for, Joe grimaced, wondering if Big Owny was enjoying his predicament from beyond the grave. Now at least Owny's name could replace the question mark written in blood on his amends list.

Chapter Ten

Roselea Gardens had slowly returned to some semblance of order. Jim Cassidy had seen Margaret Logan returning from hospital. With her were the two woman detectives he'd assumed were fellow students. He decided to allow them twenty minutes to settle in before paying a visit. He was more interested in getting information about Joe's situation, but he did have genuine concerns about the injured girl's welfare. It was that "getting old" thing again - that was the problem. That dreaded thought of becoming a pain in the arse, of feeling like an interloper, which was really just a polite way of saying, nosey bugger.

He was thinking of going for counselling. One minute he saw it as a brave move, something he needed. He just wanted to tell someone how much he missed her, how much he missed hearing her breathe, how much he missed her taking up more than her fair share of the bed. How much he missed her scrutinising his attempts at cooking. The next minute, the counselling idea was just another example of how far he'd let himself go. He needed to boot his own arse into gear.

'Oh sod it,' he sighed and phoned Stewart Street again. The unexpected answer threw him off tack. He'd been looking for a bit of an argument and had even rehearsed the list of questions he was about to ask.

'Joe Ray is no longer in custody,' the Desk Sergeant said in a wearied, monotonous tone.

'Why was I not told about this earlier?'

'We are not at liberty to disclose that information unless you are a memb...........'

'Is the robotic attitude really necessary?' Cassidy complained and waited for a reply, until he realised the line was dead. He grabbed his mobile and his car keys.

*   *   *

Joe decided against asking the cops for directions back to Roselea Gardens. He rummaged in his pockets and retrieved the all-day ticket purchased this morning. He finger-pressed it until it looked somewhat legible. On the verge of boarding a number 237 First Bus, he heard the blast of Jim Cassidy's horn.

'You OK?' Cassidy asked as Joe clicked the seatbelt into place.

Joe nodded, snorted a lungful of air and asked, 'So do you think they're going to put me back inside?'

'I don't know for sure, Joe.' Then Jim Cassidy spoke with a little more conviction. 'Not if I can help it. Look, try not to worry, I'll make a few phone calls.'

'The strange thing is this, Jim, I don't think I am worried - I'm not feeling sorry for myself - I might be as well be back inside.'

'Do you really mean that?'

'I don't know what I mean. I tried to help a lassie, that's all, just stop what was happening from happening. Then you find there's a connection – like it's meant – like your requests have been granted. Banged up for a couple of years for doing the right thing, knowing it's deserved, knowing there's a sense to it.

'You're not making any sense here, son.'

'Oh there's a sense to it Jim, that's for sure. Harry used to say "think about the shit you got away with".

'Don't take his advice here, son. He was institutionalised, he'd a different agenda.'

'It was meant, that's what I'm talking about. He was right. Harry was smarter than anybody I've known. Why be out, why put yourself through this shite?'

'You're no' Harry! Give yourself a break here, you've had a horrendous day, but you did do the right thing and I know that.' Cassidy then lowered his voice again. 'I believe you and I've got belief in you.'

Joe's head and heart struggled to find a response to those words. 'That lassie's related to a ghost, somebody I helped fuck up, years ago, before I went inside'

'Well, if you can make amends, then make amends.'

'He died years ago.'

'If you can make amends, make amends,' Cassidy persisted.

Joe looked around at Cassidy. He had respected the man for years, now he was beginning to realise why.

'Jim, do you think that Henderson will pull me in again?'

'It's a real possibility. He's trying to find out who murdered that lassie's wee sister. However, he'll know you could not have murdered the sister because there's at least twenty prison staff that can testify where you were that day.'

'That could go for nothing if they want to fit you up.'

'Henderson's not like that.'

'They're all like that, Jim.'

'I worked in prisons a long time, never heard anybody claim Henderson fitted them up.'

'Well, I'll take your word for that, Jim.' Joe's expression lightened up a bit.

'Joe, why don't we forget the painting and decorating lark today and I'll take you on a wee tour of the city?'

Joe consented and settled in his seat.

'I'll talk and you can try listening,' Cassidy joked

'What are you trying to say?'

That's exactly what they did as they sped along the Clydeside, through the new parts of the Gorbals and then onto the new quayside luxury apartments at Finnieston. Everywhere Joe looked, he saw rejuvenated parts of the city.

'Do you know where you are?' Cassidy sported a wide, cynical smile.

'No,' was the bewildered response.

'The Broomielaw.'

Joe was stunned.

'Remember Betty's Bar?' Cassidy said, bringing the car to a standstill and looking to his left. 'That's where it used to be.'

Joe followed Cassidy's gaze along the impressive riverside apartments. He'd his own memories of Betty's Bar, Sweaty Betty's or Swee B's as it was sometimes called. Fuck, it was infamous. It was full of prostitutes, cut-throat sailors from every port on the planet and, the lowest of the low, journalists. You could get hooky gear from five continents in there in five minutes; it had also served as a buckshee Bureau de Change to sailors from South America and Eastern Europe.

Now that Broomielaw was gone: those gigantic black, wooden, dingy warehouses - flattened, erased. Replaced with new money, virgin white apartments and blue, smoked-glass fronted office blocks had taken root on the banks of the old river.

'Look around. Things can change, eh? Even the worse characters can reinvent themselves.'

Joe looked around at all those pristine white facades, knowing the same old shit was going down. People's throats were being slit with the touch of a computer button. But he was impressed. The Broomielaw looked respectable. There was no getting away from that fact - the old place had dressed up nice.

'What are you thinking about, Joe?'

'Harry.'

'Why?'

'Christ, what would the world have looked like, if he'd got out?'

'Different planet. But, Harry never wanted out.'

Joe nodded and looked ahead. He could see they were heading for the old Clyde Tunnel, something at last familiar. Something was niggling at him and he knew what it was. He was jealous, jealous that the old prison officer must have been really close with Harry.

Joe castigated himself for being so petty, so fucking childish and struggled hard, keeping his emotions in check.

'Did you know the wee man was a really good football player? Should've played for the Celtic?'

'No – he never mentioned it,' Joe said, feigning interest.

'Played for Bridgeton Waverley Amateurs. Don't let the name fool you. They were Parkhead through and through.'

'He told me he enjoyed playing fitba' when he was young.'

'Should've played for Celtic. Did you know he was playing on Celtic's top lip?' Cassidy said with a knowing glance and a wink.

'Eh?' Joe looked perplexed.

'Playing right underneath Celtic's nose – the Waverley played at New Barrowfield - Celtic's old training ground.' Cassidy gave a heavy sigh.

'Thank God you never took up a career in sports journalism.'

'I thought that was quite good.'

'No, Jim, that was piss-poor.'

Cassidy feigned injury holding his hands to his heart.

'Could you please keep your hands on the wheel, Jim? You've got the makings of a half decent taxi driver there.'

'I should have let you get the bus.'

'You're better than the bus drivers.'

'That's no' much of a compliment, but I'll take it just the same.'

'So how come he never made it with the Celtic?'

'Army!'

'Army?'

'National Service; the Army started a lot of good football players' careers – but it finished Harry's.'

'Finished his marriage, as well, didn't it?'

'Aye - and Shepton Mallet nearly finished him.'

'Was that the Glasshouse?'

'Aye. Military prisons were brutal and they frowned on lewd conduct.'

'Frowned the shit out of you, I'll bet,' Joe surmised.

'He spent eighteen months there – so did the boyfriend.'

Joe looked annoyed at the inference, but Cassidy stood his ground. 'C'mon Joe, Gavin Goodwin was his boyfriend.'

Joe thought for a moment, and then asked, 'Do you think if they'd never met up again, things would have been a lot different?'

'Four people might still be alive,' Cassidy said.

'He told me that Goodwin had followed him from England.'

'Harry would have gone off with another guy at some time.'

Again Joe looked hurt.

'That's what he told me, son, he would know, eh?'

Joe stared ahead.

'How do we go about reinventing Joe Ray?' Cassidy grinned.

Joe laughed. The laugh wasn't cynical, but it sounded that way. For the moment, he was free. If they revoked his licence, it was meant to be. He would accept it as Owny MacNee's "fuck you" from beyond the grave.

Chapter Eleven

McGuire never believed his own hype. He knew nature was a far crueller killer than he could ever be. He thought cancer could not take any more from his mother, but cancer did. He would not let her look in the mirror. He became her mirror. He told her the opposite of what he saw. *I don't want people being mirrors around me. I want true mirrors, I want a real friend, I want Joe.* Then he thought back to the day when he had to hurt someone so that he would not have to hurt Joe.

It was the day that auld Mr Jack left James Wallace in charge of the classroom. He gave Wallace permission to write up the initials of anyone who misbehaved on the blackboard. Offenders would be dealt with on the teacher's return.

Wallace was an entirely different entity from everyone else at school. He was fascinated by science and all things technical, and he also excelled at mathematics. Wallace was the really clever guy at school who did the really stupid thing and wrote John Joseph McGuire's initials on the blackboard.

Six minutes after school that day, Wallace stood silent; in shock and tied to a tree. The implements of torture lay used, broken and strewn all around. They had all came from Wallace's crammed briefcase. He'd been pierced with every pencil, pen, compass and set-square he possessed. His precious schoolwork was destroyed, as were his library books.

'I told you I would hurt you,' McGuire said. But Wallace could not speak and would not speak for a very long time. McGuire continued. 'I think I'll scrape your eyeballs out.'

'I'll never tell a living soul,' Joe said.

'Good,' McGuire said.

The torture stopped and James Wallace kept his eyesight.

*   *   *

Whitey was late but he knew his "dinner date" wasn't going anywhere. The new suit's second fitting had taken longer than expected. He was impressed by his own reflection in the shop windows he passed on the Maryhill Road. A persona needs cultivating, he thought as he turned into St George's Cross and entered the newly refurbished Cross Café, now re-titled Rejuven8. Whitey thought using the number 8 in the name was cool. The man sitting at table five did not.

'Vhat happened?'

Whitey could not be arsed with the pimp's fucked up accent today and snapped back.

' Are you telling me the full story here?'

'Course I am. You were given a simple task.'

Whitey reached over and took the older man's manicured, emaciated hands in his. 'There was a wee surprise when I tried to grab her.'

'Vee surprise?'

'Aye, not that vee actually, and we'll not mention the alarming amount of police in the vicinity of that wee cow's house.'

'I told you about the possibility of surveillance.'

Whitey tightened his grip on Wagner's frail hands, performing his version of the polygraph machine. He was feeling and looking out for the slightest variation in pulse or facial response to the information he was about to feed Cornel Wagner.

'An old pal of McGuire's stopped me getting her.'

'Who?'

'Name's Joe Ray. Heard of him?'

Wagner broke free from Whitey's grip. 'You sure it vas Joe Ray?'

'Double sure, Mr Wagner - Mr McGuire introduced me to him last week.'

'This changes everything,' Wagner flustered.

'Too right, it changes everything,' Whitey agreed.

'You think he might have recognised you?'

'I would not think so. I had my hood up. Soon as he put a hand on me - I decked the cunt.'

'It could make things really difficult, complicate everything,' Wagner said more to himself than the killer who sat opposite him.

'Could it be a coincidence?'

'I can't afford to believe in coincidences.'

'Then just fucking kill her, like I said you should have, and I'll fucking kill him as well,' Whitey beamed.

Cornel Wagner slowly pondered his next move and left Whitey with these words, 'I have to go away for a day or two. I'll call you later. Be available, please.'

Whitey shrugged, rolled his eyes and thought about ordering an espresso.

*　　　*　　　*

On Edinburgh's Royal Mile, not far from Advocate's Close, sits a quaint tartan affair of a Scottish restaurant called The Wee Windaes. Secluded away from the small windows, sat two men well known in the legal fraternity, seemingly enjoying lunch. Lord Bullock was advocating that Scotland's leading solicitor, Thomas Brodie, plump for the Cockaleekie soup.

The meeting was casual; they were discussing final preparations for the upcoming Bullock enquiry into abuse in care homes throughout Scotland since 1975. The decision to make 1975 the cut-off point was twofold. Firstly, perpetrators of abuse were less likely to claim they couldn't remember the dates in question and secondly, though highly unlikely, a certain amount of sympathy could be engendered in the public eye as a result of vociferous questioning of OAPs.

Rameses Bullock was deemed an excellent choice to handle an enquiry of this magnitude. Thomas Brodie had no role in the enquiry. His presence at the table had more to do with who he knew, rather than what he knew.

'I guarantee it will collapse. So will he do it?' Bullock whispered calmly.

Brodie nodded towards the back of the room, making eye contact with a tall, lean man sitting alone at a small table, overcrowded with bottles of salad dressing and salt and pepper dishes.

The man rose and made his way over to their table. He looked like a garish American tourist decked out in loud checked shorts and an absolute screamer of a tartan bonnet. However, he seemed far too pale to come from that continent.

Up close and personal, Maurice Golightly measured six feet eight inches tall, mostly made up of sinew and bone. Everything about him was angular and stretched. It was almost impossible to make out the colour of his deep-set hooded eyes, and both decks of long gnarled teeth jostled for better position under taut pencil-thin lips.

He stopped in front of the table, stooped and stared deep into Rameses Bullock's eyes for little more than a second and then headed downstairs to the cramped gents' toilet next to the kitchen.

Lord Bullock struggled to keep his top set of dentures inside his head and exploded at Brodie. 'He's here. You actually brought him here!'

'His request - he's not the type you refuse.' Brodie shrugged

Lord Bullock started sweating profusely, giving Brodie some cause for alarm, as he dreaded having to call for medical assistance. Bullock gradually regained his composure.

'Does he need a photograph?'

'Unnecessary. He knows him of old - and he never forgets a face.'

69

Chapter Twelve

They'd discussed it, weighed up the options and came to a joint decision. If they needed anything, Jim Cassidy would get it. Joe Ray and B&Q did not get on. Joe thought the DIY superstore outlet still harboured a grudge against him. A long time ago, Joe was on the good end of a conveyor belt of hooky gear departing from their Thistle Street branch.

Joe was on his knees, undercoating the skirting boards in Jim Cassidy's spare bedroom. He didn't know it yet, but the retired prison officer was about to ask him if he fancied lodging here. However, the doorbell stopped that particular conversation before it got started.

Joe could hear female voices coming from the landing. Adjusting his position to hear better, he swung around on his knees, looked up and saw her. Cassidy peered over the girl's shoulder and said, 'I'll leave ye'se to it,' as he ushered DC MacCallum back into the kitchen.

Joe stood up awkwardly, wiping his hands on fresh white overalls. He hadn't really done enough yet to actually get his hands dirty. However, it gave him time to compose his thoughts. One thought was paramount. *She's absolutely beautiful.*

'I'm sorry you got arrested. Ah did try and tell them.'

'Don't worry about it. It happens,' he said.

'When did they let you out?'

'About quarter to three, I think. I'm not sure,' Joe mumbled and then almost as an afterthought asked, 'Are you OK?'

'Oh aye, nothing that a wee bit of good foundation can't fix'.

'Did they get the guy?'

'I don't think so. Marian's not said anything.' Margaret gestured towards the kitchen mouthing silently, 'Marian's CID. Watch what you're saying.'

'You don't know him?' Joe said quietly.

Margaret shook her head and enquired, 'He hurt you, didn't he?'

'That's another thing that.......'

'Happens,' Margaret finished Joe's sentence and they laughed nervously.

Joe stretched open the collar of his polo-style top, revealing a healthy bruise travelling from the left side of his neck down to the hollow of his breastbone.

'Could a good foundation fix that?' he asked.

Margaret Logan stepped forward, undoing the two top buttons of her white lacy blouse. She tucked the collar inside the garment exposing her neck and shoulders to show Joe her injuries. She turned as gracefully as a toy ballerina in a music box, exhibiting the dulling yellow and blue marks that her assailant had left.

Joe did not know if her scent was cheap or expensive. All he knew was that her aroma was exquisite. He did not know if she was a good person or a bad person. He just knew she was exquisite. One thing he was sure of was this. Something was happening. It might not be love, but it was the best he'd felt in a long time. His eyes traced the small blonde hairs that tapered into the nape of her neck. He felt he was coming over all Christopher Lee, fighting tremendously hard to prevent his mouth from making contact with her neck. There was a definite stirring in his groin, and he was becoming jittery and agitated. He wasn't entirely sure if he mentioned something about the colouring of her bruising, but he could not be certain because he was lost in a good place.

She turned around to face him and, as they made eye contact, Joe went bright red.

'Are you OK?' she asked.

Joe didn't know how to respond, so he went redder.

'Are you OK?' she asked again. When there was a lack of reply or even a visual response, she hollered, 'Mr Cassidy, is he alright?'

Jim Cassidy hurried in from the kitchen and quickly succeeded in making things worse.

'I think you've given him a "reddy", hen,' he surmised and DC MacCallum readily agreed with that assessment.

'Why's he got a "reddy?"' Margaret asked, genuinely astonished. 'Why's he got a "reddy", Marian?'

DC MacCallum was reluctant to say anything and looked to Jim Cassidy, hoping his next answer proved better than his first. It did not.

'I think he fancies you, love. That's obvious, but he just doesn't know how to say so. Therefore he's getting all hot and bothered, trying to hide his feelings, eh?' Cassidy said, seeking validation from DC MacCallum. All Cassidy got in reply from one half of the police surveillance team was a look of pained disbelief.

'Fancies me, he fancies me. Why does he fancy me?'

Joe Ray barged past them and stumbled his way through the hallway. He closed the toilet door behind him and locked it, sat down, placed his hands on his head and willed himself to die.

* * *

Grassing people up never bothered him. What's the point of having information and not using it? All that honour among thieves was puerile.

71

He'd learned that fact of life, very early on, when Slab Martin offered up Joe Ray's head on a paper plate. Everything came down to practicalities. You're only as good as your last shift, Slab Martin had stated, and Joe's last shift had been a particularly poor one. That cost Joe a minimum of twenty years and let John Joseph McGuire see clean through all that gangland, bravado bullshit about buying judges and juries - getting the super lawyer on board, who elicits the technicality that gets you a Not Proven or a reduced stretch. The only reason you got off with anything in this game was because you offered the Law something better.

He intended flooding the market with what he had. The Police clear-up rates would be that good they'd come under the same suspicion the jobless figures had under Margaret Thatcher.

McGuire knew he was spitting out the dummy, but he still relished the thought of the mayhem that would ensue. However, right now, he had to think about the future, look at the bigger picture and make sure that his wife and children could not be GOT.

*   *   *

Nell Hannah let Henderson into the flat and followed him into the kitchen to join their colleague. It was 8.55 and just over two hours since Margaret had mentioned a name.

'Well done, ladies,' Henderson said. 'I'll say a quick hello to our girl before we get down to it.'

'It'll have to be quick,' MacCallum said. 'She's just about to watch Bad Girls.'

'Irony's wonderful, isn't it?' He smiled and made his way to the living room.

Margaret sat cross-legged on the sofa with the remote perched precariously on her knee.

'How are you?'

'I'm OK,' she smiled pensively. 'I know the girls are working, but the company is nice.'

The old detective approached her and tenderly placed the knuckle of his hand on her cheek. 'Enjoy your programme, darling. I'll speak to you later.'

*   *   *

He widened his eyes a little more, and then grimaced for effect. The two young detectives looked at each other; willing the other one to speak. DC Hannah ended the confusion and explained the events earlier that evening.

'The television was on but we weren't really watching.'

72

'We were getting the dinner ready. It was just on,' MacCallum chimed in.

Nell Hannah scowled at her colleague.

'I've not got a problem with the TV being on. Just tell me who Uncle Vanya is?' Henderson demanded.

MacCallum obliged. 'Lord Rameses Bullock; his face was on screen, something to do with the enquiry, I think.'

Henderson's head was a blur. *Don't get too ahead of yourself here – nothing's certain.*

'She just said: "That's Connie's Uncle Vanya",' Nell Hannah stated.

'By the time we'd got the sound turned up, the item had finished'.

'Did you question her?'

'Marian asked her how she knew him. And she said he was a relative of Connie's.'

'Who is Connie?'

'Somebody she knew years ago. She said she wasn't even sure now if Connie was still alive'

'Did you ask how she knew Connie?'

'We felt it best to talk to you first, sir,' DC Hannah said.

'It was a joint decision,' MacCallum piped in.

'A nice joint reply,' Henderson smiled to himself. 'Whoever she is, we'll get to her later.' He screwed his face up, questioning himself, 'Uncle Vanya?'

DC Hannah threw her hat in the ring, 'He's the main character in one of Chekhov's plays.'

'Really,' Henderson said.

MacCallum recognised Henderson's sarcasm instantly. Nell Hannah did not.

'Yes sir,' she paused, before saying in a hushed tone, 'I can't really picture Margaret knowing that.'

Henderson and MacCallum exchanged "no shit Sherlock" glances.

'Why don't I look up the Net and get a recent photograph of Bullock and we can take it from there, boss?' MacCallum said confidently.

'No, not right now.' Henderson scratched at his head. 'Did she give the impression she knew who he was, what he did?'

'Like I said, boss, she just recognised his face on screen.'

Henderson's mood became sombre. 'Listen, we can't tell anyone about this, not right now.'

"Mr Henderson's Girls" struggled to match their boss's hang-dog expression. They were salivating at the magnitude of this case.

Henderson made his way into the living room, determined to keep an eye on the "bad girls", both on screen and off. He sat down next to Margaret on the white leather sofa. Far from recoiling from his presence, she moved closer to the old copper. He smiled fondly at her, desperately hiding this thought. *By Christ you're in a world of TROUBLE, lassie.*

Chapter Thirteen

He felt good, and it showed. He'd worked far longer than he'd expected to. Jim Cassidy had proved a man of his word, never questioning Joe's work. A time-served tradesman would've gone about things differently and would have been far speedier. Joe was painstakingly diligent in the preparation of every surface that needed painted. This resulted in the room looking super-professional. And as he stood there rubbing margarine into his hands, he felt proud. He remembered back to when he had learned the margarine tip. The tip came from Nimble George, the tutor on the painting and decorating course. George's first day teaching in prison had got off to a bad start when he started rubbing a tiny amount of margarine into every pore and crevice on his hands. 'You'll thank me for this, boy,' he stressed nervously. 'Do this before you start and after you finish and you'll not have birds looking down their noses at your grubby hands when you're on a night out. Gloss and undercoat are really difficult to wash off.'

The majority of the class were lifers and they turned on him as one. 'Are you trying to be a pure bastart, eh?' and 'Are you taking the cunt out of us?' were just two questions asked by the class of twelve, circling their tutor. George made a bolt for it, neatly ducking under the pasting table and emerging on the other side of the room - hence the title, Nimble George.

Jim Cassidy caught George up at the workshop door and brought the wind-up to an end. 'You're no allowed to escape either, mate.'

Wee George turned out to be one of life's good guys and they all learned a lot from him. The quiet way he went about his work impressed the cons. 'I'm just showing you what somebody showed me,' he would say.

Joe made his way to the bathroom and passed Jim Cassidy.

'Is it OK if I have a look?'

'Sure, go ahead.' As he scrubbed his hands he heard Cassidy's appraisal.

'That's a job well done, Joe.'

Later as Joe relaxed, sucking slowly on a chilled Budweiser, he asked casually, 'Have ...... you seen the lassie?'

'What lassie?'

Joe refused the bait. 'Have you seen the lassie?'

'Oh, thee lassie......'

'Yes, have you seen thee lassie?'

'No,' said Jim.

'Oh,' said Joe.

The pause in the conversation seemed staged.

'Joe, are we talking about the same lassie?'

'I would presume so.'

'So we're talking about the lassie that made your face go red?'

'Yes, the lassie that made my face go red.'

'Aye, I've seen her. Sorry, I was getting that lassie mixed up with another lassie.'

'Did you talk to her?'

'Talk to whom?'

Joe Ray stood up. 'Jim, I'm in serious danger of my licence being revoked.'

'Why's that then?'

'Because Jim, I'm about to strangle you.'

'Get me a beer and I'll let you into a little secret.' Jim Cassidy smirked.

Joe reached inside the fridge and heard Jim say, 'I've asked her to come for her supper tomorrow night.'

Joe felt elated but kept his emotions in check until Jim said, 'She said yes.'

Joe Ray was made up, pumped up. Even the next attempted wind-up failed to deflate him. 'I'm thinking of maybe asking you to come along as well.'

As the evening progressed, the mood changed. Both men were more than happy in each other's company. They did not talk of extravagant things. Cassidy had quite a bit more to drink than Joe; however it was apparent that he could hold his liquor. Joe curbed the urge to get hammered.

'Have you ever been in love, son?' Cassidy asked.

'Should you not issue a warning with a question like that?'

Cassidy smiled one of those knowing, concerned smiles. 'I have son; you don't mind me talking like this do you?' Cassidy did not wait for a reply and carried on with a conversation he'd been planning since yesterday. 'I'm not trying to embarrass you here, Joe, and I'm not trying to sound like I'm Warren Beatty or - oh eh - I don't know - somebody who's a hit with the women.'

'Robbie Williams,' Joe offered, not sure the suggestion was a help or a hindrance.

'He'll do,' Cassidy accepted gratefully. 'I'll tell you I'm sixty five years of age and I've had sex with three women in my entire life. Does that surprise you?'

Joe quelled the comical quip.

'The first time I can hardly remember - eighteen - a friend of mine's mother took a wee shine to me at a Twenty first anniversary party - not exactly the kind of thing you brag about.'

Joe's face doubted the last remark and Cassidy countered with, 'Well, not in those days, anyway.'

Joe gulped some lager and swallowed hard. 'Jim, I was never exactly a Casanova myself, know what I mean, and I've been banged up for twenty years.'

'That's why we're having this - discussion,' Cassidy loudly exhaled.

'Are we having a discussion, Jim?' Joe's question lightened the mood just enough.

'We're having a perfect discussion, pal. The type where I'm speaking and you're listening.'

There were similarities between Jim Cassidy and Joe's old cellmate, Harry Lawson. They were around the same age and both men rarely raised their voices. When they did, prisoners paid attention.

'Are you ready to listen, Mr Ray?'

'Oh, yes. Indeed I am, Mr Cassidy'

'Do you think she's too young for you?'

Joe was dumbfounded by the question. He was expecting to get around to talking about Margaret Logan eventually. However, Cassidy had caught him on the hop and he meekly said one word, 'Yes.'

'My wife was ten years younger than me. She's dead and gone and I'm still here.'

'Aye, but that was different.'

'How's it different?'

Joe could not come up with a different, so Cassidy offered one to him.

'Is it because you've got a past? How do you know she's not got a past?'

'I've got history, the type that doesn't need embroidering.'

'You could put an advert in the lonely hearts - triple murderer seeks similar. Must have G.S.O.H.'

'I'm so glad you added that wee bit, Jim.'

'Listen son, you know what I'm talking about. You're not stupid.'

Joe slumped forward in his chair grasping his ankles in his hands. 'D'you think she'd go out with me if I asked?'

'There is a possibility. But - and it's a big but - you do have to ask.'

Joe raised his head optimistically. 'Any suggestions?' he ventured before bowing his head again.

'Take her to the pictures.'

Optimism and pessimism surfaced simultaneously on Joe's face. 'I'm not sure I like the pictures.'

'Listen, you don't have to like the pictures. You just have to be there.'

'What will we talk about?'

'You could talk about the picture you just watched.' On the verge of losing the plot completely, Jim Cassidy saw that Joe Ray just might be about to grasp the popular concept of a first date at the movies.

* * *

One floor below, DCI Henderson rummaged for his mobile. The silent and vibrate mode always scared the life out of him. The initials A S displayed on screen also scared him. This call could not be ignored. He took the call inside Margaret Logan's toilet.

'Why's there an echo?'

'I'm not quite sure, ma'am,' Henderson said, still unsure how to address his new boss.

Anne Swinton, the new Chief Constable of Strathclyde, spoke in a clipped East Coast twang. 'I've called a meeting of all senior detectives at Stewart Street. That means now, Mark.' She didn't elaborate further.

Something substantial had happened, that's for sure. Whether it was as big as this case, was debatable. Henderson was concerned that he would have to broach the touchy subject of Lord Rameses Bullock with Anne Swinton. He fired this parting instruction to his DCs, 'slowly, slowly, catchy monkey, ladies.'

* * *

Approaching Stewart Street, Henderson became aware of a huge press contingent camped outside the station. Soon he would be inundated with over-eager coppers, desperate to impart their views on Glasgow's day of madness. He knew before he got to the meeting that three of Glasgow's major crime figures were on display in the city morgue and that seasoned hacks at the Evening Times, Glasgow Herald and the Daily Record were thinking all their Christmases had come at once. He also heard that the Scotsman's editor had sent his chief crime reporter through from Edinburgh by helicopter.

The meeting of senior detectives was being held in the Incident Room and, as he walked in, Henderson realised he was last to arrive. On a hastily arranged bulletin board were "before they were dead" and "after they were dead" photographs. He quickly scanned them but decided against offering an opinion on his preferences. Introductions were unnecessary as everyone in the room was well acquainted with each other and with the parade of dead villains.

Anne Swinton motioned Henderson to take the seat allotted him and began speaking in her usual no-nonsense tone. Most of those present preferred this. Those that didn't, kept the fact to themselves.

She simply read out the names. 'Daniel Brogan, 36. Robert Duncanson, 42, and his business partner, William Tonner, aged 51. It's been what you could call a busy day.' The phone, in front of her, began ringing just as she finished speaking. She took the call, showing no emotion whatsoever and never said a word in reply. She placed the receiver back on the handset and said, 'Billy Davis is dead.'

One of the detectives sitting up-front quipped, 'Has he been shot as well?'

'No, he's been decapitated,' the Chief Constable stated.

This news was as big as anything that had preceded it; bigger, when you considered how high Davis' profile had been of late. It had been reported a lot recently that Davis would not leave his house without wearing a bullet-proof vest.

Billy Davis' body was parked underneath the number two ramp at Coyle's garage, just off Alexander Parade in the city's Dennistoun area.

On the second floor of the police station, young geeks were super-busy, assembling computer software and turning the Incident Room into the Major Incident Room. On some of the more modern computer screens, selected images of the crime scene at the garage were coming through thick and fast.

The harsh lighting made the yellow four-post ramp look as if it was luminous. The ramp's bed sat at a strange angle. One side was pushed down into the floor while the other side was raised by four or five inches. The posts remained perfectly upright. Between the running boards, the vague outline of Billy Davis' right leg poked through the gap.

On the right-hand side of the ramp, a huge roll-top Snap-on toolbox stood with three of its drawers open. An almost life-sized poster of the model Jordan adorned the side of the toolbox. She was holding two giant ring spanners in her hands, and rivulets of black motor oil streamed between her breasts. Her white hot pants weren't very practical but the sensible, steel toe-capped work boots were spot on.

The oil that smeared the model, perfectly matched the congealed blood pooled under the ramp, surrounding the bright red toolbox. A hacksaw lay horizontally on the ramp's right-hand running board. Behind the hacksaw sat the head of Billy Davis. It looked staged, like a piece of technical wizardry or a magician's illusion. His face looked restful, but expectant, as if he'd been asked to close his eyes before seeing a big surprise. There was a huge protrusion just above Davis' right temple. The mash hammer used for that purpose was not visible because it was being used to prop the head up and stop it from rolling over.

The forensic photographer on duty was impressed by the theatrical presentation of the scene and he continued sending shots through to HQ showing that the "Great Pretender", Billy Davis, remained a ham, even in death.

The Chief Constable took her jacket off, and neatly positioned it over her chair, like she meant business. If there was any lingering resentment about how she got the top job, it wasn't being shown today. She'd only been in charge of Lothian and Borders Police for just over two years. The results she'd achieved in that time were seen as impressive. Forces throughout Britain sent scouts sniffing around to see if she'd be interested in a move down south. All received the same answer. She wasn't interested. Strathclyde had come calling and would not take no for an answer. Anne Swinton had got what she wanted. She was forty-nine years old, and, as they used to say in the old days, she had a bit of meat on her. She was attractive, the cameras liked her and that helped a lot in her presentation of the difficulties facing the modern police force. She was the constabulary's version of New Labour. The difference was, she was the real deal.

She'd cut her teeth as a beat cop in small East Lothian towns like Tranent, where diplomacy was needed on a regular basis. Those small towns were as wild as Glasgow in many ways, where claustrophobia and paranoia went hand in hand with a populace crammed into one main street at the weekend. Her advice to big-mouthed, drunken nuisances was to speak politely to her, then follow her advice and go home. They got one chance and if they did not take it, they were lifted. Then, it wasn't a case of being let out when they sobered up. If she lifted you, you went to court. And she made sure you paid the fine or you went down for it. The rest of her career followed that principle. Every colleague was allowed one mistake, but Swinton clamped down on repeat offending.

Henderson decided today was not the day to make his one mistake; he would drop that hot potato on her lap tomorrow.

Chapter Fourteen

Downstairs in the kitchen, Big Yogi brought an abrupt end to a heated discussion. 'I don't give a fuck how specific he was, he'll want to be told now.'

'But he was insistent,' said young Scooby.

'Insistent, specific, what's wrong with you cunts?' The big man grabbed the pile of newspapers off the kitchen table and rapped both men over the head with them. On his way upstairs, he bellowed down, 'If I see anybody fucking about with phones, I'll break thumbs.'

Scooby slipped his mobile back into his jerkin.

Yogi rattled his boss's bedroom door and walked in.

'Why the heavy knock? You think I was having a wank?'

'Read that,' Yogi said, throwing the papers onto the huge bed 'and you'll cream panties.'

McGuire clocked the front page of the Record, showing the four faces of major underworld figures. Underneath each photograph was one word, "deceased".

The giant headline said "WAR". The footer read, "Full story, pages 2, 3, 4, 5, and centre pages". The Scottish Daily Express was calling for the Army to be brought in.

'Somebody sawed Billy Davis' head off.' Yogi grinned excitedly.

McGuire smiled. *Rab Hutchinson had relished squaring his financial obligation. He'd been instructed, 'Make sure he's dead'. My God, the wee man was thorough. Perhaps I should put Wee Rab on the payroll permanently if that's what he does for eight grand.*

'What's the score, JJ?' Yogi pleaded.

'The game's just started,' McGuire said flatly.

Big Yogi stood up and asked, 'Are you wanting your breakfast now?'

McGuire nodded.

'There's something else,' Yogi said hesitantly.

'What?'

'Wagner wants to see you. He's been pestering me like fuck.'

'Tell him to come to the Tavern at four o'clock,' JJ smiled contentedly.

*   *   *

Stewart Street was actually busier than the previous evening. DC MacCallum and DC Hannah had managed to get a decent cup of coffee at the top end of Hope Street. They were scarcely noticed as they made their way into the station. The story of the gangland slayings was growing arms and legs. Both ITV and BBC had big-name reporters from down south covering the story, much to the chagrin of regional reporters who'd spotted a prime slot for self-promotion.

'Nell, do you think we've backed the wrong horse?'

DC Hannah looked at the trucks of the media's technical crews. 'Who knows? We might all be at the same race meeting.'

'Oh my God, we're starting to sound just like him'

'Look, MacCallum, don't just speak cliché, live it - breathe it.'

Inside Stewart Street, cleaning staff were losing the battle tidying up after an infestation of coppers. The planned press conference, to be held inside the station, had been cancelled and the car park at the rear of the building was hastily being rearranged to serve that purpose.

Hannah and MacCallum sat in Henderson's office, more confident than on their previous visit.

'Anything?' Henderson asked despairingly.

'Connie is not a she,' MacCallum beamed.

Henderson nearly fell from his executive swivel chair. 'Go on, go on,' he said, frantically wiping his eyes.

'Connie is the nickname Caroline gave Cornel Wagner.'

'Why are all the good apples falling on me?' Henderson sighed.

The two junior officers dared each other to laugh. Then Hannah broke their version of a Mexican stand-off. 'We showed Margaret three different photographs of Lord Bullock. She's adamant he's Cornel Wagner's Uncle Vanya.'

'Uncle Vanya, the dirty bastart.'

Marian MacCallum took over. 'Margaret said, years ago, they stayed at Bullock's cottage in Dumfries for a few weeks.'

'Did she say how they got there?'

'We did not delve too deep, Boss. That's the reason we're here. How far can we go? Who are we allowed to question?'

Henderson looked impressed as he walked over to his window and looked down on the organised chaos in the station car park. The press conference was in full swing now and a multitude of cameras flashed incessantly. 'We have to get away from this circus, sit down somewhere where you can hear yourself think - go over everything we've got - formulate how we proceed with this investigation.'

'Sir,' Hannah said, 'we could use the flat tomorrow night, Margaret's having dinner upstairs at that man Cassidy's.'

'That sounds like a plan. OK?'

'Boss?'

'Yes, DC MacCallum.'

'We've looked at criminal records. – and eh, we're not quite sure Cornel Wagner is actually foreign.'

'Not quite sure?' Henderson quizzed.

'He changed his name by deed poll in 1962. His real name is Francis Collins, from Partick.'

'They're all pretentious up that way. Half of them sound posher than you do, Hannah.'

Nell Hannah declined the bait and let the comment ride.

'Who's at the house now?' Henderson asked

'Two uniform - so we need to get back soon,' DC Hannah confirmed.

'Get back there now. Try and find an official link between Bullock and Wagner, Collins, or any other name he's gone under. Try and find out more about the cottage; see if she can give any names, friends, acquaintances of Bullock or his nephew.' Henderson gave a derisory snigger. 'Try not to be too direct. Keep it cosy, keep it low key.'

The two DCs frowned, unsure of Henderson's logic.

'Girls, I'm not sure what we've got here. When you start poking your nose into the fallibilities of High Court judges, the wise poke tentatively.'

'Should we be taping her?' DC MacCallum asked.

'No, no. Keep it casual for the moment.'

As the detectives got up to leave, Henderson asked, 'Do you know what they're calling you at the station?'

'Mr Henderson's Girls,' they both answered as one.

'You don't mind, do you?'

'Not really, it's not that bad, not when you consider what they're calling you.'

Henderson's astonished expression posed the question.

'Dame Judi,' MacCallum answered.

'As in Dame Judi Dench, sir,' Hannah expounded.

'Really.' Henderson slowly sunk into his chair. 'See you tomorrow.'

As they closed the door behind them, Henderson made a mental note to thank Tank Williams again. He lay back in his chair, put his feet on the desk and did a woeful impression of Tony Curtis impersonating Cary Grant. 'Judi, Judi, Judi – Dame Judi.'

Chapter Fifteen

Jim Cassidy pursed his lips and loudly tutted.

'What?' Joe snapped at the bait.

'You think we'll have to hire a van from Arnold Clark?'

'What for?'

'Bringing your stuff round here.'

'Thank fuck you never cracked that kind of shite when you were working. You'd have been done in years ago.'

'I'll give you a run round now, if you want.'

'If you don't mind, Jim, I'd rather go myself.'

'Not wanting to be seen consorting with the enemy?' Cassidy nodded.

Joe apologised instantly. 'It's not that, Jim. I don't want to end up cracking somebody's jaw.'

'There's a good chance some of your fellow tenants will recognise me.'

Joe smiled, grateful that he didn't have to spell it out any more than that.

*   *   *

The "Sore Thumb" on Abercrombie Street was about to become a sore point. Joe's intention was to drop in, get his clothes, say thank you and goodbye and leave. Anything in the locality of the Gallowgate is never easy. His prime concern was that someone in authority would block his move out of this shithole. He nodded acknowledgement at the two young men sitting on the stone steps outside the front door.

Joe entered the mish-mash of a building and turned right into the smoking room. The sunlight blasting through the massive bay window highlighted the horrendous amount of smoke in the room. Joe painfully readjusted his eyes, trying to discern who sat at the giant dining table. There were about eight men in the room. A few of them started hollering rebukes about him being a dirty little stop-out. Joe answered them when he was able to focus on who he was actually talking to. The room was full of ashtrays and scattered newspapers. Normally most red-tops would be opened and folded at the racing sections. Today, however, all were displaying pictures of the Glasgow Underworld's not-so-dearly-departed.

The smallest of three young chavs standing at the top of the table spoke. 'You've not been up to yer larks again, have you, Joe?'

'Sorry?' Joe looked bemused.

The wee guy became a little bit more vociferous. 'Were you out shooting about the other night there?' His two pals thought this was hilarious and collapsed onto their mate's shoulders. He shrugged them off and strode forward. 'You're JJ McGuire's main man aren't you?'

'What the fuck are you talking about?' Joe asked, sounding more perplexed than angry.

The two pals suddenly stopped laughing and became inquisitive, as one of them asked:

'We've heard all about you. Just out and players are going toes up left, right and centre...'

'Funny, I've no heard about you,' Joe cut in.

Unexpectedly, the three men became friendly. Then, Joe found out why.

Val Deveeney entered the room and asked Joe into her office. Joe followed meekly behind, shit-scared of his own reaction as he passed by his three tormentors, who, on cue, mocked, 'Oh, you are in big trouble, mate.'

Joe sat with his back to a glass partition. These partitions were everywhere in this place. Members of staff always stressed that anything you said would be treated in the strictest confidence. When you pointed out to them you could hear toenails growing next door, they gave you that "you're being awkward" look. All Joe wanted was to get out of there without killing some cunt. He was beginning to wish that he'd brought Jim Cassidy with him.

*   *   *

On Westmuir Street, Johnny V sat, fed up, listening to how young Whitefield would bring the lid down on some major crime figures.

'Some cunts throwing their hat in the ring, that's for sure'

'Any ideas who?' V asked sarcastically.

'I have my ideas. The boys in Paisley are getting far too cosy with the Russian fucks.'

'Is it not the Albanian Fucks?'

'No it's definitely Russian, V, they just sound Albanian.' Whitey laughed a little too manically at his own joke.

'Speaking of accents,' Johnny V said, 'what do you make of Wagner meeting the boss today?'

Whitey's mood changed instantly. He tried to remain jovial, but inside his head, paranoia took a foothold.

'Is that who he's meeting in the pub?' Whitey asked, sounding upbeat.

'Been pestering us for days, wanting to speak, wanting a word,' Johnny V replied.

'Why here?'

'Vhy Shettleston? Vhy the Tavern? I don't know vhy,' Johnny V mimicked Wagner's accent.

Whitey fought hard trying not to be too inquisitive, although he was desperate to know exactly what Wagner wanted from McGuire. A question that had been niggling Whitey was answered. Now he knew why Wagner had failed to contact him. Now paranoia took a stronger foothold.

*　　*　　*

Cornel Wagner parked his Silver Lexus just off Shettleston Road and walked into the Tavern in the Town, giving off the impression he was slumming it. He was dressed impeccably, every garment tailor-made, including the buff coloured rain-coat draped over his arm. He was alarmed that their meeting was in a public bar when he considered it prudent to be discreet.

McGuire beckoned Wagner over to the snug. 'Are you eating? The steak pie's superb.'

'I don't think so,' Wagner said as he shuffled his body along the back panel of the snug partition.

'Is this not a bit too public, Mr McGuire?'

'You can call me JJ today. We're not at work.'

'JJ, I need a very big favour.'

'Whatever happened to wee favours? They just seemed to go out of fashion.'

Wagner failed to see the humour. 'I am in serious danger. This is serious, most serious.'

'You work for me, you're safe.'

'There's a chance I could be put away for a long time. I cannot do prison, Mr McGuire.' Wagner's eyes sought succour, understanding. They received neither.

'Don't even make the vaguest hint of threat or you'll be killed where you sit, even in front of these witnesses.'

Big Yogi appeared from nowhere and sat cosily next to Wagner - much too cosily. Wagner felt as if he was about to become embedded in the wall of the lounge bar.

McGuire spoke very quietly. 'I think you should discuss your difficulties, right now.'

'It's private - rather delicate.'

McGuire looked across the table. 'Yogi can do delicate. Can't you, Yogi?'

'At a push Boss, at a push,' the big man replied as he squeezed himself into Wagner.

Wagner struggled to get some air into his lungs before saying. 'I need your help, Mr McGuire. My situation's desperate.'

McGuire glanced at Yogi and the pressure on Wagner's rib-cage eased.

'It's a desperate predicament I find myself in, Mr McGuire - I vould never bother you othervise.'

'I take it that a desperate solution's required for this desperate situation?'

'I've never asked for anything before.' Wagner paused and took a nervous look around the pub. 'I need someone taken care of.' His voice trailed off as his head sunk into his torso.

'Permanently?'

'I'm afraid so, Mr McGuire.'

'Mr Wagner if you want me to kill someone for you, then I'd prefer you to be completely honest with me. OK, Franny?'

The colour drained from Wagner. 'How long have you known?'

'I've always known.'

Wagner struggled finding his former accent. 'S-s-sorry,' he stammered quietly, 'It's been a long time since I was Francis Collins.'

Chapter Sixteen

Margaret forced her head into the pillow and forced herself to stop crying. She ran to the bathroom and faced the mirror. She'd have to keep it together if she wanted to get Nicola, Emma and wee Cheryl. She'd learn how to live properly, study how to bring up children correctly. She'd ask for help, take all the help. Anything they told her to do, she'd do, because that's how it's done - you do what they say and things go right. She'd go to college. The adverts on the telly said you could go to college. They said it was easy. She would go to college, study, study like fuck, learn how to be a good parent. It cannot just be about love because nobody could love anyone any more than she loved her sister and her children. When they were young, she'd forcibly cradled Caroline in her arms and told her how much she loved her and told her she'd always look after her.

She dried the tears from her eyes and thought about the man who came to her rescue. He'd probably be there tonight. Well, she hoped he'd be there tonight.

She looked into the kitchen and saw the laptop sitting on top of the table OPEN. She'd watched Marian use the machine a lot. If she wasn't using it, then Nell was. They were her friends, now. She could say that. She knew it wasn't just work with them.

Margaret was terrified of breaking it. It had looked easy when she'd seen them fire it up. That's what they said when they used it. 'Fire it up.'

She skipped through to the living room and had a quick look-see at the street. Back in the kitchen, she took a huge breath to stop her heart pounding so much and leaned forward and pressed the last elongated button on the right that Marion called the hibernate. At around about eleven o'clock she'd say, 'C'mon Nell, hit the Hibernate. Let's get some shut eye.'

Margaret jumped, startled by a jarring machine-gun sound and the high-pitched beep as the computer woke from slumber. A little square white box with a picture of a tiny white rose appeared in the middle of the screen. Next to the box, it said "three programmes running". Margaret gently touched the black pad and the white arrow on screen went haywire. She stood back, took a deeper breath and then tried again. She manoeuvred the arrow onto the white box and pressed down. She kept her eyes on the screen as everything seemed to happen so fast, she barely had time to read as bands of text swam across the screen and instantly disappeared.

Then the screen became a beautiful shade of blue and a face from the past appeared magically. That's the photo they showed her last night, but now she could see the words written below the photograph. The caption read, "Lord Bullock at the opening of the Scottish Parliament". There were more words on display, lots of them.

Margaret Logan never had that much schooling - she was considered sub-standard in most subjects. However, she could read. It might take her a while, but she could read.

Hesitantly, Margaret scrutinised the keyboard again and saw four little arrow shapes pointing different ways. She touched the one pointing downwards and held it down. More and more photographs began rolling on to the screen. Margaret jumped back again, holding her breath, terrified she'd broken the machine. She returned and gently pressed the upward arrow and stopped at an old photo showing a young Rameses Bullock playing rugby at Oxford University. The next page she scrolled to, proved the most fruitful. It gave a brief résumé of Bullock's career. She took her time reading it, making double sure she took it all in.

It did not take long to realise just how powerful and influential the man Connie had described as really special, really was. It said he'd be heading an enquiry into abuse in the Care System. Funny, when he was just Uncle Vanya, he'd helped them escape from the care of Maranatha House.

A plan began formulating. Lord Bullock had helped out once before. He could help her out again. Underneath one of the more recent photographs it read, *Lord Bullock outside the refurbished Crown Office in Edinburgh's Chambers Street.* She made the decision. Lord Bullock would help her get the children back, all of them, even wee Cheryl. It was simple, he would help, or she would tell, and she had lots to tell.

*   *   *

Fuck it, Henderson said to himself, it's only a job.

'Any time soon,' Chief Constable Anne Swinton said impatiently.

'Ma'am, the enquiry I'm leading is progressing slowly, I've thought all along - right from the very start - that there's something very seedy about this case.'

'Understandable, considering the background,' Anne Swinton reasoned.

Henderson reached inside his jacket, produced and unfolded an A4 print-out of Rameses Bullock. Painstakingly, he flattened the piece of paper onto Anne Swinton's desk.

He turned the image around 180 degrees so that the old judge glowered up at her. Swinton's face froze, she unbuttoned her tunic, stretched back on her chair and looked at the ceiling, barely stifling a scream.

'Bullock knew Caroline Logan. I've got two detectives keeping Caroline's sister Margaret under 24 hour surveillance. Last night Margaret caught a glimpse of Lord Bullock's face on Reporting Scotland.' Henderson paused, not just for dramatic effect. He wanted to make sure he phrased what he was about to say properly. 'She knows him as simply Uncle Vanya – we checked – she does know him.'

Swinton had moved from her desk before Henderson had finished his sentence. She walked over to her door and quietly locked it. She returned to her desk, sat down and inhaled deeply, 'Weegies,' she slowly exhaled; 'Uncle Vanya.'

Henderson took that as his cue to proceed. 'Margaret Logan says Lord Bullock is a relative of Cornel Wagner – the same Cornel Wagner who runs JJ McGuire's knocking shops.'

Swinton remained silent, although she started tapping the nails of her right hand onto the highly polished oak desk. The tapping rose in intensity, then she snapped, 'You think McGuire's connected with the girl's death?'

'It's more than a possibility. I have reliable information that Margaret Logan definitely knew Cornel Wagner in the early 1990s. Seems she might have been working as a child prostitute at the Palms Sauna in Anderston. Cornel Wagner and McGuire were an item then - that I do know.'

'You've not brought her in, have you?' Swinton asked, looking distressed.

'No, we've not really questioned her yet. My "girls" are taking their time building a rapport, especially since the abduction.'

'Attempted abduction,' Swinton snapped. 'Still, your assessment of the situation proved correct.' She seemed to mellow.

'I'm probably going to question her tonight after I've discussed it with MacCallum and Hannah.' Henderson dispelled the concerned look on his Chief Constable's face. 'We're questioning her at her own home - I'll be able to let you know more later ma'am.'

'Mark,' Anne Swinton said softly. 'I need to downsize your enquiry.'

'Much?'

'Drastically, I'm afraid - Mr Henderson, I hope you're happy with your "girls" because - that's all the help you are going to get.'

Henderson was impressed with Anne Swinton. He hoped it was mutual. Even with everything on her plate, she still knew the score, knew the interactions between her officers and had a grasp on the pulse of the force.

'You don't seem too upset, DCI Henderson?'

'I'm happy, Ma'am. The fewer people who know about Bullock the better.'

Anne Swinton took the hint perfectly. She nodded and asked, 'Joseph Ray, anything there?'

'I don't think he's part of the equation here. I believe he genuinely came to the girl's assistance.'

'He's linked with McGuire, though. I'm told they used to be very tight.'

'Once upon a time – but he's been away for twenty years. I don't believe he's a player now.'

'You think Ray may be involved in this Underworld War One? That's what the media's calling the Glasgow situation.'

'No, that's purely McGuire.' Henderson paused, shook his head, scratched it and then said, 'There is another link with Caroline Logan and McGuire.'

'Oh?' Swinton edged forward in her seat.

'The MacNee case - you might have heard about it, Ma'am?'
Swinton had heard about it. 'That's the closest Glasgow has ever came to getting a conviction on Mr McGuire.'

'McGuire and Ray both got a Not Proven. They would have walked anyway. The case was riddled with inaccuracies and the Crown Office had left files open and unattended. There were major discrepancies concerning evidence gathered at Tobago Street and London Road. It was shameful seeing the corruption rampant in the Procurator Fiscal's office.'

'They tortured him?' Swinton asked.

'For four days. McGuire became a legend on the back of what he inflicted on that poor cu...' Henderson caught himself just before he spoke out of turn. 'Thing is, Owny MacNee was the uncle of Caroline and Margaret Logan.'

'Was?'

'He's dead, killed himself - went skinny dipping in the Clyde as the bells chimed in 1986.'

'How big a part did Ray play in the MacNee case?'

'McGuire was the senior partner, but Ray was no slouch when violence was required.'

Henderson had been anticipating the Chief Constable's next question for quite a while.

'Who presided over the MacNee case?' she asked.

Henderson shook his head very slowly. 'It wasn't Bullock, Ma'am.'

'Maybe bent judges are just like bent coppers. When their back's itchy, they know who'll scratch it.'

'Judge Healey was not like that. He tried like f –, he did all he could to make sure the case proceeded. In the end it was embarrassing - for him, for us, for anybody concerned with justice.'

'Well, this murder inquiry seems to be throwing up some very influential coincidences - Bullock, Wagner, McGuire and Ray.'

'Like I said before, Ma'am, I don't think Ray is a player these days. When I questioned him, he was more scared of his licence being revoked and he was gob-smacked when I pointed out the MacNee connection.'

'I would not discount anybody, right now. We've been asking discreet questions about Joe Ray regarding the three players lying in the morgue.'

'I know he's got previous, but I'm positive he's not part of this - McGuire's orchestrated that. I'm certain of that, Ma'am.'

Swinton stood up from her desk and walked around to where Henderson was standing. Her mood seemed to change. She spoke a lot more softly and, for the first time since Henderson had known her, she looked unsure of herself.

'I could have waited for Greater Manchester – They were definitely interested - but I took Strathclyde, grabbed at it if you want to know the truth. You expect tough, but you don't expect Dodge City. Christ, Sir Trevor MacDonald's people are badgering the hell out of us for an exclusive interview with me.'

'Anne - please - just hang in there, the clever money's on you.'

Anne Swinton straightened her tie and tugged her tunic into its rightful position and returned to her desk. The mask was back in place. 'I met Lord Bullock several times when I worked at Lothian and Borders – always courteous – too courteous, you know – patronising.' She steadied herself. 'Still, that does not necessarily make him a bad man. It just makes him a man - and a standing cock has no conscience. Is that not the old saying?'

'Yes, Ma'am, it is.' Henderson felt ashamed for some reason and looked down at his feet saying, 'I've had discussions with Bullock and he wasn't courteous to me.'

'Well, hopefully you might be able to return the compliment - High Court Judges consorting with gangsters, pimps and prostitutes. It's just not on, Henderson.'

Mark Henderson was taken aback at her little outburst of joviality.

'Any progress, keep me posted. Text first and I'll get back to you. Make sure you're alone when I ring.'

Henderson took a final look at the frenzied activity in the station car park as camera crews jostled for position. 'What do you think of the circus?'

Anne Swinton finished putting her face on, clamped the compact mirror shut and placed it in her bag. 'I'm looking forward to the circus leaving town,' she sighed.

Chapter Seventeen

The flat was quiet. Obviously his new landlord was out. It was a fair assumption he was out buying the food for tonight's meal. Joe had managed to get his stash from his mother's house without too many questions being asked. He'd never felt good about leaving it with her, but it had been out of necessity. There was no way he could have left any money at Abercrombie Street.

He started getting himself set up in his new home. There was more than enough wardrobe space and there was no need to hide stuff here. Cassidy's days of searching were over. However, Joe did not want Jim Cassidy knowing about McGuire's contribution to his lifestyle fund. Not for the moment, anyhow.

It was just a relief to be out of that fucking place. All the time he'd been at Abercrombie Street, he'd been making excuses for his fellow residents - misguidedly thinking they were no different from him. They were different all right - they'd no fucking class, just a bunch of opportunist thieves, who'd steal anything that wasn't nailed down.

Every time you talked with them, they'd be looking through you, beyond you, looking at you and scrutinising what was available or could become attainable. The thing that perturbed most was how obvious their intentions were. They did not even have the mental capacity, or could not draw up the physical effort, to deceive.

Joe thought about the joker he'd engaged with only last week. The boy had told him about the time he was out in Garrowhill at half past one in the morning, tanning cars for anything he could get. His first pick of the evening, a brand new Volvo estate, proved fruitful. He opened the glove box and found two and a half grand stuffed in a brown paper envelope - but still the cretin stole the spare wheel and the radio.

The clown had got away with it, that's what disturbed Joe most. No-one had stopped him. No nosey neighbours and no patrol cars passing by. There was no rhyme or reason to it. Thinking about scenarios like that could only lead to madness. They could get you thinking you can get away with that shit - being bold, not giving a fuck, just doing crimes because that's all you knew.

Harry and Jim Cassidy had shown Joe that he could be bigger than that. Now, he desperately wanted to live a different life. Joe was actually terrified that people might realise how much he yearned to be an ordinary man. He knew, in his head, that he'd probably left it too late to lead the 9 to 5 life. However, his heart was reading a different story.

He thought about what he should wear tonight, what he should wear for her. Minutes after unpacking and putting his clothes away, he had most of them sitting back on the bed as he attempted different combinations. He was after that look of not trying to impress. That certain look was proving to be extremely trying. He settled on a pair of Levis and a tailored white shirt, hanging loose outside his jeans.

*   *   *

It looked like Jim Cassidy had bought Marks & Spencer's. Every inch of space on every kitchen work-top was taken up with fresh produce.

'Brilliant, eh,' he joked. 'Bung that in the microwave for two minutes and they think you're Jamie Oliver.'

'Who's Jamie Oliver?'

'Gordon Ramsay?' Cassidy offered a substitute.

'Fuck's Gordon Ramsay?' Joe said, puzzled.

'Good one, Joe. Like it,' Cassidy giggled as he started putting the meal into the fridge in the order it would emerge later this evening.

Joe scratched his head, wondering why his last remark was thought to be so funny. 'Can I help?' he asked, feeling redundant.

'Stick the kettle on, son,' Cassidy said, as he scrunched up some of the food wrapping and forced it into the huge mirrored pedal bin.

Joe was filling up the jug when Cassidy caught him unaware. 'When will you ask her?'

Joe's face was totally blank, so Cassidy persisted. 'When will you ask her to go to the pictures?'

'As soon as she walks in the door,' Joe snapped.

'That's not actually such a bad idea. Let's her know right away that you're interested.'

'Jim? I was being sarcastic.'

'I know you were, son - so was I,' Cassidy revealed, then said, 'But it is not the worst idea you've ever had. Tell you what, play it by ear.'

'You know for definite she's coming?'

'Oh aye. I saw her earlier. She's definitely coming. That's why I got blueberry cheesecake. That's her favourite. She doesn't seem the complicated type – that's good, son. Believe me that's good, Joe.'

Joe's eyes lit up at that last statement although he tried hard to hide the fact.

The see-through kettle started boiling and Joe watched the pressure subside as the cut-off switch did its duty. *I wish I had a cut-off switch in my stomach*, Joe thought.

*   *   *

96

He was very specific about the number. He wanted twelve. Johnny V was told he could be selective, pick his own preferences. In the end it had taken five cars over twenty separate journeys, trawling through the giant housing schemes of Drumchapel, Castlemilk and Easterhouse before reaching their quota. Pushers seemed reluctant to get into cars with anyone - understandable in the current climate. Apprehension hung over the city like a wet shroud. People were going out tooled-up just to buy tenner digs of Blow. If it could be harnessed, the national grid could be powered by those frequent surges of electrical paranoia gripping the bowels of those dealing recreational drugs.

*   *   *

There they sat - bound, gagged and mystified. A few had shat themselves. Those that hadn't, soon would. For the moment, they just looked round at each other and tried to communicate through terrified eyes. Empathy for one another's plight only heightened the intensity of their fears. The workshop they sat in looked immense - this was an optical illusion created by the two weak light bulbs, spaced about twenty five feet apart, that hung high above their heads. There was activity aplenty going on all around them. The voices were muffled, although they still echoed. The footsteps traipsing back and forth on the cold concrete floor did likewise. However, some voices carried a little more clarity.

'Many will we need?'

'More than one would be a start.'

The man spoke into the mobile 'Bring three – I don't care, bring three, I don't want to be here all fucking night.'

The men tied to the chairs knew each other or knew of each other. In all probability, they had bought from each other at some point over the last couple of years. It was just as probable that they'd ripped each other off. Some of them were getting bold and beginning to struggle with their restraints. This came to an abrupt end when a large hooded man walked over and slammed a mash hammer into the face of the first man in his path. The chair toppled and the recipient lost consciousness, unaware of his good fortune. The struggling stopped and the tethered men looked at each other with renewed fear. In the hazy darkness, curious voices became audible again.

'How's he going to do it?'

'Chisel.'

'Chisel?'

'Bolster chisel.'

'Oh …….. right.'

97

'Aye, you know - the big flat one. Panel Beaters call it a spade chisel.'

*   *   *

You just don't get a better exclusive. That was the opinion of a traumatised News Desk at the Daily Record. Janet Todd had broken all protocol by bringing the package in from the street. The heavy duty cardboard box measured two feet square and stood nine inches high. The gaffer tape lapping it had been put on haphazardly. Scribbled in black ink-marker on one side was, "FOR THE RECORD".

It was only minutes ago that Janet, scalpel in hand, had delicately sliced at the khaki-brown gaffer tape. The first incision brought forth such an intense aroma of grilled bacon that her stomach rumbled in anticipation. As she freed the lids of the box from their bonds, her eyes focussed on the little parcels covered in bubble wrap. She took the first of these packages out and placed it on her desk.

'Somebody's being good to themselves,' a passing sub commented.

Janet just smiled, keeping her eyes on the prize. She gently rolled the package on the desk, making helpful incisions, freeing the wrap from the cloying Sellotape. She could see grease swish between the folds of plastic and she was careful not let liquid fat escape onto the table surface as she unfurled the parcel. THEN, she froze. It felt like a fist had been pushed through her chest and had clamped around her heart. She could not scream, not straight away. She had to touch it first. She did not know why, but she touched it and then she was able to scream. Then she could not stop screaming.

Her colleagues fought hard to subdue her. Then somebody else saw what Janet Todd was screaming at. There, sitting on the desk, was a small cooked hand.

The hand was split in lots of places, like an over-cooked roast. Yellowed knuckle bones stood proud from the contracted flesh that used to cover them, and shafts of bone protruded through the finger-tips. It was difficult to tell if the hand had been trying to make a fist or releasing itself from one. It had the gnarled grasp of a spin bowler. The remains of a ligature were visible near to where the hand had been severed. Pieces of burnt twine were embedded and encrusted into dried out, overcooked flesh.

'This is a crime scene,' someone said. Nobody knew who.

'We need to be careful – don't touch anything,' said someone else.

'This is a fucking golden opportunity,' Rab Cowan, the Chief Sub, said and immediately took charge of the situation. 'Get the snappers in here.'

'There's more in the box – lots more,' Janet mouthed, realising she might be missing out on her own exclusive.

Within seconds, the room was crowded. Within minutes, every one of the packages had been placed on the cutting-room table. Photographers were taking snapshots of them from all kinds of obscure angles. One of the older journalists was placing his hand amongst the cooked hands highlighting the extent of shrinkage during the cooking process.

There were five tiny hands openly displayed, and seven others still bubble-wrapped. One hand was being photographed more than the others. The palm was flat and the ligature looked similar to the others. What was different about this hand was the way the fingers were bent back on themselves. The splits, caused by cooking, were more pronounced on the folds of the fingers and around the contracted knuckles. Somehow, the extreme pain of detachment seemed more visible.

Those handling the hands, at least had the foresight to wear latex gloves. The empty cardboard box was now being photographed. Spotlights were being shone on the box and quickly repositioned to give a better view of the pool of human grease that had congregated and soaked into one corner of the box.

Rab Cowan looked towards his editor for guidance. There seemed a long pause, but it was actually only a couple of seconds. The editor scanned the cutting-room table three times before saying reluctantly, 'Phone the police.'

Chapter Eighteen

Marian MacCallum displayed the same look of approval as her colleague Nell Hannah. This was the third outfit Margaret Logan had tried on. The previous two had been impressive, but this outfit was the best of the bunch. She was wearing skinny, dark blue jeans with a short, lime-coloured smock. To boost her height, she wore a pair of light, wedged sandals. The two detective constables had helped out with hair and make-up in turns during the afternoon. Both officers were now aware that seeds of confidence were taking root inside Margaret Logan. Every little victory in Margaret's makeover that day was interspersed with rogue waves of guilt that washed over her. She'd be ecstatically happy one minute at the results of technical adjustments to the application of her eyeliner; next minute she'd be hit with an intrusive reminder that she wasn't allowed to be happy. How could she be happy when her sister was dead and her children were gone? How could she have the nerve to smile? How could she have the brass neck?

Nell Hannah had come into her element then. 'Listen,' she said, 'your children will be back with you, Margaret - all of them. The people responsible for killing Caroline will be put in prison where they belong. You will have a decent life. You know why? Do you want to know why?'

Margaret Logan had never ever thought of that question before, but she did now.

'Why?' she asked. Her eyes rolled upward, fearful of the answer.

'Because you deserve it. You deserve a decent life. Look at yourself - you're beautiful. You're beautiful on the inside, too. What's happened in the past does not have to happen in the future. You can have a say. You're entitled to a say.'

'How can I have a say?' Margaret asked.

Marian MacCallum took over. 'Course you can have a say. You can do the stuff we talked about the other night. You can go to college. Margaret, it's about time you gave yourself a pat on the back.'

Before Margaret could speak, Nell Hannah resumed the psyching up process.

'Go for your meal, go and enjoy yourself. We'll be here if you need us.'

'What will I say?' Margaret asked.

'Looking the way you do, you'll not have to say too much. Will she?' Hannah looked at Marian MacCallum for confirmation.

100

'Just be yourself, Margaret, you'll be fine. Remember it's only a dinner, but it'll be better than the stuff I've been dishing up, eh?' MacCallum laughed at her own joke.

Margaret Logan walked into her bedroom and quietly closed the door. She opened the door of the wardrobe and looked herself up and down in the full-length mirror. It had been so long since she thought she could look that good. She spun around on the soles of her sandals and stopped herself perfectly in front of the mirror. She stepped back and admired the handiwork of the two police women. She started crying for different reasons, now. It was so nice just for somebody to take the time, to be a pal; to take the time, just to take the time.

*   *   *

This was surely the shortest police escort in Strathclyde's history. DC MacCallum put a reassuring arm around Margaret and walked her up the two flights of stairs to Jim Cassidy's flat. Just before Marian knocked on the door, she said, 'If the food is not that good, don't mind, I'll make you toast and scrambled eggs later.'

Margaret smiled, although it could have been confused with a wince. 'Thanks Marian, I'm absolutely starving.' Then her nerves came to the forefront again. 'Ah hope my stomach doesn't start making noises again.'

'You'll be fine,' Marian assured her.

*   *   *

A beaming Jim Cassidy opened the door. 'Come in, my wee darling.'

Margaret Logan gave her escort a forlorn look as she was ushered into the house. She looked around in a nonchalant sort of way, taking in the furniture of the flat. Then she saw him sitting nervously, crouched on the armrest of the sofa. She was so glad he was there. And so glad he looked the way she felt inside.

Joe rose up and kind of stood to attention. Hesitantly he edged himself a little closer to her and shook her hand.

She did not know why, but as he took her hand in his, she curtsied. He did likewise.

'Joe, show Margaret where she's sitting.' Jim Cassidy yelled from the kitchen.

Joe seemed lost in thought as he led Margaret Logan to the table. It was only when she attempted to sit down, that he realised he was still holding her hand.

*   *   *

101

Whitey was surprised how homely McGuire's house was - every wall in the huge lounge was covered with photographs of the two boys. They looked like McGuire. "Boys from Brazil" like clones with lighter hair. There was a huge framed photograph of Eileen McGuire, showing her sitting relaxed, cross-legged like a front row child in the school group-photograph. She wore white satin pyjamas, her hair was swept to one side and hung gentle and loose, and her face glowed as she smiled heavenwards. Eileen was a looker alright, though he'd never mention it, not even in jest. JJ walked in from the kitchen with two huge mugs of coffee in his hands. He was wearing the most luxurious white towelling dressing gown Whitey had ever seen, and a pair of brown leather slippers. Everyone else in the house was dressed for business. At least two of the men present were wearing bullet-proof vests and everyone else, Whitey included, wore stab vests under their bomber jackets. Even with the proliferation of gun crime in Glasgow in recent years, you were still more likely to get stabbed. Those in the trade still clung on to that old "hands on" approach. Everyone still carried a blade as back up.

The massive plasma screen was on but the sound was turned down to a minimum. McGuire was watching Sky News. Underneath the big screen, a small portable had been rigged up to play Teletext. The news snap at the bottom of the plasma screen kept repeating these words: "POLICE CONFIRM THE 12 SEVERED HANDS FOUND IN GLASGOW HAD BEEN MICRO-WAVED --- THREE VICTIMS SUFFERING THE EFFECTS OF AMPUTATION ARE IN SEPARATE HOSPITALS - ONE MAN HAS DIED DUE TO COMPLICATIONS - POLICE ARE EAGER TO FIND ANOTHER EIGHT PEOPLE----- POLICE CONFIRM THE 12 SEVERED HANDS FOUND IN GLASGOW HAD BEE------- "

'Said earlier that the police hadn't ruled out a racial motive. That's what you wanted, eh boss?' Whitey looked for acknowledgement, and received none. 'I'm putting it about that an Afghan warlord is not too happy about product distribution in this part of Europe.'

McGuire smiled. 'It's amazing the devastation a few choice words can invoke.'

'Will we be doing devastation as well, boss?' Whitey eagerly enquired.

'It's a possibility, son.'

Whitey approached the full-length peach curtains that ran the entire length of one side of the lounge. He pawed at them as he walked along, gauging their weight and thickness, as he sought their opening.

'Whitey,' McGuire said, 'don't look out the window. Somebody might shoot you.'

Johnny V was in the room in an instant with a pump action shotgun aimed at Whitey's head.

'I'll shoot you right now if you go near those curtains again.' He pressed the barrel of the gun against Whitey's forehead. 'You're not normally that stupid. Why be stupid now?'

'V? C'mon, it's me. I'm just looking at the curtains.' Whitey remained calm, almost assured.

'Leave it, V, we're all edgy,' McGuire said softly.

Johnny V removed the gun and walked away grunting. 'The curtains are shut for a reason.'

JJ McGuire sat back on his chair, thinking Young Whitefield wasn't as scared as he should've been.

Moments later, Big Yogi came into the room, smiling. McGuire stood up and made his way into the kitchen. Yogi followed. Two complete outfits lay out for his perusal. He opted for the one on the right. 'Are we being watched?' he asked as he started dressing.

'We were, but you're somewhere else at the moment, boss.' Yogi failed to suppress a cynical snigger. 'The police got an excellent tip-off from themselves.'

'What about the press?'

'Not a problem, they're playing catch-up in Maryhill and Barmulloch.'

'Many people at the farm?'

'Enough. Everything's cool, boss, honest, cross my heart and hope to die.'

JJ McGuire raised an eyebrow.

*   *   *

The farm was about two miles from High Blantyre, just off an old "B" road that snaked close to the main East Kilbride road every now and again. Two Shoguns sandwiched McGuire's Land Rover Discovery. The armour-plated Discovery had been shipped over from Baghdad two years ago, although it had never been used that much. It was purchased as a precaution during the dispute over who controlled the security industry on Scotland's building sites. At an informal "I'll tell you what" session, JJ McGuire had designated control of the industry to four men. Their success was guaranteed, BUT greed's always greedy, whatever way you fanny it up.

The three vehicles stood silently behind a broad wooden gate at the foot of a badly rutted, single-track road. High above them, a torch-light beamed on and off six times. After a pause of ten seconds, it flashed twice more. The gate was opened and three engines roared into life as the vehicles crawled up to the farmhouse. They must have known the road well because their headlights remained switched off.

This was the best JJ had felt since his consultant had told him what was what. Now, sitting silently in the back seat, he looked across a black horizon. Sporadic bursts of flickering lights blinked through gaps in darkened hedgerows, as traffic sped relentlessly downwards on the Glasgow Road. He wondered how long he could go on without people noticing. Perhaps they were noticing? He'd been told that in some people, the lucky people, the decline is swift. Some people were unlucky enough to get nine years. He'd always prided himself on knowing his enemy, and this fucker was formidable.

The research he'd done today on the internet had been scary, but he needed to know. Suddenly, four words read earlier today made a wake-up call inside his head. "Characterised by mood swings." He recoiled violently in his seat as if hit in the face with a brick. Is that what all this is about? A mood swing?

His driver gently eased on the brakes and asked, 'Are you OK, boss?'

JJ composed himself. 'Carry on.'

Now he thought about the five men already dead and the four others who'd soon join them. In Glasgow, Lanarkshire and Renfrewshire, street crime in general had increased by almost twenty per cent and physical assaults had risen by twenty four per cent since his bad reaction to being told bad news. If this was a mood swing, then Glasgow better watch out because, according to the literature he'd read earlier today, more would follow, and they'd increase in severity.

JJ McGuire had worn protective vests in the past; however, he was not wearing one today. This bravado instilled confidence in his men, and they showed no fear as they pulled into the courtyard of the farmhouse complex.

Scooby opened the door of the Discovery and McGuire was surrounded and escorted by five men towards one of the outbuildings. A crack of warm light appeared in a set of double doors. Then the doors were opened and shut in quick succession. The inside of the old barn was surprisingly hot. The reason for this was a huge space heater, based at the rear of the building, blasting heat towards the throng of heavy-set men congregating around four men, who lay naked and trussed on the barn floor.

JJ McGuire made his way through the throng and stared down at the flabby middle-aged men that wriggled uncomfortably at his feet. One of the men screamed up at JJ, 'I've got money, lots of money.'

'Déjà – déjà – déjà vu,' McGuire grinned as he took the pump action from Johnny V. He placed the barrel against the man's mouth and slowly squeezed the trigger. Nothing happened. McGuire looked around, his face filled with petulant boredom. Johnny V stepped forward, took the shotgun and replaced the missing cartridges.

'Sorry, I didn't want it going off on that fuckin road,' V mumbled.

If McGuire accepted the apology, he never showed it. He pressed the gun against his victim's mouth and pulled the trigger. 'Don't worry it'll be just as quick for you,' he sneered at the other men lying rigid on the floor. Laughter erupted as JJ repeated the same actions twice more. The fourth man had somehow managed to wriggle onto his side. JJ shot him at point-blank range through the ear and then fired another shot at what remained of the head. He handed the shotgun back to Johnny V, saying, 'Use the revolver for the send-off. We don't want the place caked in shite.'

McGuire went towards the other end of the barn and started stripping off. Young Scooby diligently followed. He had fresh clothes hanging from both arms and a box of wet wipes resting on them.

'Ah wish Joe was here,' McGuire said with hurt in his voice.

Scooby was almost positive that his boss was crying but he remained silent and shunned eye contact. He was unsure how to respond and he was frightened, very frightened.

Chapter Nineteen

Henderson had a key cut for the outside door, but he still pressed the buzzer as he entered the building. He only had ten minutes or so to talk to his officers before Swinton's arrival.

A mug of coffee was placed in his hands as he entered the flat. Henderson frantically took small sips from the mug before sitting down on the armchair next to the window. His eyes were fixed on the street as he spoke. 'Is there anything I should know before she gets here?'

The two Detective Constables looked at each other for reassurance before shaking their heads.

Henderson appeared to relax visibly and gave the impression of a concerned father. 'How'd she look – for her dinner date?'

'She looked beautiful, sir - but nervous as a puppy on bonfire night.'

'I've not heard that expression before; very good, MacCallum.'

'I just made it up, sir. Came to me when I left her at the door.'

Nell Hannah spoke, 'She's been up there a good hour and a half – she's obviously over her nerves.'

Henderson didn't respond because he'd caught sight of the black Mini Cooper convertible parking in the street. The woman emerging from the car looked like she was setting off on a mountain walk. Her purple Berghaus was fully zipped and its hood up. A lime-coloured woollen tammy pulled down low, kept most of her face hidden. But Henderson recognised the elegant gait. Anne Swinton waved at the window before heading up the path, and Henderson went out to let the Chief Constable in personally.

Swinton took no time settling in. She took her mobile from her jacket and deliberately switched it off, saying, 'I can give you twenty minutes tops. It'll be a bloody miracle if I'm not missed.'

Henderson passed her a mug of instant coffee with one sugar and took her jacket from her. The lady took a tentative, heat-testing sip and then a sizeable gulp before speaking, 'We are only days away from the start of the "Bullock Enquiry", facing the distinct possibility we may have to question Lord Bullock in connection with the death of Caroline Logan.' She paused, looked around the room. 'It's bloody melting in here,' she stated.

'The heating is switched off, Ma'am,' DC MacCallum answered.

'I could be sitting in the fridge and I'd still be roasting.' She threw the young DCs her most condescending look and said, 'Cheer up, girls, you've got the menopause to look forward to.'

The DCs looked to Henderson for a sign, a look that asked if it was OK to speak their mind.

Henderson took the task on himself. 'Ma'am, there's a good chance that Margaret looked at the data we have on Bullock – DC MacCallum is positive someone has been scrolling through the file she has compiled on Bullock.'

DC MacCallum stood like a game show hostess with her laptop held open in front of her. On screen was the image of Bullock outside the Crown Office. 'Ma'am, there was a different image on-screen when I put the computer into sleep mode.' MacCallum scrolled down until she reached a photograph showing Bullock entering Glasgow's old High Court.

Henderson stood up. 'I think it's safe to say Margaret knows who and what "Uncle Vanya" really is.' Henderson paused, formulating his next words. 'Even if he isn't involved in Caroline's murder, we should be asking what went on at his little bolthole in Dumfries.'

'I wonder what kinds of thoughts are going through Margaret's head?' Swinton asked.

*　　　*　　　*

One floor above, Joe was plucking up the courage to ask for a date. Jim Cassidy was making tea, after Margaret had stated she could murder a cup. Joe nudged closer to her and kept his voice very low. The worried look on his face showed as he prepared for disappointment. Just as he was about to speak, she spoke.

'Would you like to take me to Edinburgh sometime?'

Joe nearly fell off the armchair answering, 'Of course I would. When would you like to go?'

'How does tomorrow grab you?' Margaret flashed a smile that both mesmerised and confused.

'OK,' he said, before mumbling, 'Jim's gonny want the house – ah should ask – ah need to ask.' Joe rose from his chair, 'Give us two minutes - Ah need to ask him a question.' He mimed the words "ask him for time off" as he headed for the kitchen.

'Joe?'

He turned around, and she said, 'Tell you what, let's make it Friday, makes it easier for everybody.'

Margaret was surprised by how well she'd handled this situation. She could hear Jim Cassidy vociferously agreeing to her request.

Joe gave a smile and the thumbs-up sign, jauntily strolling back into the living room. His smile was not returned. Margaret looked pensive. 'You've not changed your mind, have you?'

'No, of course not, it's just that I need to ask permission as well.'

'Ask who?' Joe asked.

Margaret whispered dramatically, 'The two policewomen who are looking after me.'

'Oh' Joe nodded his head, feigning abject despair. He was about to say 'another time maybe' when Jim Cassidy came into the room laden with two mugs of coffee and a small tea set.

Cassidy placed the tray on the coffee table in front of where Margaret sat, and picked up the coffees and handed one to Joe.

Margaret's eyes fixed on the bone china tea-set, and she picked up her tea-cup and placed it on the palm of her left hand. Her right hand slowly and carefully pirouetted the cup around. Her eyes followed the floral design that crept over and around the delicate handle. 'This is beautiful,' she said, putting the cup down and picking up the sugar bowl ready for similar consideration.

'It was my wife's,' Jim Cassidy said softly.

'Oh, I shouldn't be using it.'

'Of course you should. It's good to see a beautiful woman using it again.'

Margaret took her time using the tea-set. Both men said nothing. They just watched. There was something childlike about the way Margaret went about pouring herself a cup of tea. The sugar tongs were gently put back in place before the tiny milk jug gingerly dribbled slightly too much milk into her cup. Margaret looked up apologetically before pouring her tea. Then her eyes started darting around the bone china objects on the tray.

'Hold it,' Jim said. He scurried into the kitchen and returned with a tiny ornate silver spoon. 'Enjoy.' He handed Margaret the spoon.

Margaret slowly stirred her tea, gradually becoming aware Joe was watching her. Their eyes met for a moment, and that moment was enough.

Joe felt it, she felt it and Jim Cassidy observed it.

Joe dared himself to stare a fraction of a second longer. Margaret held his gaze before reluctantly bowing her head to taste her tea. Joe's mind was already reliving the moment when Jim Cassidy began speaking.

108

'So you're going on a date to Edinburgh - lovely city, plenty to do there. What do you want to see?'

'The castle,' they said in unison and started laughing.

'It's dear,' Cassidy stated.

'How dear, dear?' Joe asked, failing to suppress a fit of the giggles.

The older man became slightly tetchy, not really feeling part of the joke. 'Well I don't know the exact price – but take my word, it's no' cheap.'

Joe's head was elsewhere. She had not corrected Jim Cassidy when he had said "date", so that's what they must be going on.

'Do you know Edinburgh well, Jim?' Margaret asked.

The older man mulled the question. 'I used to go through there quite a bit when I worked in the service - involved in quite a few transfers - Saughton and Barlinnie, but I know the city well – because of Freda.' Cassidy's eyes watered as he continued. 'We used to drive through there for our anniversary – stayed at the Wee Ivanhoe B&B on Dalkeith Road. The city is gorgeous in May – it's gorgeous all the time, but it's better in May. That's when the flowers really flaunt it in Princes Street Gardens.'

It was obvious to Joe that Jim Cassidy had a tear in his eye, and it was even more obvious just how much he missed his wife. They'd talked the other night and Cassidy's thoughts had registered, but Joe had no comprehension of how you could stay with the same woman for forty years. He was baffled as to why his own parents stayed together for so long. They had family to bring up and that keeps you together, supposedly, but Jim and Freda Cassidy only had each other and yet their love had endured. And that love had grown, even after death.

Joe could see that Margaret was hanging on to the older man's every word. Her eyes looked tearful and there was weariness in her face. The age difference he'd worried about earlier, did not seem so apparent now.

Jim Cassidy's head was down and he stared directly into his coffee. Margaret Logan rose and approached the older man. She gently lifted his head and thumbed the tears away from his eyes. Neither party said a word as Margaret slowly returned to her seat.

The room fell silent. However it wasn't one of those uncomfortable silences. It was as if a time had somehow been set aside for remembering loved ones.

*   *   *

The image came slowly. He wasn't even sure at first if it was a genuine memory. He could see the glowing embers of a small fire just beyond the entrance of the faded indigo tent. A pair of soggy, tan coloured, work-boots were drying next to a small, stone-circled camp-fire. Joe could feel the warmth of that fire now.

He was standing outside the tent feeling elated, knowing the rain was having a Kit Kat (taking a break). His father was stretched out on the canvas fold-away chair, his feet propped as close to the fire as was humanly possible. Joe could see his friend sitting enthralled.

'Your feet are steaming, Mr Ray,' Joe's friend blurted out.

'They're totally steamboats,' Joe screamed and the two boys went into hysterics. Joe's father merely pulled his feet apart to witness better the plumes of vapour rising from his sodden socks.

'D'you think my feet sneaked down the pub and forgot to tell the wife?'

The boys took a pause from their laughter, looked at the older man, then each other and then screamed together, 'Oh Aye,' before resuming their infectious laughter.

His dad had called the holiday "The second summer of Lola" because it was Joe's turn to take possession of the old Dansette portable record player. Joe also inherited numerous classic sixties singles. The record player went on holiday too, accompanied by Joe's best friend John McGuire. The Kinks' classic, Lola, had taken both of them hostage. They played it at every waking opportunity. They'd liked songs before, been smitten by a tune, but this was different. Lola was love and Lola was the real thing.

His dad had told them, 'Lola's going to burn out the batteries.'

'We know the caravan's wired to the mains, Da,' Joe had said.

'Lola's going to burn out the mains as well.'

Then Joe remembered something. It had been his father who'd given young John McGuire his nickname.

'My mum and dad call me John Joseph,' McGuire had said rather formally during dinner on the first night of the holiday.

'Is that no' a bit long-winded, son? Why don't we call you JJ? That's got a nice ring to it, JJ.'

*   *   *

Another street name from the past promptly brought Joe back to the present.

'Chambers Street.'

Joe was confused. Why was she asking about a street?

Jim Cassidy answered her question, 'The museum - d'you want to visit the museum?'

'Is that where the museum is?' she asked, interested.

'Aye - National Museum of Scotland - well worth a visit.'

Joe brought himself into the conversation with a hefty cough.

They both turned to look at him.

'Oh you're back with us - you were on planet Joe there,' Cassidy said.

'Sorry - I heard you mentioning Chambers Street,' Joe said.

'You're going to see the big whale, Joe,' Cassidy scoffed.

'Big whale?' Joe looked more confused than before.

'In the museum, you're going to see the big whale in the museum.'

Cassidy was making reference to the complete skeleton of a blue whale housed in the museum.

'There's a museum in Chambers Street?' Joe said.

'Aye, it no just High Courts, judges and lawyers. There's also stuff worth visiting – is that not right, Margaret?'

Margaret's eyes sought the floor and she made no attempt to answer.

Joe noticed the change in Margaret's demeanour but said nothing. He was just happy to be going on a date.

'How will you be going to Edinburgh – bus – train?' Cassidy never gave them time to answer and he made the decision for them. 'Train's better, you'll be there in three quarters of an hour. Everything you want to see is in walking distance – that's what's so good about Edinburgh – got a compact city centre.'

Joe caught Margaret's attention and they both smiled as the older man divulged his opinions on Scotland's capital.

'Do you want to go home?' he asked quietly.

She nodded and her eyes took a stretch, 'Would you like to walk me home?'

Joe pursed his lips. 'Will I need an umbrella?' he asked pensively.

'Only if you're going to use it as a parachute. I just stay downstairs, Joe.'

Joe turned around, showing his back. 'Jump on and I'll get my brolly.'

'We'll walk, daft arse, we'll walk,' she said.

Margaret went over, kissed Jim Cassidy's cheek and thanked him for his hospitality.

As they left, Jim Cassidy began searching for his Edinburgh A to Z.

The short walk to Margaret Logan's apartment was the highlight of the evening. Joe felt like a lovesick schoolboy, shy, awkward and more alive than he could remember.

They stood outside the door of her apartment in complete silence, for what seemed an eternity. In reality, they stood there for two minutes and seven seconds before a word was spoken. There was nervous eye contact, as if they both knew the other's fragility.

Joe broke the silence, 'So we'll get the train for our date?'

Margaret merely nodded her head.

'Did you hear what I said – our date.' He emphasised the D in date.

'And your point is, caller?' Margaret said dryly.

Joe was taken aback by her nonchalance, but he smiled none the less. 'It's been a long time since I've been on a date.'

'You should get out more, mate,' she replied in the previous tone.

'Where I was, you didn't get asked out too much.'

'That's not what I heard. I heard it's rife in there.'

'Are you winding me up?'

'Do you need to ask?'

Joe glowed from the heat this little bout of cerebral foreplay generated.

Margaret was also aware of the effect her behaviour was having on her admirer.

He bent forward and ever so slowly made eye contact. And then he gently kissed her on the lips. She pulled back slightly before returning his kiss.

'Goodnight, Joseph.'

Joe turned and slowly walked upstairs. At the turn of the staircase he heard her say.

'I'd quite like to go to the pictures sometime.'

Then he heard the door of her apartment close and he said one word out loud. Well, not too loud. He said, 'Yippee.'

Chapter Twenty

He got up on Monday morning feeling more elated than the night before. He was on his way to purchase half a dozen morning rolls. They'd be well-fired and they'd definitely taste terrific. The papers would be filled with horrific events, gangland slayings, probably perpetuated by JJ McGuire and associates. As a civilian now, he'd relish reading about them. It was amazing how the moist touch and taste of a pair of lips could change the world. Helen of Troy's face launched a thousand ships. Well - Margaret's kiss had rocketed him into a sublime orbit. He stopped momentarily, admiring his own bravado in a shop window. She could have pulled away but she didn't; she kissed him back. Not too much, just enough, just enough to change the world. He nearly bumped into the door mirror of a white Transit van. As he steadied himself, he realised there was something familiar about the huge bulk of a man making his way from the rear of the vehicle.

'Get in, Joe, don't give me an excuse.'

Suddenly, horse-drawn coaches turned back into pumpkins.

'Do you need an excuse, Yogi?'

'You'll probably not believe me, but I always did.'

The reply startled Joe.

Yogi's eyes gestured towards the van's rear doors and Joe accepted the request. He was relieved to find no-one was inside. Yogi shut the back doors, noisily banging the dodgy latch back into position before applying the padlock.

That's fucked that escape plan, Joe thought. He turned towards the cab and saw it was blocked off with a grille. The grille in itself did not look that strong, but crucially you had to be wary about what sat on the other side of the grille.

'Don't pish your pants. If I was going to hurt you, you'd be hurting now,' Yogi said, easing his giant frame into the driver's seat.

Joe stared at a pile of dust sheets on the floor that failed to reassure him of Yogi's intentions.

The engine started. 'Joe, sit down and fucking relax, JJ doesn't want anybody seeing you going into his house.'

The big man's attempt at placating Joe failed abysmally. His next proved more fruitful.

He turned around laughing, 'The place is hoaching with paparazzi.'

Joe heard two separate car horns blow at once and then Yogi braked violently, veering the van to the right. Yogi casually opened the door of the van, leaned out and said. 'Oops,' as he stared back at some disgruntled drivers. Toots of horns went silent as Yogi sat blocking the street off for about a minute, before slowly pulling the door closed and resuming his journey at a sedate pace.

Joe felt relieved by these actions. If he was about to be killed, he was sure that his killer would not want so many witnesses to the event.

Big Yogi seemed more convivial than before. 'Where was I? Oh aye, the paparazzi. We are all starting to feel like Britney Spears these days. Every time I get out of a motor, I'm thinking of giving them a money shot, but it's getting too cold not to wear knickers.'

Joe knew the big man was only repeating someone else's crack; JJ's, more than likely. 'How is he?'

'Busy. D'you not read the papers? He's very busy.'

Joe piled the dust sheets together, fashioning a comfortable seat. He was hoping there might be something heavy tucked away under the dust clothes, like a car jack or a wheel brace, but there was nothing. Using something like that would only irritate the big cunt anyway.

The journey went a lot quicker than anticipated. Once or maybe twice, he bothered to stand up to catch glimpses of scenery. They entered Mount Vernon from the tail-end of Shettleston. Joe recognised the Railway Tavern when Big Yogi slowed to toot recognition at some pedestrian. The van sped up again and the driver started talking.

'Get yersel under those covers, Joe.'

'No fucking way, they're bogging.' Joe declared, hoping the tone of his protestations would somehow convince Big Yogi to change his request.

The big man spoke without any emotion. 'Look he doesn't want the press seeing you. The sheets are clean, they just look used.' Big Yogi paused, checked to see if his words were having any effect. They weren't. 'If need be, I'll truss you up myself and I don't do delicate.'

Joe slunk under the sheets like a scalded puppy.

If a bullet is going to come, is it better not to see it? Is it better not to know why you're being killed? Would a reason really make a difference? These were some of the recurring thoughts swirling around inside Joe's head. Bobbing up amongst those thoughts was one beacon of hope. They were friends or used to be best friends. But he'd rejected that friendship, publicly rejected JJ's protection. That must have hurt JJ.

The van started speeding up and began swerving erratically from side to side. Screams of protests could be heard outside. Suddenly, the van screeched to a halt.

'Keep the fuck out my road. Next time, I'll flatten you!' Yogi shouted.

The van lurched forward three times amid more squeals of protest, then the voices dissipated and the van slowed to a steady crawl. The sound under the wheels changed and Joe sensed the tyres were travelling over gravel. The van took a sudden right, braking violently and quickly reversing before coming to an abrupt stop. The doors were pulled open and successive dips in the suspension told Joe that at least two men were now inside the back of the van. He could feel hands pulling at the pile of dust sheets, but they were not unwrapping him. A hand grasped his ankle and pulled him along the floor.

'What end's up?' a voice asked abrasively.

'Who cares?' a different voice answered.

Joe did not recognise the voices. He didn't struggle as they pulled him from the van. He groaned with pain and fright as he was dropped onto gravel. His left arm became free and he felt cold fresh air breathe against it. Two hands clamped onto his arm and he was dragged up some stairs.

'Shut the door,' he heard Big Yogi bark.

Joe heard a door close and then he felt as if he was being pulled in ten different directions at once. He came to, free from the cloying dustsheets, sitting bedraggled and befuddled on cold black floor-tiles. He looked up to see JJ McGuire offering him a mug of warm tea.

'Don't worry; it's not poison,' McGuire said with a touch of endearment in his voice.

Joe took the mug with both hands and sipped slowly at the tea, relieved to see Yogi and the others leave the room.

'Don't think much of your kitchen.'

JJ laughed. 'This is what we call a utility room, mate.'

Joe looked to his left and saw sunlight bounce off a peach-coloured toilet seat behind a rustic looking, black glossed door. 'Don't think much of your toilet, either,' he said.

'That's for the help; saves them from coming into the house - that does Eileen's nut in.'

'Can I see her?' Joe asked between sips. 'It'd be nice to meet her.'

'Sorry, she's away, got the boys with her.'

'What boys?'

'She has my two sons with her.'

'Where are they?'

'That's a secret,' McGuire laughed.

Joe blew slowly onto the mug of tea, creating a series of ripples. He looked up and asked, 'Am I going to be killed?'

'No.'

'Hurt?'

'No.'

'Then why am I here?'

'I wanted to show you around the house.' McGuire paused before saying, 'I also wanted to ask you a big favour.'

Joe's eyes filled with tears. He wasn't sure if they were tears of joy, relief, exhaustion or gratitude. He wiped his eyes, realising they were all of the above.

'I'll never ever understand you, JJ. I thought you could not surprise me any more.'

McGuire just smiled, 'C'mon see the house. You'll love it.'

Joe stood up, looked around the worktops for somewhere to rest the mug of tea. He placed the mug next to two huge Belfast sinks that looked as if they had never been used.

'What's the favour?' Joe asked with a glimmer of sarcasm.

'I want you to kill me.'

Chapter Twenty One

It seemed to take an eternity for the train to clear Queen Street station. The 9.47 to Edinburgh crept forward in fits and starts. Conversations inside the second carriage were hushed. Most of the talk was concerned, in some way, with the bodies of dead gangsters sprouting up in the "dear green place" called Glasgow. Clichés bounced around like a pinball. 'If you live by the sword,' or 'You don't get killed for nothing,' swiftly followed by that old chestnut, 'As long as they're only killing each other, eh?'

If you believed the general conversation, then Glasgow was a city where only one degree of separation distanced you from the criminal underworld. People talked openly about where the blame lay for the bloodshed. "McGuire." Some claimed to know him personally, the majority knew someone who knew him, and a few implied, "They just knew." These conversations were rampant in a city gripped by fear and curiosity.

Sitting at one of the highly sought after table seats was the one man in Scotland who knew for certain who was responsible for what the papers termed "Street Carnage." Better than that, he knew why. Joe felt like sneering at them like a wounded child. "You'll never get it in a million years." Christ, he was finding it impossible to get and he'd got it, explained straight from the horse's mouth. My God, even Yogi and the hired help don't know and they're blowing away dubious businessmen, mutilating low-order pushers with archaic forms of punishment and they haven't a clue why.

The discussion, that's what he termed the conversation he'd had concerning McGuire's predicament; that discussion had kept him up most of last night and he was determined not to let it spoil his day. Problem was - it was spoiling his day.

'You don't look too clever,' Margaret had said, greeting him at her door.

'I could say the same thing about you.'

She threw her eyes back in her head, saying louder than necessary, 'My guests have been asking questions, a lot of questions.'

'Least you've got an excuse,' he sighed, as she let him into the flat. He immediately said hello to the two detectives. He felt no animosity, even though they were police. He was happy they were looking after someone he cared about. The detectives seemed friendly enough, but he knew they had reservations about today's trip, even though Henderson had OK'd it.

'Would you like some coffee, Joe?' DC MacCallum asked.

'That would be nice.' He hesitated, then said, 'You're Marian, eh?'

'Oh sorry,' she said, seeming a touch nervous. She leaned forward, offering her hand. Joe shook it warmly. 'This is my friend and colleague, Helen Hannah. We call her Nell.'

DC Hannah stepped forward. 'It's very nice to meet you.'

Joe was instantly bowled over by DC Hannah. She looked pure class and sounded like she was minor royalty.

'Joe, it's rude to stare!' Margaret stressed.

The slight rebuke stung Joe. He rubbed his eyes and step backwards. 'Sorry, it's the accent. I wasn't expecting it.'

Margaret flung her arms around DC Hannah.

'Ah told you, Nell, you're too posh for the likes of us.'

DC Hannah returned the affection and said in a really bad Glasgow accent, 'I'm wan classy lassie, by the way.'

Margaret Logan shrieked an exaggerated laugh that somehow shocked any residual tension from the room.

Joe found the situation strange, but pleasant. It was the first time in his life when meeting the police was not a decidedly frosty experience. But they were working and never ever forget - a copper is always a copper. He stopped himself mid-thought. He was being a touch hypocritical. He was sharing a house with a prison warden - a man who'd been a turn-key for forty odd years.

Well, he'd changed. He felt more comfortable in their company than he did with those arseholes back at Abercrombie Street or with McGuire's cronies. Anyway, it was plain there was genuine affection there. It was more than just a job. That was obvious.

'We've made you some sandwiches – nice ciabatta bread,' DC MacCallum said.

Joe had never heard of it, but he'd eat it anyway.

'We'll drive you to the station,' Nell Hannah declared.

*   *   *

'If you're prepared to wait for about quarter of an hour - you'll qualify for the Away Day special.' The counter assistant was giving off a working-class hero vibe as if constructing concessions on the hoof. 'There's stipulation's regarding return times...... that's the only drawback......,' he mused.

'We'll just pay full price, mate, if that's OK. We're not quite sure when we're coming back.' Joe smiled, handing over two crisp twenties.

Margaret was impressed and she looked it. She detested stinginess in people as much as she detested someone who flashed their cash too much, and she'd seen plenty of that during harsher times.

They sat there like a mirror image of each other as they both slowly blew into the lids of the coffee cartons.

'They're meant to keep it nice and warm.' Margaret smiled, keeping eye contact.

'They're keeping it roasting. It's burning the mouth off me.'

'Blow harder,' she suggested.

'I'm not sure about that.'

'Why?'

'It's going to bubble up, come out the wee hole and burn my nose.'

'That could be a problem - that could be very painful.'

'It could also be very embarrassing.'

'Why don't you give it a wee go, take a chance,' Margaret said, super-serious.

Joe returned the sombre look. 'If you're sure,' he said as he leant over the table and tentatively pursed his lips. He cast Margaret a look of mock terror and then blew into the lid with sustained pressure until hot liquid spurted from the only escape route available and landed on his lips, chin and nose. Joe sat there, white coffee dripping from his face, trying to appear philosophical.

'It's not as hot as I thought it was going to be.'

'Still hot though?' Margaret enquired.

'Oh yes,' he said, placing the paper cup on the table, moving it a couple of times, leaving rings of liquid on the pearl-grey Formica top. He wiped at his face and then stopped as his companion opened a fresh pack of tissues and tenderly wiped his face.

Joe leaned back, thinking how beneficial an act of stupidity can be. As she finished wiping his face, she took his hands in hers. Her hands felt slightly rough, although they looked as smooth as marble. She wiped his hands clean, then brought them to her lips and blew gentle breath across his fingers. The heat from that breath cooled as it passed over his white knuckles.

The heat inside Joe was intense, so intense, he could feel it bubble up inside him, seeking an outlet, rising, swirling around his neck and surging into his head. He tried to keep his eyes clamped shut, tried to endure that feeling a moment longer, but his eyes sprang open.

She noticed straight away, but did not say anything; there was no need. They knew silence was required. Words would only interrupt this moment. Both knew their souls had touched. The moment was fleeting but intensely powerful. They both looked a little scared, and a little confused.

Joe attempted to remove the lid from the coffee carton as he placed it on the table. At that moment of contact, the train violently surged forward. Coffee went everywhere and they both sat vibrating, stifling laughter that spasmodically spat itself out from their clenched mouths.

*   *   *

'Where's Chambers Street?' she asked.

'Oh my God, a Scottish tourist,' the girl looked confused. 'Sorry, hen – ma sense of humour. Just carry on across the bridge and it's the third on your right,' the old man said.

Margaret took Joe's arm in hers and led him across the North Bridge. They stopped a couple of times. It couldn't be helped; the scenery demanded attention and admiration. The weather in Glasgow had been good, but today, it proved a poor second to Edinburgh's. The Castle stood impressively silhouetted against a vibrant sky. They turned in unison, their eyes panning across impressive architecture before resting on Arthur's Seat, and then seeking and settling on the cool Prussian Blue of the Firth of Forth. In the distance, they saw the Kingdom of Fife. This October day, Fife's coastline was making a plausible impression of the Mediterranean coast. They felt as if they could taste the sea air above the exhaust fumes of the relentless heavy traffic trundling across the old stone bridge. They joined some of that traffic and headed for the National Museum of Scotland.

Joe was walking too fast for her liking. She was struggling to keep up, and struggling to read a succession of blue plaques fixed to the walls of the University buildings. She was getting too hot and she shouldn't have been. She knew it was down to panic. Fuck, she swore silently, I should've stuck in better at school. Fuck? I should've gone to school. Her eyes scanned up and down the street. At the far end, she saw a more modern type of building. It was fawn, tan coloured - she was never sure if fawn and tan were the same colour.

'I think that's the new bit of the museum,' Joe said helpfully.

She smiled, trying to appear calm as they were crossing the road now, going in and around the islands of cars parked in the middle of the street. Still she could not see it, but spotting some police cars parked gave her optimism.

'There we go.'

Joe's voice startled her and she muffled the word, 'Shit.'

'You OK?' he asked, as he led her towards the huge broad sweep of stairs leading up to the museum entrance.

'Sorry – I was in a wee world of my own there.'

'Wait till you get inside. There are loads of wee worlds in there.'

Just as she was about to enter the revolving doorway, she turned for one last scan of the street. Her gaze followed the roofline of the building opposite until it stopped at a solitary stone cherub, a baby, a child angel, with a hammer in its hand. The building looked familiar, reminding her of Buckingham Palace; the sandstone was clean, very different from the charcoal-coloured buildings they'd scurried past earlier. Just underneath the cherub, in huge lettering arching across the front of the building, were the words "Crown Office" and her heart soared. She bobbed left and right, trying to get a better view of the statue. However, the glaring sun made that impossible. She moved slightly to her left, trying to see if the child angel had little wings on its back. However, it was impossible to tell due to the sun's brightness. Wings or not, this baby looked as if it meant business. It held a judge's hammer in its hands. This was a sign, a sign she was doing the right thing. In her head, she said a solemn prayer to the Stone Angel, imploring it to grant all her children protection. She asked for one thing more. She asked for Justice.

She pulled Joe through the museum's revolving doors, whispering gleefully, 'Let's go see the big whale.'

*   *   *

The eye contact between the guards was subtle, but clearly hinted that they should approach with caution. As they walked, the taller of the two men spoke discreetly into the mouth-piece of his radio head-set he held slightly away from his face. 'There's a problem with the porcelain.' Seconds later, four other men responded to the code that took them to the stairwell leading down to the ladies' toilets.

The man standing at the top of the stairwell seemed very agitated. 'Please - check again.'

'I've checked twice, son - there's no one in there,' the old lady said apologetically.

Joe bounded down at least ten or twelve steps, cursed to himself, spun around and raced back upstairs saying, 'Shit, she's gone.' He looked about frantically. There were shoals of schoolchildren everywhere, mingling dolefully around exhibits in the great hall.

The teachers shepherding the children could be heard placating kids with names like Jessica, Francesca and Justin, or sarcastically telling their charges that if they didn't take an interest in the pottery section, they would not be visiting the Jurassic section. 'That's correct, Colin, no dinosaurs.' Little Colin looked stunned.

Joe waltzed by little Colin and the others as fast as he could, niftily dodging pillars and rounding free-standing exhibits, ducking down every now and then to look under the huge display cases, scanning along the ground, hoping to see the one pair of legs he could recognise. There was no sign of her. He stopped, played an instant playback - she definitely hadn't passed by him – no way. He about-turned for a third time to make his way back to the stairwell, only to find his progress was halted by two sturdy men in blue blazers.

'Can we be of assistance, sir?'

Joe decided against knocking them out the way. 'No, everything's cool.' He turned and met two more blue blazers. His eyes sank to the floor and he let out a pitiful howl of dejection, 'I've lost her.'

The security men looked relieved. One asked, 'What age is your daughter?'

'She's not my daughter.'

Joe knew it wasn't an arrest, but they were escorting him to the security office. He did not want to cause trouble or offence. He wanted help from these men, and he wanted help from God so that he could get his concerns across in the proper manner.

He wanted them to turn the museum upside down so that they'd find her quickly. He wanted a phone so that he could talk to Henderson, and he wanted help to remain rational. Less than a handful of people knew where they were today. Three were police and the fourth was Jim Cassidy - someone he trusted implicitly. She could be lost somewhere in the museum, she could have taken a wrong turn and she could be just as frantic as he was.

*   *   *

'What's your business here?' the doorman asked for the third time and waited for an answer.

'I'm here to see Lord Bullock, it's a personal matter,' Margaret said in her best, "To the Manor Born" accent.

'What department does he work in?'

'Oh, this is so embarrassing; you know I can't remember, it's completely gone from my head.'

The doorman remained stone-faced.

'Is there a judges' department, I just know Rameses is a judge, quite a good one I'm told.'

'Well, darling, all the good judges are round at the Court of Session, so I suggest you go there, because you will not get into this building.'

'But I know he works here; I saw a photo of him standing right at this doorway....' Margaret began crying and went into distress mode.

'Lord Bullock worked here a long time ago. Please go round to the Court of Session.'

'I don't know where that is, mate,' Margaret said as her posh accent malfunctioned.

'I'll show you,' the doorman said as he walked out onto the pavement.

*   *   *

Margaret clutched the doorman's hastily drawn map to her chest and hurried onto George IV Bridge. She hoped and prayed that Joe would understand. She liked him, but this was something she had to do. He'll realize I was right when he meets the children.

Why's he drawn a bridge? She asked herself as she looked ahead. I can't see a bridge. She wasn't an expert on bridges, but they were usually easy to spot. Then she saw an iron fence spanning a gap in the buildings. She was beginning to think she'd been played for a fool, when she turned and saw the unmistakable sight and shape of St Giles Cathedral through the railings. She looked at the map again, thinking the doorman must have been a good drawer at school. She threaded her way through the tourists congregating on the Royal Mile.

*   *   *

Mark Henderson peeled the little yellow post-it from his left hand and pressed it onto his desk; he punched the number written on it into his phone.

'National Museum of Scotland,' a male voice said.

'This is a DCI Henderson phoning from Stewart Street Police Station in Glasgow.'

'Thank you for returning my call so promptly, Mr Henderson. We seem to have a bit of a situation here.'

Henderson could hear a man shouting, 'Let me speak to him,' in the background, then the voice became muffled.

The man on the phone apologised saying, 'Could you give me just one second, Chief Inspector?'

'Detective Chief Inspector.'

There was a pause of a couple of seconds and then the man spoke again.

'Would you be aware of a young woman called Margaret Logan visiting Edinburgh today?'

'Yes, I would,' Henderson butted in. 'What's happened?'

'It appears she has disappeared whilst visiting the museum. My name is Hanlon, Chief of Security at the museum.

Henderson butted in again. 'How long has she been missing?'

'About an hour and a half, we think. We have a chap here who has told us that the girl's life may be in danger.'

'Put him on, Mr Hanlon.'

'She's gone,' Joe spluttered. 'She went to the toilet and that was it.'

'Was anyone following you?'

'No – I don't think so.'

'Don't think so,' Henderson growled.

'I'm certain nobody was following us, least I never saw anyone. We've searched the museum high and low. The security guys have been brilliant, but she's gone.' Joe stopped talking; hoping Henderson might know what to do.

'Stay where you are in case she comes back. I'll get in touch with the Edinburgh police.' He paused before asking, 'Have you looked in the street?'

'That was one of the first things we did,the guards said that nine out of ten adults who get lost are usually sneaking out for a cigarette.' Joe looked to the Head of Security man for verification and received a glazed look in return.

'What's your phone number, Joe?'

'I don't know. Hold on, you must have it or you couldn't have phoned here.'

'No, your phone number – your mobile number,' Henderson rasped.

'I've not got a mobile.'

'Well, take a note of this number and keep it with you.'

Joe gestured for a pen, and a guard sprang to life, offering a pen and grabbing a blank sheet from a dilapidated printer tray.

*   *   *

She was positive everything metallic was in the tray. The man smiled and motioned her through, and the alarm went off. 'You're OK, darling.' He ran a hand-held scanner over her. She froze in an unstable stance.

The scanner beeped again and again when in close proximity to the very broad belt buckle that hung from her hips.

124

'In you go,' the doorman said.

If relief showed on her face, no-one mentioned it. She quickly pushed through a set of double doors and found herself in a huge hall, even grander than the museum's. Intricately carved, wooden beams stretched dramatically across an incredibly high ceiling. They looked like snowflake shapes turned in on themselves.

The room was full of lawyers, advocates and clients, pacing up and down the giant hall, deep in muffled conversation. It looked more like an art gallery than a court, but she felt she was in the right place. A few people in mid-mumble wore judges' wigs and black cloaks, but she could not see her judge. She walked past larger-than-life statues of men in flowing robes. On the massive walls of the Old Parliament Hall, men, similarly attired, peered down at her from huge paintings. These were important men making important decisions. She'd seen a lot of that in her life. They always had that serious look, the look that said - they knew what they were doing. Even when the decision was wrong, and they were usually wrong – they had to look like they knew what they were doing. She'd seen men like these in different situations. When the robes were off, the mask remained in place. She'd heard them berate her in a public court, and then she'd seen them beg her to hurt them in private, imploring her to degrade them as they pled and paid for ridicule.

She took an exit and entered a corridor filled with smaller paintings of learned men. They might have been painted hundreds of years ago, but one thing was certain - it all came down to size with them and that had never really changed. She turned left and entered the Box Corridor. Running along the length of one wall was a series of two-tiered shelving stacked with small, varnished, wooden cases. They had little brass nameplates on them. She scanned the names, hoping to find Lord Bullock or plain old Rameses Bullock.

She sniggered. Then she saw quaint old telephone boxes, with framed glass windows, like the ones in 1930s Hollywood movies. Next to them, a series of oak-panelled doors with words written in gold, stating who could enter them: Solicitors, Counsel, Private; and the court's Public Entrance.

The next corridor seemed promising. She saw a clutch of legal people looking at a cluttered notice board. A long brass plaque ran above the notice board, giving the court numbers, and more importantly, it gave the names of the judges presiding. Margaret waited patiently for the legal people to finish their business. One of them, a man, turned around and smiled at her.

'I do apologise,' he said.

Then he dramatically swung a cloaked arm up in the air and, like a bullfighter, ushered Margaret past him and allowed her access to the notice board.

'I won't be long,' Margaret returned his gallant smile.

Lord Breaslie, Lord Bryce, and "Oh" *lady judges*, Lady Gaellen and Lady Forrester-Smith either side of Lord Bruce, but she could not see Bullock's name there. She slowly back-tracked until she saw an old church pulpit standing at one of the entrances to the Great Hall. As she walked towards it she felt her hand brush against stone. She turned to her right and saw an alcove. Inside the alcove stood two statues that were just about her size. She stood back slightly and read the small notice that described the statues. They were the sisters Justice and Mercy and they'd been lost for a long time, a couple of centuries in fact, before being rediscovered in 1910 at a house in nearby Drummond Place. The sisters showed the scars of their time on this earth, their noses were missing and their right hands were also lost. It said that the scales of justice were missing from Justice. Margaret felt buoyed. If she needed further proof she was doing the right thing, then this was it. The Stone Cherub had led her here. Of course, Joe would be worried, but there was nothing she could do about that. She would make up for it later. She knew she was in the right place. This is what she'd come looking for - Justice and Mercy, and here they were standing right in front of her. Looking at the figures, it was obvious they'd never had the same attention lavished on them as the men carved in stone that looked down their noses at people finding their way about this place.

*   *   *

Queen's Counsel Thomas Brodie would have recognised Margaret Logan even without the description from Albert, the doorman at the Crown Office. She was the spit of her sister Caroline. Maybe it was time he distanced himself from Lord Bullock. The doorman called him first, but Albert is useful and he is discreet. He smiled as he switched off his mobile and gently tapped her shoulder. 'Please don't be frightened,' he said.

She spun around and looked up at the imposing frame. The man's skin looked as if it was highly polished and drum-tight. Little lines of blood vessels could be clearly seen, following a weak jaw-line. Just as she was about to speak, he spoke.

'If you want to meet Lord Bullock, follow me.' With that, he turned and walked away.

Margaret ignored any thoughts concerning her safety and followed. He stopped half-way along the Box Corridor, fumbling beneath his gown. His face showed exaggerated pain as he eventually produced a small Yale key. He quickly opened the plain oak door with the word PRIVATE on it.

Margaret looked inside. It was small, just a tiny cubicle, like Doctor Who's Tardis in reverse. She'd expected it to lead somewhere. It didn't, but it at least had a light.

'In you go. You will be quite safe,' Brodie smiled.

Margaret looked and sounded sceptical. 'I don't think so.'

'Look dear,' he said patronisingly, 'Counsel has briefed clients in these closets for years – privacy is assured, no prying eyes and no pricked ears.'

Margaret remained unconvinced and it showed.

'Lord Bullock has asked me to find out why you are looking for him.'

'I don't have to go in there to tell you that – I need his help; simple.'

Brodie tempered his anger, muttering. 'It'd be good to know exactly how many little niggerettes are likely to clamber out from under the woodpile.'

'Scuse me, what did you say?'

'If you don't do as I say, you'll be removed from this building and will have no chance of meeting the old boy.'

Margaret's body language complied with the instruction.

Brodie brought out a mobile from a side pocket and waved it. 'You can talk to him just now.' His eyes again motioned her into the cubicle.

Reluctantly, she stepped inside. A shelf about six inches wide ran along the three walls of the cubicle. The wooden panelling had many marks and blemishes on them, varnished over countless times, but still discernible as language.

Brodie stepped inside the box and the situation became very uncomfortable. The position of the shelf forced Margaret's head into his chest. She could smell rancid sweat vying to overpower expensive cologne. She'd smelled similar battles many times before. Personally, she preferred good old-fashioned body odour.

Brodie pressed against Margaret and looked down smugly. 'When these closets were built, people, in general, were a tad smaller.'

Margaret backed herself further into a corner as she felt Brodie press his groin into her stomach, manoeuvring the tip of his erection into the hollow of her belly button.

'For a big man, you're not very big.' Margaret thought derision would debilitate Brodie's ardour. She was mistaken.

Brodie welcomed ridicule. He pressed further against her stomach and handed her the mobile. She took the phone from him and scrutinised the onscreen instructions.

Brodie wrapped an arm around her and pressed the speak button.

Margaret held the phone with two hands, succeeding in keeping Brodie's hanging arm away from her breasts. 'Hello,' she struggled to say.

'Hello, Margaret. It's a pleasure to hear your voice again.'

'I don't know what to call you.'

'I don't mind Vanya.'

'But that's not your real name, is it,' she asked before lashing out at Brodie who'd taken one liberty too many. 'Pack it in, ya dirty bastard.'

'Is everything all right?' Bullock asked, concerned.

'Your pal here is getting a wee bit too friendly.'

'Put him back on.'

Margaret handed the mobile back to Brodie, who theatrically pulled his hand from his cloak like a second-rate magician.

Seconds later, Brodie handed the mobile back, his demeanour completely changed. He quickly backed off, leaving some breathing space between him and Margaret.

Margaret looked Brodie up and down. 'Maybe people were bigger than you thought years ago?'

Brodie said nothing, but his face made a big show of being bored.

Margaret just grinned, delighted with a small victory. 'I need your help, Vanya. My kids are in care and I want them back.'

'I'm not sure if I can be of much assistance there, my dear.'

'Surely someone as prominent and as powerful as you could have some influence.' Margaret did not know where the words were coming from. She was just glad to snatch them from somewhere. She did not want to threaten Bullock. She knew from her time at the cottage how much the old man loved flattery. That would be a better road to travel.

'If I could be of assistance, then it would have to be discreetly. You do understand that my dear.'

'Oh, of course, I just want help, any help; I want Caroline's wee girl back as well. You did hear about Caroline? Somebody killed her, drowned her - held her head down.'

'It's a vile, wicked world, dear. I was heartbroken at her demise.'

Margaret started crying and Thomas Brodie took a worried look at his watch. He was due back in Court 7 shortly, and he knew his clerk would soon be nervously scouting the corridors for him.

'Could you not get the police to buck their ideas up?' she asked.

'If only I could, dear.' Bullock sighed as if he'd answered that question too many times before.

'We were supposed to be your children – kind of – but it's not the same. If we really were your kids, you'd be devastated if somebody took us away. And you'd do anything to get us back,' Margaret stressed. 'Every day they're away from me feels like my Caroline's been murdered again.'

'Margaret, please stop crying. I'll meet you and we'll discuss any help I can give you. Mr Brodie will arrange it, but you have to promise me that you won't discuss it with anyone, especially not Mark Henderson or the officers staying with you.'

'How did you know that?' Margaret asked, shocked that Bullock knew so much about her situation.

'I have been trying to help behind the scenes, making enquiries, not too successfully I'm afraid, but I have tried to keep up with any progress regarding Caroline's sad demise.'

'I thought maybe you or Connie might have been at the funeral. I looked around a couple of times, hoping that you'd make it.'

'I sent flowers,' Bullock lied, 'but I had to be in Edinburgh that day.'

Thomas Brodie cleared his throat and signalled he wanted the mobile back.

'He wants to speak with you, Vanya.' Margaret said.

'I really must hurry up this conversation,' Brodie said tersely.

Margaret could hear Vanya's raised voice reverberate around the small cubicle.

Then Brodie handed her back the phone.

'You're not angry with me, are you?' Margaret asked timidly

'Oh, of course I'm not angry,' Bullock lied again.

'And you will help me?'

'Yes, I'll help in any way I can. Please pass on the children's names and any relevant details to my associate and we'll get things moving this end.'

Margaret let out a strange sort of nervous laugh. 'Oh I'm so glad you are going to help me. I didn't want to get heavy. I know how much you helped us both in the past – the past is in the past, eh?' Margaret stared straight through Thomas Brodie.

'Don't fret, dear. I'll help, but it must remain private. We'll meet soon. Hopefully, I'll have good news.'

'I just want them back. People think they're doing things for the best, putting them in care, but we both know that's not always the case.'

'Please put my associate back on,' Bullock asked.

Margaret passed the phone back to Brodie and she observed his facial expression turn from a hurt child back to the smug bastard who pushed his wee hard cock into her belly.

He scribbled a number onto the back of a plain white card and handed it to her.

She looked at it and knew instantly that it was a mobile number.

'Give me the names of the children.'

He handed her paper and pen.

Margaret carefully printed out the names as Brodie laboured his breathing. She handed pen and paper over and received a plain white card in return.

Devoid of emotion, Brodie instructed, 'Call this number on Sunday at exactly five past five. If you mention anything that's happened today to anyone, then any help on offer is off, and both the judge and I will deny all knowledge of you.'

Margaret nodded agreement, although her face hinted at something else.

Brodie clamped his hands onto her breasts and twisted hard. 'Do you honestly think anyone would give a two-penny fuck about your version of anything?'

Margaret did not give Brodie the satisfaction of seeing pain or fear on her face. She forcefully pulled his hands from her and looked towards the door and waited.

Brodie opened the door of the cubicle and Margaret Logan stepped out, then she coolly and slowly made her way through the Great Hall. She had one last look around at the Men of Power peering out from those dark broody paintings. She left the Court of Session far happier than she'd entered it. She hoped Joe would understand.

*   *   *

Brodie swaggered towards Court 7, his chest puffed out, making a big show of letting an extremely attractive female pass by him. DC Nell Hannah returned the smile.

Chapter Twenty Two

Joe sat there, very still and very ill at ease, with only two security men for company. The others were back patrolling the museum. They'd assured Joe that they'd keep their eyes peeled for Margaret. The two who remained, encouraged Joe to make himself at home and suggested he make himself a coffee.

Joe took them up on their offer. As the kettle slowly started to make perceptible sounds, indicating that it actually worked, Joe Ray made a decision. He felt inside his jacket for a tiny strip of paper. The paper had curled up on itself. Joe straightened it out and pulled it between thumb and forefinger. The fold ensured the paper stayed rigid.

He asked, 'Is there a private phone I can use?'

The two security men looked at each other, hoping the other would make a decision.

Joe spoke from both heart and head. 'Look, I'm really worried. Her sister was murdered not that long ago. It's not that I don't trust the cops, it's just,' he stopped as an icy chill shivered inside his stomach. He steadied himself before putting his cards on the table. 'Look, I need all the help I can get.'

The security men nodded at each other and slowly made their way to the door of the office. 'We'll give you two minutes,' the smaller of the two men said.

'Do you use a dialling code if it's a mobile you're phoning?'

'No, just dial the number,' they answered, mystified.

Joe could tell they were having second thoughts about him using the phone. He quickly dialled the number. The dialling tone seemed strange to Joe. He wasn't exactly sure if he actually had a connection. Then a voice said, 'Hmmppph.'

'It's me,' Joe said.

'Where are you?'

'Edinburgh. I'm at the National Museum of Scotland.'

'You're where?'

Joe clamped the phone closer to his ear, trying to muffle out any bad language, 'I need a favour,' he asked.

'I need a favour as well.'

'There are favours and there are favours,' Joe remonstrated.

'That's exactly the way I see it.'

'Look, are you going to help me here? I'm desperate.'

'What is it?'

The floodgates opened and words spewed fast and furious. 'The lassie I'm with has disappeared. Somebody tried to abduct her last week. Her sister was murdered not that long ago. I've told the cops she's missing and I'm waiting on them getting back to me. I'm in Edinburgh. I don't know a fuckin' living soul.......'

'Name?'

'Pardon?' Joe took a huge gulp of air.

'Ah need a name, Joe.'

'Her name is Margaret - Margaret Logan.' Joe waited for a response and then he snapped, 'Hello, are you still there?' The urgency in Joe's voice was apparent to the guards at the door. They turned around, staring vacantly at him, unsure how they could help.

'Who's dealing with the case?' McGuire eventually asked.

'DCI Henderson. He's meant to be getting back to me.'

'He questioned you the other day, didn't he?'

'He thought I had something to.......'

'And you were only doing your All Action Hero stint.'

'Aye, something like that.'

'What have I always told you about women?' McGuire joked.

'I've forgotten,' Joe answered.

'Join the club.' McGuire paused before adding, 'Are you an item?'

'No, it's not like that – don't get me wrong – I like her - she's younger, quite a bit younger.'

'You're hoping to itemise her?'

'No.'

'She's not got a close-up of your wrinkly coupon and went Joe the Toff, Joe?'

'Look, I know you're pulling my chain – but I'm dead serious. I think somebody has grabbed her – and I've not got a fucking clue why.'

McGuire changed tack instantly.

'Tell you what,' he said. 'I'll make a few calls, see what I can find out – and you can phone me in an hour – OK.'

'Do you know who she is, JJ?'

'No. Should I?'

'She's Owny MacNee's niece.'

'No-Strings Owny?'

'Aye – "No-Strings Owny".' Joe failed to hide the resignation in his voice and had to hold the phone away from his ear as JJ McGuire manically burst into song, Pinocchio's song.

'I've got no strings to hold me up.'

'JJ, it's not funny – it never ever was FUNNY.'

'Well, it's still fresh with me - perhaps that's the only bonus I get these days, so I might as well enjoy it – I've got no strings to hold me up....'

Joe was powerless and waited until McGuire finished his jaunt down memory lane.

'Finished?'

'Not as finished as that cunt was...'

Joe cut in angrily. 'We know he's finished, but what about the people he left behind. She's part of that and I feel responsible for her.'

'So that's you being responsible, asking me to find her?'

'We're both responsible, that's a fact.' Joe tensed, waiting for the retort that stayed put.

'Phone in an hour and I'll see what I can do.'

'Thanks JJ.'

'Buy a mobile, ya miserable bastard.'

*   *   *

McGuire hung up and sat back in his leather easy chair, mulling over the name Margaret Logan. This was the second time he'd heard that name in a matter of days. 'Yogi.'

'Aye.' the big man popped his head just inside the room.

'Get Wagner and take him somewhere quiet.

'Now?' Yogi asked.

'Yes, now.'

*   *   *

Joe fumbled the phone onto the receiver as the security men came back into the office. 'That was some two minutes,' the taller one said.

'I'm really sorry about that. There's a good chance the guy I called can help.'

'Who knows, she might just walk back into the museum as right as rain,' the smaller man suggested.

Joe attempted a smile, unsure if it was successful. His head was somewhere else. He was in a dark place, and Pinocchio's song was being sung over and over again.

Chapter Twenty Three 1985

Out-of-puff breezes wheezed through the tenement closes on Wellshot Road. The day was beautiful. Streams of cherry blossom nudged up against the pavements, obliterating all signs of litter. The petals had recently migrated from Tollcross Park. Most kids were barefoot today and mostly wearing swim wear. Soon they would find the huge T-shaped water keys they'd planked last summer, and burst water mains would be erupting and cascading, regulating the temperature of every kid in the East End.

Two young men strolled into the close of number 48. According to the fashion of the day, their jeans were pulled high on the waist, and the bright pastel shirts were baggy at the belt-line and opened to the navel. The sleeves were rolled high and tight, strangling the biceps. Oddly, they wore steel toe-capped work boots below their fashionable apparel. In their hip pockets, each had Ball Peen hammers, their shafts shortened to the width of an adult hand. At the far end of the close a tall, well-built young man stood, silhouetted, staring onto the back court. He seemed to be enjoying himself, yelling words of encouragement at two toddlers a wee bit scared about stepping into the small paddling pool he'd filled up earlier that day.

The two men approached hesitantly. They had their hands in the air signifying that they were unarmed.

'Owny – can we have a word?' asked the man with red hair and blonde highlights.

Owny MacNee turned around confidently. The foot pump he'd used recently was close by and would be a useful weapon. On top of that, anywhere he ran to in this vicinity, tried and trusted help would be close at hand. 'Aye – what can I do for you?' he smiled.

'We just want a friendly word,' JJ McGuire said.

'It's too hot a day to be rolling about the floor. Besides I'm not wearing my hard shoes.'

'We've got a sweetener for you.' The man with the highlights tweaked a manila envelope apart revealing the bundle inside.

'Much?' Owny asked.

'Five hundred.'

'What have I got to do for that?'

'You don't have to do fuck all,' JJ said.

'I charge a wee bit more for doing - fuck all.'

Joe stepped forward, hand outstretched, offering the envelope.

Owny eventually took the package. 'I take it this will be a regular thing?'

'How regular is regular?' JJ asked.

'Weekly,' Owny said, pointing towards the children splashing about in the paddling pool. 'I've got the upkeep of an outdoor swimming pool to think about.' Owny turned his back on them and suddenly he felt cold, fresh air on the back of his legs just as they crumpled beneath him. However hard he tried, his legs stayed crumpled.

They dragged him into the hazy darkness of the close and pummelled him about the head and arms amid the sounds of splashing and children's raucous laughter.

Joe grabbed the envelope from the ground and stuffed it inside his shirt, as Owny took the opportunity to take two handfuls of Joe's pink cotton shirt.

'Haw Pinocchio, let go of my mate's clobber.'

Owny ignored the request and tried to pull Joe down to his level.

'I'll no fuck yer shirt up,' McGuire assured Joe as he dragged the Stanley knife slowly across Owny's knuckles. As each tendon was cut, the corresponding finger meekly released its grip.

*   *   *

The roller door of the former British Telecom Sherpa van squealed open and quickly screeched shut. The van sped off, leaving criss-crossed lines of fresh blood to bake on hot tarmac. Three men now inside the cabin of the van smiled at each other, a task that had seemed formidable had turned out to be a piece of piss. McGuire sat in the middle with his feet resting on the dashboard.

'You've got to hand it to the old-timers,' he said, 'Freddie was right, cut the fucking hamstrings and it's penalty kicks all the live long day.'

He then battered his fist against the panel separating the cab from the body of the van.

'You hear that Owny, it's going to penalties. What's Pinocchio's song again?' he asked, but an answer was unnecessary as he'd been rehearsing it in his head for days. He began to sing, 'I've got no strings to hold me up.'

*   *   *

In the back of the van, Owny MacNee was doing his sums; aware he was dying or soon would be. He knew why they'd set about him, and he was pretty sure who they worked for. He hoped desperately that someone had

135

reported the incident. There was absolutely no chance of escape. He could not even pull himself along the floor of the van. The blood loss looked horrendous, his trousers were saturated and the delighted screams he heard coming from the driver's compartment meant life was about to get even worse.

*   *   *

Bannock Street, Lilybank, had been due for demolition two years ago. However, four roughcast three-storey tenements remained. Their windows were all boarded up, and steel doors had been erected to stop junkies and vandals accessing the buildings. The steel doors with their industrial padlocks had not worked. That day, vandals and junkies were pretty thin on the ground. They'd been well warned, 'Stay away or return at your own peril.'

Big Owny entered the tenements in Lilybank the same way he'd exited Wellshot Road. The only difference - a couple of old army blankets cocooned him.

JJ McGuire had been as good as his word. The kicks were fast and frequent. Owny soon realised his attacker was enjoying his work. The other guy was different, not really up for the task at hand. Owny knew why he was being punished. He stopped some drug deals in Tollcross, battered a couple of pushers, took their fucking blades off them and even slashed one of them across the arse. He'd confiscated their drugs and their money. He was the leader of the Tollcross Wee-Men, and no cunt was dealing smack in his part of the city. He did not mind them touting speed, and they could throw dope about like a custard pie fight. But he had a thing about heroin. That particular drug had fucked up his sister, and he was fucking committed to ensuring that others would not tread Katherine's path.

*   *   *

Night came and night was fucking cold. Orange street lights shone through the dull yellow plastic sheets that covered the smashed window. The room stank of urine and excrement – and his toiletry needs only added to the stench. All around, remnants of furniture that had been set ablaze long ago still filled the air. His legs felt like ice, but he was sure the bleeding had stopped. Maybe the saturated cloth had dried onto the wounds on his legs. If he did not move, and it was very hard to move, then he might not bleed to death this night. Luckily, the blankets he'd been wrapped in like some Beirut hostage, remained. His arms were aching and he could not grip, but somehow he could still use his thumbs. He pulled the army blankets around him as best he could and passed out.

136

He awoke and looked about the graffiti-strewn walls. He could see the outline of where mirrors and photographs or small paintings used to hang. Small nails protruded from the walls of ripped wallpaper. He tried to imagine what kind of trinkets dangled from them. He could still scream for help, but what kind of help would come? It would probably be a continuation of the violence he'd endured the previous day. He was sure of one thing: his body could not take much more. He somehow managed to crawl along on his elbows towards a warm patch of sunlight that shimmered on the litter-scattered floorboards, and lay there waiting for his adversaries to return. He did not have to wait too long.

* * *

McGuire announced his presence with a forceful kick to the back of the head. He had someone else with him - an older man, say around the thirty mark, and both men were drinking. McGuire was supping straight from the neck of a big bottle of Whitbread. He smirked, saying 'See, when I finish this, I'm going to stick it up your fucking arse. You're going to be an example. A wise man told me, there are no good or bad examples, there are only examples.'

Owny said nothing in reply. Whatever energy remained was reserved for staying alive.

'Strip him,' McGuire barked.

'I'm not touching him, his clothes are bowfin,' the older man winced.

'Cut the clothes off the cunt. Nobody will hear you.'

The wounds opened instantly as McGuire forced and screwed the neck of the bottle deep into Owny's bloodied anus.

Joe Ray walked in just at that moment. 'What the fuck are you doing?'

'Enjoying myself,' McGuire said, smearing patches of blood across his own sleeves.

Big Owny pleaded hard with himself not to cry, but his tears weren't listening. He willed himself to live, even though he wanted to die, wanted to leave this world there and then. He tried to crawl away, but that option was physically impossible now. There was no strength left in his arms. He couldn't even roll into a ball. He thought about the next life, if there was one, and then he saw them, saw them clear as day. It was their fourteenth wedding anniversary celebration. Mum and Dad giving it "big licks" posing by the fireplace, fancy wee whisky tumblers pinched between finger and thumb, toasting each other the way the toffs do. The image left and was replaced with something stronger. Vengeance. He thought about a meeting with God or Satan. It did not matter who, as long as one of those higher powers could grant him another audience with John Joseph McGuire when both men were on their toes. Then Owny heard words of respite.

'Enough, he's had enough.'

McGuire looked up but remained silent.

'Let's go,' Joe said and McGuire's sidekick desperately complied with the command.

McGuire whispered, 'It was quite tricky getting that fucking thing up there, but it's going to be a lot more difficult getting it back out.' He pulled a claw hammer from his belt and, two-handed, brought the hammer down on the base of the bottle protruding from the bloody mess that was Owny MacNee.

Joe stood frozen as McGuire brushed past him and slowly descended the stone stairs, and a song echoed off the walls of that graffiti-covered close.

'I've got no strings
So I have fun
I'm not tied up to anyone
They've got strings
But you can see
There are no strings on me.'

Astonishingly, Joe found a working phone-box in Lilybank, and six minutes later an ambulance drew up at 24 Bannock Street. Three days later, the junkies and the glue-sniffers returned to their playground.

Chapter Twenty Four

Joe had stopped fidgeting, stopped trying to look hopeful, and the security men had given up the consolatory glances. Then, just like the guard had said, Margaret Logan walked back into the museum.

Joe just did not look relieved. He looked beaten, and questions formed a disorderly queue in his head. He rose from his seat and put his arms around her. 'OK?'

'Sorry, Joe.'

He held her close to him, returning knowing glances at the throng of security personnel. She broke away momentarily. She began crying. 'I just had a freaky. I just had to get away for a bit – I just had to think – I just had to get away and think, Joe.'

Joe held her close to him again, asking Mr Hanlon, 'Could you call DCI Henderson and tell him everything is OK?'

Hanlon seemed happy to oblige, and seconds later he handed the phone over to Joe. 'He wants a word.'

'Aye.'

'What's the story – anybody try anything?' Henderson asked.

'No, nothing like that. She just had to be on her own for a bit – she freaked. Her words, Inspector, not mine.'

'Do you believe her?'

'Of course, why wouldn't I? There's not a mark on her, but she is upset.'

'Get her back home straight away. I'll arrange an escort.'

'What do you mean?'

'I'll arrange for a couple of police officers to make sure that she gets back to Glasgow safe and sound.'

'I'll do that.'

'You've lost her once today already.'

'Well, there won't be a second time.......'

'Put Hanlon back on,' Henderson insisted, and Joe reluctantly handed over the phone.

*   *   *

Inside Stewart Street police station, DCI Mark Henderson slowly blew onto a mug of coffee handed to him by DC MacCallum. He winked at her, and was touched to see his wink returned. 'Tell DC Hannah to make sure she's on the same train as they two.'

DC MacCallum made the call.

The contrast between the two journeys was significant. The mood was sombre, and both their faces were sullen. They sat beside each other as opposed to smiling at each other across a table filled with treats. This time, the table was empty and it seemed like they lacked the energy to look out the window and take in the scenery. Both stared vacantly at the empty seats opposite. Joe had stopped asking questions. It was pointless. He wasn't getting anywhere. He knew she was lying, that was obvious, and she was a bad liar. Joe knew the difference between a good and a bad liar. He knew because he'd just spent twenty years among brilliant liars. His head was crammed full of questions.

Did she meet somebody or did somebody get to her? He thought back to the day he first met her. *She was being taken somewhere. They weren't fuckin' around. She'd be taking the same fucking exit route as her wee sister. That's why the police had her under surveillance. They detectives are babysitting her for a reason. She must know something? She must have seen something? Fuck sake, the cops aren't exactly setting the heather on fire here – probably waiting for someone to show their hand.* Then it slapped him. They were waiting for someone to show their hand *again*. The word jumped about his brain like a demented puppy. *Why would they let somebody like me take her to Edinburgh?*

Joe looked around the train compartment. It wasn't that busy, there were roughly twelve other people in the carriage. *How many of them were working undercover?* Joe's eyes darted from face to face. He could see a couple of candidates ticking all the boxes. However, the more he looked, the more paranoid he became. Diagonally to his right, a man sat with one of those big bastards of a newspaper almost stapled to his face. The pen in his right hand hinted that the man was doing the crossword puzzle. The hint was subtle. Joe could not remember seeing the man put pen to paper. Maybe the guy was just stupid. Joe imagined two eye-holes cut into that huge newspaper. Perhaps they were female, same as the two working surveillance. Or perhaps they came as an item? He leaned slightly to his right and caught sight of a middle-aged couple four rows in front of him. They looked affable enough, and they looked as if they were actually in love. *That's really mixing business and pleasure.*

He cast a cursory glance at Margaret; her eyes were down, her demeanour flat and her lips were petted. Fuck, she looked good grumpy. He wanted her so much, but his major problem was this. He just did not know what to fucking say to her.

Paranoia kicked in again. *I might be glad that undercover plods are close by. What if there is a cunt, or cunts, on board who want to end her and any silly fucker stupid enough to get involved?* His eyes darted around the carriage, looking at faces that were becoming familiar and were now having the audacity to re-invent themselves.

*   *   *

She could see he was agitated, knew he was annoyed, although he hadn't said so. She felt guilty about tricking him. He didn't deserve it. She gently edged closer to him, apprehensive in case of rejection. She slipped her hand into his and looked into his face. She smiled timidly and rested her head on his shoulder. She closed her eyes and pretended to sleep, but she would not sleep.

The image of the stone cherub was inside her head. The child angel with the judge's hammer in his hands was dishing out justice. Then another thought crept in. It was Connie's instructions from 1994 that directed them to the small petrol station where Uncle Vanya picked them up, sitting as promised inside the old, burgundy Rover, waiting patiently in a small lay-by four hundred yards from the petrol pumps. Neither of them had ever heard of that colour before. When they saw the car, they realised it was the colour of cheap red wine.

He'd wanted to help, wanted to help so much, but he had concerns. He hinted at "restraints financial" and said "space was at a premium" and that the sleeping arrangements would be cramped, finally stressing that perhaps he could not look after both of them at the same time. Margaret had taken the hint. Uncle Vanya had been kind, gentler than Connie, when it came to that.

The cottage looked as if it had come straight out of a fairy tale. He'd said his Aunt had bequeathed him the property and, 'It's my solemn duty to return the cottage to its former glory.'

Margaret remembered the wee blue post box, the same as the Americans had, far away from the house.

'There will be no letterbox-rattling, noisy postmen rudely awakening our slumber,' Vanya had said with a knowing wink.

She had loved the way Vanya talked. He sounded like he was playing a posh person in Oliver Twist. The house was filled with really old books. Strange ornaments kept them company. A wee brass telescope perched on the sill of the small living room window. She'd loved the furniture, the scuffed old leather couch and armchairs that seemed to hold the shapes of occupants from long ago. At the back of the cottage was an old, red brick outbuilding. The roof was made of rough concrete about four inches thick, just like the roofs of middens found in the backcourts of Glasgow's tenements. There were four windows running along one side of the outbuilding. The windows were more like grilles, separated into twenty four small window panes, four rows of six. Margaret remembered Caroline counting them. You could see the impressions of thumbs pressed into putty on the wrought-iron frames, even under all those coats of white, flaky paint. The window glass was covered in dull, black paint, baked graphite by countless suns.

Vanya said his "Hobby House" had been painted like that during the war. But now, it was his workshop and a strict no-go area. Thick, rubber extension cables stretched from the cottage into the end wall of the workshop, disappearing through a hole where half a brick had been removed. A heavily padlocked green door sealed the building. The door looked expensive, as if it came from a fancy house and had been shortened to fit. Four bolted lengths of reinforcing timber strengthened cropped, ornate door panels. Deeply embedded bolts ducked inside the thick timber.

The "Hobby House" did not remain secret for long. On their third night there, Vanya announced, 'We're going to the pictures.'

'Where are the pictures at?' Caroline screamed, as Margaret peeled her from the low ceiling of the cottage.

'Here,' Vanya said with a mysterious smile. 'It won't take long to set up.' He wagged a finger at Caroline, 'So you'd better be patient.'

Caroline did not need telling twice.

Minutes later Vanya had erected a huge screen and was busy adjusting the range and scope of the projector shining upon it. The projector sat on a small wooden sewing table. Vanya moved the table back and forth to get the adjustment "spot on" as he called it.

'I thought you two girls would like to see how we made movies long before we had video. This is proper film, 8mm Kodak colour.' He seemed elated as the first images flickered on screen. They looked as if they'd been shot from a moving car and you could tell it was harvest time. Bales of hay stood in clusters in cropped fields. Then the picture changed to show three men grappling with a heavy bale of hay that swung wildly from the arm of some huge tractor-like contraption. The men tugged and pulled violently at the straps. They had long iron hooks in their hands that glinted with the sun's reflection. They pulled and jerked with hooks in one hand while pushing with the other until, finally, the bale gave up the fight and slowly dropped into position alongside the other bales that half-filled the lorry trailer. Then the picture changed to show three men with their shirts off standing at the very end of the trailer. Perched between them, a little blonde-haired girl sat with her bare legs dangling off the back of the lorry. The men towered over her, laughing hysterically as they went through a variety of strongman poses. The camera ignored their antics and focussed on the girl, slowly zooming in until her face completely filled the screen. The girl delicately pinched blonde curls away from her eyes, smiling shyly at the camera.

Margaret turned and faced Caroline. 'She looks like us.'

'I know,' Caroline said, sharing her sister's stunned expression.

The camera jerked and slowly panned downwards. It stopped and focused on a small cut visible on the little girl's knee. It looked as if she was trying to push the camera away, then her other hand joined in and she seemed determined to block the camera from looking at her injury. Her fingers gradually obliterated the entire screen and then huge numbers, in countdown, flickered across the screen before old motor cars could be seen travelling along a busy main street. The people's clothes looked really funny. Then two cars could be seen approaching an old stone bridge. A green car with wooden beams on its side, stopped and parked at the bridge.

'That's Connie,' both girls screamed. There was something strange about him. He had hair - dark brown hair latticed his forehead. Every now and then it attempted lift-off, seeking a different direction. He smiled at the camera, nervously patting his wayward hair into place. He was wearing a light brown check suit that seemed miles too big for him. He went to the passenger's door, opened it, and the little girl took his hand and stepped from the vehicle like a fairy tale princess. Her dress was bubble gum pink and she looked like a doll suddenly brought to life.

Margaret thought the girl must be about nine or ten years old, although she was dressed to look much younger. Her hair colour had been changed to a golden blonde and, as her face drew nearer, you could see thick mascara cake her eye lashes. Her eyes sprung open, revealing ice-cold, blue pupils. The eyes were so strange, like the hypnotic eyes of the snake in "The Jungle Book", revolving and unable to focus.

'Is she drunk?' Caroline blurted out.

'Very perceptive,' Vanya said, peering down into the projector with a huge smile spreading his face. 'She was a very bad girl that day - drank a whole bottle of wine cordial.'

'What's wine cordial?' Caroline said, casting a cursory glance at her sister to see if she knew.

'I might let you have some,' Vanya said. 'But you have to promise not to be a little greedy guts, like Anna.'

'Is that her name?'

'Yes, that was her name.'

Margaret sensed a powerful emotion in the old man's voice. Caroline did not. She was more concerned with trying wine cordial.

'When can I try it?'

'Tut, tut.' Vanya wagged a mocking finger, 'I would have to get your big sister's permission, Caroline.'

'No you don't. She's not my boss.'

'Yes I am, Caroline.' Margaret stretched across to try and grab Caroline's arm, but the younger girl was too swift and agile. She leapt from the couch and ran towards Uncle Vanya, who placed a conciliatory arm around her.

'Caroline, you have to listen to me – I want you to promise me that you will always do what your big sister says.' His arm remained around her as he waited patiently for an answer. As Margaret rose to her feet, he gestured that she remain seated, with a benign smile.

Gradually, Caroline removed her head from under the old man's arm. The petulance in her voice was put on. 'I promise,' she scowled and begrudgingly stated, 'Whatever you say – goes, Margaret.'

As Caroline slowly returned to the couch, she saw familiar sights on screen. The green estate car was parked outside the cottage.

'The tree, the tree - there's the tree, Margaret,' Caroline screamed again.

Margaret stood up and went to the living room window and stared at the remains of the tree. It looked like a giant old-fashioned catapult. A Big Y about seven or eight feet tall. On screen you could see the two huge branches filled with foliage before they'd been cut. Now, two stained sawn discs peered skywards from the trunk by the gate.

'I don't like her claithes, they're minging,' Caroline said scathingly.

The girl on screen could be seen walking around the side of the cottage and then straight into the "Hobby House". Connie was close behind her, smiling patiently into the camera before pulling the door of the outbuilding shut.

There was something odd about the door; it was painted bright pink, the same colour as Anna's dress. Caroline looked towards Margaret before turning her eyes to Vanya.

'How come she gets to go inside the Hobby House?' Caroline asked, labouring her resentment.

'Ah, poor little Caroline, you see injustice everywhere you look. Anna was the same.' Vanya pointed at the screen. 'She always fought the good fight, fought for liberty.'

Caroline let her head fall into her chest, mumbling, 'I'm not fighting, I just don't think it's fair.'

Margaret smiled up at Uncle Vanya, hinting at both pride and embarrassment over her sister's sullenness.

The film suddenly stopped and the old man began speaking. He appeared distant, lost somewhere. Both girls noticed it, but remained silent.

'The "Hobby House" is a mess now. It could never be the way Anna had it, it was her little palace.' He wiped tears from his eyes. 'It's all still there – but she's not, she's gone.' The tears were streaming down his face now as the empty film reel clattered with a constant rhythm.

Margaret stood up and walked over towards Uncle Vanya, led him away from the projector and sat him down beside Caroline, while she returned to switch off the machinery.

'Her things are all there. She's not, she's not,' he kept repeating.

Caroline reached over and took the old man's head in her arms and he became quiet.

*   *   *

Now Margaret nestled into Joe's side and wondered if Rameses Bullock still had that sadness about him, and did he still think he'd wasted his life.

Chapter Twenty Five

He watched the tall gaunt man struggle to find the correct path in the rabbit warren of corridors of the Palms Sauna. There seemed to be something fragile about this poor lost soul. His arms were raised above his head as he tentatively felt his way round the cramped interior of the building. You could see why he paid for companionship. For a split second, he pitied the poor girl who'd serviced this grotesque individual. But then again, a job's a job, and if they wanted to keep that job, they needed to make sure no-one entered his private space. He stood up and slid open the small glass partition.

'I'm afraid you have entered the private area, sir. You have to go back to the girl at the desk and she vill show you the vay out.'

The big man slowly stooped until his deep-set eyes could stare through the gap in the sliding glass.

'This is a private area, sir........'

When Cornel Wagner came to, he was back at his desk but sitting higher up than usual. It slowly dawned on him that he was being held like a ventriloquist's dummy. He tried to speak, but found it difficult and extremely painful. Every breath was agonising. He tried to feel his ribs and discovered he could not move his arms. Stronger arms than his were wrapped around his torso He tried to kick his legs out only to find them clamped between long, bony limbs. He managed to pull his head back slightly and focused on hooded eyes staring impassively beyond him. He saw sinews undulating under the taut skin of an elongated face he was beginning to remember. He could detect the outlines of long misshapen teeth, still prominent underneath closed, pencil-thin lips that squeezed out excess saliva. Breathing was becoming more difficult. His body tried to break free from the vice-like grips that held it. He tried to stretch but every attempt failed, using up whatever oxygen remained inside his lungs.

He looked beyond the face, hoping one of the girls or a lost punter would come to his aid. 'Please stop – please.' These whispered words took the last breath from his body.

Maurice Golightly sucked his lips dry before saying, 'Night, night.' And then he placed a hand over Cornel Wagner's mouth and sat for ten minutes, relishing the quiet time.

*   *   *

A small piece of cardboard hung from the door of the Straw House with the words "Private Function" written on it. Inside, JJ McGuire sat quietly, watching four of his men playing Bastart Brag as news filtered through about Wagner's death. Gangland reprisals are seldom so reserved he thought, and this one rang hollow.

'Whitey, you need to throw one card away and pick one up from the middle,' Johnny V said, trying to temper his feelings.

'I don't want to throw one away, I'm happy,' Whitey replied as he turned and showed McGuire the three threes he held in his hand, (the highest hand in Brag).

'That's why it's called Bastard Brag, son,' McGuire said sombrely.

Whitey threw a three of clubs onto the table and picked up a nine of diamonds.

'That's wiped the fucking smile off yer face, eh?' Johnny V smiled.

Whitey did not respond.

McGuire's thoughts returned to Wagner and to Joe Ray. *What a coincidence, those two wanting my help in finding Margaret Logan.* He looked at Whitey playing cards, still fizzing at having to throw away an unbeatable hand. *Now I have to ask you about the other hand you've been playing, Whitey.*

Chapter Twenty Six

The other day there, back at JJ's

'Has your arse stopped making buttons?'

'It's settling down a wee bit - but who knows what damage your next request might provoke.'

'I'm only asking you to kill me.'

'There you go again and there goes my bottle.' Joe stood up just in case he really needed to find the toilet sharpish.

'I'll make it worth your while. I've got a tidy nest-egg set aside for you.'

'I'm not sure if you're going a wee bit daft in your old age - but I'm out on licence.'

'I am going a bit daft, but the money is kosher, totally legit - my legal teams spent weeks scrutinising it.'

Joe fought the urge to make some sarcastic comment.

'I am going a bit daft,' McGuire persisted

'What are you talking about, JJ? I don't need this. I don't want anything. In fact I'm glad I'm away from all this shite.' He took in a huge gulp of air before saying. 'The best day I ever lived in this life was the day I realised I could not do this – I can't do this, I honestly can't'.

'Finished?' McGuire asked.

Joe nodded, sniffing air into his lungs.

'Have you been doing drama courses in there?'

'No,' Joe answered, genuinely hurt by the last remark.

McGuire sensed that hurt, and snapped his fingers and indicated that Joe sit down. Joe sat, sinking slowly into the plush leather armchair.

'What have I always told you, eh? What have I always said?'

Joe said nothing, his eyes seeking solace in the carpet pattern.

'C'mon, what was it? C'mon Joe, remember.' McGuire's stern façade forced an answer.

'You can't be a nice gangster,' Joe mumbled.

'Exactly!'

McGuire rose from his chair and began pacing around his spacious living room.

'I'm going to tell you something quite pertinent.'

'I'm not sure that I want to hear it.'

'Joe! It's advisable that you really communicate, so clamp your mouth shut and wedge your ears open.'

Joe heeded the advice.

'Your problem, Joe, wasn't the misguided belief that you could be a nice gangster. What the fuck is that anyway? Oh I say, I simply must break your fingers, it's not personal, it's just if I don't, then I'll be accused of sending mixed messages to the plebs, and then it will all turn rather frightful and ghastly for everyone and lots more fingers will have to be broken, perhaps even tiny little fingers.'

McGuire paused and invited a response. None came.

'Joe, your problem is that you could not be me and that's why you got banged up. You couldn't hack it stone cold sober - you needed a wee charge in you. When it came to the crunch, when it got right down to the nitty gritty, the dirty stuff, the real shite, you could not hack it. All you had to do was drive by and open fire. Job done as they say in "Cockneyland", bish bosh, collect the dosh. But no, not you, Mr "they called me a wanker".'

McGuire's face took on a look of overwhelming disbelief.

'What you did was prove what a wanker you really were, a complete and utter fucking tosser, a fucking tosser.' McGuire lunged at Joe, screaming, 'Stand up, get on your fucking feet.'

Before Joe could move, Big Yogi and two others were inside the living room.

'Fuck off,' McGuire screamed at them.

Joe sat frozen to the spot with two handguns being pointed straight at his head.

'Is everything OK, boss?' Big Yogi asked cautiously, as he gently placed his huge mitt onto his employer's shoulder. This act brought McGuire back to his senses and he eased himself onto one of the long sofas.

'Everything's cool, we were just discussing old times. In fact, we're going to continue. Could somebody make a pot of tea?' He gave Joe a reassuring smile. 'That's tea for two, Yogi. And Yogi,' he added, 'I'm delighted with the response time, shut the door behind you.'

He turned to Joe, 'Hungry?'

Joe remained stunned and silent.

'Organise some food for us,' McGuire said catching the big man as he pulled the door closed.

Yogi popped his head back in the room, 'Will he be able to eat?'

'I won't be holding a gun to his head.'

'It's not that bad,' Yogi protested.

'Tell you what, Yogi, I fancy some corn dobbie. Aye corn dobbie, on well-fired rolls',

'Ah don't think there's anyth.....' Yogi tied to answer.

McGuire cut in, 'Send out. I'm in the mood.' He turned to Joe. 'That's the good thing about Eileen being away, I can eat any old shite, even Yogi's.'

Yogi laughed, as he pulled the door closed.

A full charge of fear jumped around Joe's insides. Every time he tried to speak, another surge of terror jolted through him. Seconds ago they were about to blow him away. Now they were sniggering about bad cooking, being all palsy walsy, and sending out for corned beef.

'Where were we?' McGuire asked.

'You were calling me a fucking tosser, and I was sitting like a fucking tosser, just taking it.'

'That's better, Josie Boy - more like your old self.' McGuire lay back on the sofa. 'You're here for a while, be prepared, more criticism will follow.'

'Superb, well-fired rolls, corn dobbie and copious amounts of censure, it just doesn't get any better than this.'

'I always could wind you up.'

'What the fuck kind of reply do you want here, JJ?'

'Just say it's true.'

'This is fucking outrageous.' Joe laughed.

'Just say it's true.' McGuire remained raised up on one elbow.

'True.' Joe's smile feigned resignation.

McGuire lay back down.

'After we eat, I'll tell you something really outrageous.'

'I can hardly contain myself.'

'You'll just have to.'

The laughter that followed was real and Joe felt buoyed that he'd spoken up for himself. Gradually, the fear in his stomach subsided. Joe was puzzled with the conversation. It reminded him of how they used to speak when they were kids growing up. JJ always could wind him up. He'd put up with it until a certain point, and then he'd snap and bite back. McGuire seemed to always relish that moment. Joe could never work that out. If anybody else ever snapped back, they'd receive a severe beating. But they were grown up now, the severe beatings bar sat at a loftier level. Snap back at McGuire nowadays and the likelihood was you'd be dead, or certainly fucked up in a major way.

'You want a whisky?'

Joe's stomach muscles went into spasm and he lost the power of speech again.

'Whisky, I'm making a whisky, d'you want one?'

'Sorry,' Joe stammered, trying to say no.

'You'll like this – excellent malt.'

Joe took a hefty gulp from the crystal tumbler placed in his hands.

'Steady, Joe,' McGuire commented ruefully.

'What?'

'You know what you're like on an empty stomach.'

'I'll be alright – anyhow we'll be eating soon enough,' Joe reasoned.

McGuire scratched at his face and spoke slowly, precisely and logically. 'I'm a wee bit concerned, Joe, bothered, worried, scared you might get pissed and say something that will upset me. Then I'll have to do you in. And that places me in a difficult predicament. Killing the one person I'm hoping is going to kill me.'

Joe headed for the drinks cabinet for a refill. 'OK?'

McGuire nodded consent.

Joe's face was pained. 'I wish you'd pack all this pish in – I cannot take it. I really can't.'

'Help yersel, have a beer as well. Drink the cabinet, Joe.'

'I'll fucking need it if you keep talking like that.' Joe replenished his glass.

'D'you believe in God, Joe?'

Joe nearly spat his drink out, 'Fuck me, I never ever expected to hear that question coming from you.'

'I'm asking, do you?'

'You're serious.'

'I'm always fucking serious. Even joking, I'm serious.'

'I do, JJ, some things happened when I was inside – and I believe, I know there's something. I asked something and that something helped.'

Now Joe scratched his head, scrutinising JJ McGuire. 'Fuck me, you're not thinking of repenting?' he asked.

'It's a thought, eh?'

'A monumental thought!'

'A monumental task as well.'

'The confession will be a stretch and a half,' Joe calculated.

'It'll take a few men o' the cloth, eh. What do you think?'

The knock on the door put the sniggering on hold. Big Yogi looked miffed. Nothing new in that, thought Joe. The big man laid two trays on

151

top of the coffee table. One tray held a plate piled with well-fired morning rolls, accompanied by side plates of sliced tomatoes and extra slices of corned beef. The other tray had milk and sugar and two white porcelain tea pots, one pot with a fresh supply of hot water. A solitary saucer with spare tea bags sat between two huge mugs.

Yogi gave the tea bags a soulful glance. 'In case it needs a boost.'

'Thanks Yogi, that was very good of you.'

'Not a problem, boss.' Yogi left quietly, although the atmosphere he brought into the room lingered a while longer.

'I would not like to bring home an empty pay poke to that big cunt,' McGuire grimaced before saying, 'He fucking hates you, always has done.'

The roll in Joe's mouth did not stop him talking. 'Why, I've never done him a bad turn?' Joe's brain kicked up a gear. 'Did I ever bad mouth him when I was pished?'

'No, he'd a fucking killt ye stone dead.'

As Joe ate and pondered past indiscretions, JJ McGuire explained the reason for Yogi Hughes' animosity.

'It's his wife.' McGuire's expression suggested they keep their voices down.

Joe looked bemused. 'I don't know his wife.'

'Yes, you do.' McGuire nodded as Joe continued shaking his head his head. 'She worked in the chippy on the Gallowgate, across from the Blue-Vale flats.

'I don't remember her.'

'You don't have to remember her. She remembers you.'

'What did she look like,' Joe asked, suddenly interested.

'Obviously, forgettable. But she always talked about you.' McGuire raised his eyebrows. 'There you go, having impacts on women and not even knowing.'

'Was she a looker?'

'Come to fuck, Joseph. You've seen Yogi. She married him.'

Joe looked slightly downhearted at that remark.

'She'd a killed you an all. Fuck, she's bigger and badder than he is.'

'I just can't place her.'

'Plaice her,' McGuire laughed.

Joe looked perplexed.

'Plaice her,' McGuire stressed the word. 'Plaice as in fish – plaice – plaice, oh for fuck sake.'

Joe suddenly got it, although he did not find it particularly funny. 'And that's why he doesn't like me?'

'Yes. You'll forever be a rival in the love stakes. I heard her mention you at a party a few years back. The big man's face was a picture.'

Joe changed the conversation. 'Eat up, yer food will get cold.'

'Joe, the food is cold – cold meat's the clue.'

'Don't be a picture straightener. You know what I mean.'

McGuire bit into a roll and began pouring the tea.

The food was great. Maybe it was the couple of whiskies that gave him an appetite, maybe it was just talking to JJ. Joe wasn't sure but perhaps it was just discussing anything other than the crazy stuff McGuire had mentioned earlier. "Kill me", that's what he'd said, kill me and I'll make it worth your while. Joe leant over and took a fresh roll. Hastily, he opened the roll up and began piling some fresh slices of tomato onto the layers of corned beef, and as he clamped it shut, a few pieces of charred crust fell to the floor.

McGuire looked to the floor, then towards Joe. 'Don't worry - the cleaner will get that tomorrow.'

'No, no,' Joe said as he placed his roll back on the tray and retrieved the fallen crumbs from the plush carpet. When Joe looked up again, it was obvious he was conversing with a very different entity. It looked as if someone had flicked an off-switch in JJ's head. He was fiddling clumsily with the mug of black tea in his hands, and the mug handle seemed to present an obstacle to him finding a proper grip.

'Are you OK, JJ?' Joe asked, fearing that McGuire was having some sort of stroke. Then, in the blink of an eye, normal service was resumed.

'Where was I – eh – oh, aye - I want you to kill me.'

'Oh, that old chestnut,' Joe failed to sound flippant.

McGuire ignored the remark as his eyes randomly scanned the room. 'I suppose you could do me the way I done my auld man.' He sat upright and placed his tea back on the table. 'Get me paralytic, hang me from a tree. Simple - fuck me - the press would have a field day with that, eh? I'll get your money sorted out a bit quick, make sure everything's proper.'

Joe rose to his feet, deeply concerned, thinking of seeking Big Yogi's assistance. 'JJ, are you all right?'

'Of course I'm not all right. I've got fucking Alzheimer's, Joe, Early Onset Alzheimer's. Why the fuck do you think I'm asking you to kill me? It needs to be you. Can you not see that?'

Chapter Twenty Seven

Joe stood patiently inside the cramped grocer's as three young workies from a nearby building site attempted to buy the shop. Then Joe's eyes settled.

His eyes settled on the pile of Daily Records on the counter. Under the big "Payback" headline were photographs of two men murdered yesterday. Both worked for McGuire. Joe bought the paper and began scanning it as he left the shop.

Cornel Wagner had been killed inside the Palms Sauna. But the other man grabbed Joe's attention. Ian (Whitey) Whitefield's badly beaten body had been found near a lay-by on the A8 eastbound. Joe leafed to page eight and saw a photograph of Whitey leaving Glasgow's High Court in 2004 after a Not Guilty verdict. There was no beaming smirk on Whitefield's face, his head was bowed slightly. His soulless eyes looked outward and upward. The pose looked rehearsed and convincing, conveying a subtle cocktail of menace and malice. Joe had seen those eyes and that look very recently, and it wasn't when JJ McGuire made the introductions at Terry's house. This was the wild-eyed fucker who had decked him when he tried to help Margaret at Roselea Gardens.

The realisation that he'd made one huge mistake was instant. The growing sense of horror was gradual and unremitting.

*   *   *

She sat with her feet tucked underneath her, and her discarded slippers lay, wrong side up, on the floor, making a bad attempt at playing "hide and seek" under the settee. The remote lay by her side, though the TV screen sat idle and blank, barely managing a dull reflection of the room and its three occupants. Margaret was trying ever so hard not to cry. The news report had hurt her, she couldn't fully understand why. Maybe she didn't want to understand why. But she knew it was all about Caroline. She was imagining how upset her sister would've been. Connie was dead, murdered, gone forever and, just like Caroline, she'd never got to say goodbye to him. She failed to stem the tears.

The two detectives watched in silence, making eye contact now and then. They were planning a strategy on the hoof. To them, Cornel Wagner's murder was a godsend. Now, they could ask Margaret how she came to know the old pimp. One line of questioning was now redundant because it was obvious Margaret had cared deeply for Cornel Wagner.

DC MacCallum cleared her throat and gently suggested, 'Do you not want to get dressed?'

'No I don't,' Margaret spat out an answer and kept her scowl fixed to the floor.

The two DCs looked at each other, with their eyes hinting and hoping the other might take the lead.

'He wasn't a bad man. Maybe he was bad - but he was good to us. That's all I know.'

Nell Hannah approached gently, crouching on the floor awkwardly, pushing Margaret's slippers to one side, before sitting cross-legged with her back resting against the couch. She raised her hand above her head and reaching backwards until Margaret took hold.

'Just talk, Margaret. It will help.' There was strength in Hannah's voice.

Marian MacCallum took that strong reassurance as her cue to join Margaret on the couch and snuggled against her. She brushed her hand lightly back and forth on Margaret Logan's lap. As her hand came to rest, a heavy teardrop landed on it. MacCallum let the teardrop stay there as her own eyes became cloudy.

All three women sat silently in the pale light and waited while God switched the world's sound system to mute --------------- then.

'Sometimes he just wanted us to lie beside him - I asked him tae help us – help get us out of that place. Connie was different - he didn't play us off against each other.'

'Out of what place?' DC MacCallum asked.

'Maranatha House.'

'Where's that?' DC Hannah asked; gripping Margaret's hands as their pulse rates merged.

'Dumfries. It looks like a fairy castle – only it's filled with Frankensteins.'

'When were you there?'

'From 1991 to 1995, they kept putting us back in there. They were bad to us – why do you think we kept running away?'

Margaret paused, anticipating another question, but the detectives' silence forced her to continue.

'Then Connie came and cut our hair. He made us laugh, made us feel good, the funny way he talked. He made our hair really nice. They said he used to be a really great hairdresser, a top stylist in London, and one time he put a bob in Judy Garland's hair, and he worked with other film stars too.' Margaret stopped, looked into DC MacCallum's eyes, seeking verification that they believed her. 'He hated the boys, lopped their hair off like an army barber – called them Cheeky Vee Bees; Caroline would go into hysterics when he said that, that's why he said it – he'd say it a lot.' Margaret wiped the tears welling in her eyes. 'They kept putting us back there. You think they'd have taken the hint.'

'I'll get you a tissue.' Marian MacCallum made her way to the toilet, froze monetarily in the hall, thinking about grabbing the voice recorder and her notebook from her coat. However, that course of action seemed somehow inappropriate. If the floodgates were opening, she didn't want the flow interrupted. If Margaret was about to start naming and shaming, then they'd rely on good old-fashioned memory, however fallible that form of data collection was considered by their superiors. She quickly pulled five or six tissues from a lemon-yellow coloured box and picked up an unopened pack of wet-wipes.

Marian MacCallum knelt beside Margaret and let the fingers of her left hand deftly part Margaret's tangled blonde locks, and curled them neatly behind her delicate ears. Four holes were visible on each ear, little red rings circled each piercing, like tiny unhealed wounds gaping open, embarrassed by, but still prepared to suffer exposure. She peeled strands of wet hair from a tired face and tenderly wiped around Margaret's eyes, cheeks and mouth. The flesh, when pressed, seemed slow to return to its normal shape, but the Detective Constable was in no hurry. She held the wet wipe delicately between forefinger and thumb and ever so gently combed Margaret's eyebrows back into shape with her pinkie nail.

'Where did Connie take you and Caroline?'

'Humph,' Margaret tensed slightly at the question.

'When you got away from Maranatha House, where did you go?'

'A cottage, just a wee cottage, it never had a street.'

DC MacCallum placed the wet-wipe on top of a cushion and began to massage Margaret's face. She used gentle movements, from the neck up, tempting colour back into Margaret's pale sunken cheeks. The tears had stopped, but Marian MacCallum knew the lull would not last.

'Whereabouts – what area was the cottage situated?' DC Hannah asked.

'I think it was in Dumfries, but I can't be certain. He picked us up near the petrol station. We seemed to drive around for ages - just wee country roads - lots of wee country roads. We ran from the big, bad castle to the gingerbread cottage in the wee enchanted forest. That's what they said.'

'They?'

157

'Sorry. That's what Connie told us.' Margaret corrected herself. Margaret's slip was obvious to both detectives.

'Anybody else there?' DC MacCallum asked casually.

'Just us,' Margaret confirmed.

'How long were you there?' Nell Hannah asked.

'Could've been a month or maybe even five weeks? It seemed for ever at the time.' She paused. 'We went to bed one night and woke up in somebody's back garden in Glasgow.'

'You don't remember getting there?' Marian MacCallum asked, very concerned.

'No.'

'Whereabouts in Glasgow?' Hannah asked.

'Don't know. It was an old woman's house because she woke us up - told us she'd phone the polis if we didn't move.'

DC Hannah looked at her colleague as she asked, 'You don't know where?'

'It's not that far from the city centre - cause we walked it there. You could look down and see a football ground from her street. Caroline asked a man if it was Rangers or Celtic and the guy burst out laughing, saying it was the fuckin Fisso's. We'd never heard of the fuckin Fisso's, so they can't be very good, can they?'

Marian MacCallum struggled, suppressing the giggles. Margaret threw her a puzzled look while DC Nell Hannah's face showed bland bemusement.

'That would be Partick Fisso's ground. You've heard of them, Margaret. Partick Thistle FC.'

Margaret began to laugh, slowly at first; little sniggers erupted between pathetic attempts at saying the word 'fisso'. Marian MacCallum was gone now, creased up with laughter; she fell against Margaret and they convulsed in unison.

Nell Hannah looked down on the helpless pair, just as MacCallum looked up saying, 'Henderson's a Fisso supporter; give us an F, give us an I, give us a So, what have you got, Fisso –Fisso – Fisso----.' She shrieked with laughter.

Hannah joined in, laughing loud and hard, not quite knowing why. As the giggles started to subside, Marian MacCallum leapt up saying, 'I need the loo.' At the doorway, she turned momentarily and made eye contact with her colleague and mouthed, 'She's lying, but we should have taped her.'

Chapter Twenty Eight

'I don't want tea, I want help.' He paused before saying, 'I want shooting, that's what I deserve; I should have a Government "stupidity" warning tattooed on my forehead.'

He held the newspaper up in front of him.

'How am I meant to respond here?' Cassidy asked.

Joe resumed walking in tiny figure-of-eight patterns again. 'I've made things worse - I'll end up getting her fucking wasted. How can I have been such a fuckin' idiot, eh?' He swung his head round, looking for an answer.

'Joe, stop the pacing, you're making me stir crazy,' Cassidy said, trying to emphasise the pun.

'I think I've fucked up, Jim. I need help. I need to.....'

'Sit down, take a breath and try inserting a few pauses amongst the dialogue. That'll be beneficial in this conversation.'

Jim Cassidy held one of the breakfast stools like a waiter seating a customer. Joe eventually twigged, and Cassidy returned to his kettle and began brewing up.

Joe flattened the newspaper on the breakfast bar, tweaked out the page with that photo of Whitey and left it protruding like a magician's hint. 'That's the guy that tried to grab Margaret. Somebody's killed him.'

Jim Cassidy put the tea cups down and sat beside Joe.

'You sure?'

Joe tugged the folded page out further and pointed at the page. 'I've met him, met him at my cousin's house. He works for JJ McGuire.'

'Why didn't you say something before?'

Joe shrugged 'It's the look in the eyes, Jim. I wouldn't have recognised him in any other picture. It's that look.'

Cassidy looked at the front page and asked, 'What about the other guy?'

'Don't know him. But he's ran the saunas for years.'

Jim Cassidy read out a short paragraph from the paper, 'A reliable source says underworld factions are grouping together in order to fight back against McGuire.'

'Paper talk, Jim; McGuire's killed both men. They've done something wrong; or failed to do something right. With JJ, the outcome's similar.' Joe's hands pulled at his face as he spoke. 'He wants to kill Margaret. When she went walkabout in Edinburgh - I asked McGuire to help find her; how could I have been so fucking stupid? I've led him right to her.'

'Has he got back to you - made any kind of contact since then?'

'I phoned him later on and told him that she'd come back.'

'What did he say to that?'

'Buy a mobile and keep in touch.'

Cassidy gave a sceptical look. Joe answered. 'He wants me to do him a "favour" – I just wish I'd never made contact.'

'What kind of favour?'

'You don't want to know, believe me.'

'Have you kept in touch – will you buy a mobile?'

'I hate them. How many times did you and your pals tear up the joint looking for those fucking things when I was inside?'

'You're not inside anymore.'

'Sometimes I wish I was. Life was simpler.'

'Why would McGuire want to kill Margaret?' Cassidy paused to rephrase his next question. 'If you think McGuire wants to kill Margaret – that would mean he probably killed her sister. Why would he want to kill them both?'

Joe could offer no reply, so Cassidy continued, 'You could ask him, straight out.'

Joe went into a kind of mini-blackout. There were just too many questions and differing scenarios competing with each other inside his head. When he regained some control of his thoughts, Cassidy was standing over him.

Joe said, 'I'm going to tell you something, Jim, and I want you to swear on your wife's soul that you tell nobody, you say nothing.'

Jim Cassidy had seen this look once before on Joe's face. When he'd persuaded him to decommission the "Mad Highlander" and bring the prison siege to an end. However, he was livid that Joe had the temerity to bring Freda's soul into the equation. There followed a bizarre bout of battling facial expressions before Cassidy reluctantly relented and said, 'I swear.'

'JJ McGuire has asked me to kill him. There, I said it.' Joe looked relieved.

Cassidy's face struggled for a why.

'McGuire has been diagnosed with Alzheimer's. That's why big-time criminals are going toes up. He's snuffing out any future threat to his family. There's a reason he picked me. I can't tell you the reason, I kind of swore an oath, long time ago, but I can assure you that there is no way that JJ McGuire is going to go slowly gaga in some home for the criminally decrepit.'

'I wish I hadn't asked the question.'

'Join the club,' Joe said. 'I wish you hadn't asked either, but I'm relieved you did. I've been walking about with this shit in my head since he told me. I actually feel sorry for the poor cunt. How mad, how sad, is that, eh?' Joe laughed as cynical tears stung his eyes. 'I'm feeling sorry for a guy who's killing people left right and fucking centre, cutting pushers' hands off, and who is probably going to kill someone I really care about.'

Joe stopped momentarily, as if a thought was just filtering through. 'Even if I was to put a bullet in him tonight, he could still have her killed. He's got people putting bullets in people's heads all over the fucking city.'

'She's got two detectives looking after her,' Cassidy said, trying to sound optimistic.

'You think that would stop him? That wouldn't stop him. It would give the sick cunt a challenge. Add to his kudos by taking out a couple of cops.'

'Will we check up on her?' Cassidy asked quietly.

'What have we got in the form of weaponry, Jim?'

'Cutlery, a couple of claw hammers – oh, and some wood chisels.'

'They'll do. If you're going to get shot, it's better to have your hands full.'

'Joe, would you consider telling the police exactly what you've told me?'

'Don't be absurd, Jim. I'd be killed violently and so would you, because if he asked me if I'd told anybody, I would give him your name. Remember, Jim. I know, first-hand, how he operates.'

'I'll see what's in the cupboard,' Jim Cassidy said.

Joe went for the knives sitting snugly in the wooden knife block. He poured them out, shuffled them and settled on the heaviest and strongest looking blade. It wasn't the biggest, but there was less chance of the blade bending when hitting bone.

Jim Cassidy returned with an assortment of tools and a telling question. 'If McGuire wanted her dead, would she not be - dead?'

Joe was stumped for an answer.

'With all the "stuff" that's going on, if he really wanted to kill her, he'd have killed her. He's probably known where she was since before that day in the street – and that was a while ago.'

161

Methodically, they placed their selection of weapons on the kitchen work-tops and sat down.

'You've got a point there, Jim. Maybe I've got it wrong here, maybe McGuire's got nothing to do with this.' Joe jumped back to his feet, 'I'm gonny phone the cunt and ask him outright.'

'That's not the best idea you've ever had.'

'What else can we do?'

'Why don't you ask her, ask if she's done something that would make McGuire want her dead.'

Joe thought about it for a split second. He was jumpy; the nerves were kicking in again. He went into the living room and looked out into the street. The street looked no different from normal, but what did that prove? What the fuck does normal mean anyway? It looked normal the day that guy Whitefield decked him. Joe wondered what weapon Whitefield had used. *Fuck*, he shuddered. It could have been a sawn-off, a slipped finger and he would have had his head blown off. It was getting dull outside; Joe was not sure if it was down to the clouds, or if it was getting late. He shouted for a time check and Cassidy told him that it was eleven o'clock. Jesus Christ, how could he think it was late? His head must be mince. Sheepishly, he walked back into the kitchen, eyes fixed to the floor. 'Will you come with me?'

'Course I will.'

'What are you carrying?'

'What do you mean?'

'Take a knife, Jim. Take a screwdriver or a hammer - just in case.'

'Joe, there are two policewomen with her - chances are they're probably armed.'

'I do fucking hope so,' Joe said icily as he edged his way into the brightly coloured stairwell of Roselea Gardens. Joe didn't want to say, not out loud anyway, but he felt absolutely brilliant inside. Every nerve in his body had woken up. The blade up his sleeve probed keenly onto the ridge of flesh formed between his wrist and the palm of his slightly inverted hand.

Chapter Twenty Nine

DCI Henderson paced up and down the stances of Buchanan Street Bus Station, looking every inch the disgruntled punter. The bus was twenty five minutes late. He walked past the newsagent's again and threw the counter assistant another dagger. 'Fucking prices you pricks charge are fucking criminal,' he muttered to himself. The wee Asian prick returned the compliment with a half-arsed snarl. Henderson smiled, glad to get a reaction. At least the skinny wee fuck was sprouting a set of balls and sticking up for his self.

Henderson made his way back to stance F and, two minutes later, the 13.10 from Ayr trundled home. The driver was animated and agitated, gesturing travel conditions to sceptical colleagues inside the station who pointed to their watches.

Bill Hoover said she'd be wearing a purple coat. My God, it was hard to miss it. It was like something the Queen wore opening a farming museum in February 1972. The shoes, a dull, tawny brown, did not match. Nothing matched. Her hair resembled a badger, an ugly badger. A black dye had obviously been used, at some point, but that some point was God knows when. Now a variety of wiry, grey and white hair competed with black hair crumpled against her coat collar. A grey skirt hung at a bad angle below the coat's hem-line. She carried a huge, green, Eco Friendly, canvas bag-for-life. Thank God they don't do a purple.

He waited until the other passengers had left the stance and approached.

'Mrs Hochnall? I'm DCI Henderson.'

Jeanie Hochnall turned a bit too abruptly, nearly falling over. Henderson caught her by the shoulder. She felt bony and frail under garments that unkindly bulked her out.

'Is that you, Inspector?'

'Yes,' said Henderson, thinking she could call him anything she liked, 'I hope your journey was not too tiring?'

'Oh no, I loved it. I've not been through to Glasgow for ages.' She looked around the station. 'Big changes, eh?' Henderson agreed as she whispered, 'It's nice to get your bus fare paid.'

The policeman nodded and smiled again.

'Next year I'll have the free travel pass and I'll get out and about again.'

She looked a hell of a lot older than fifty nine, bad hairdo or not.

'I thought we could go to the hotel next door. Maybe get some refreshments?'

'I could murder a cup of tea!' Jeanie Hochnall froze and recoiled in horror.

Henderson gave a little snigger, saying, 'its no' a crime to murder a cup of tea in Glasgow. If they ever make it law – I'm emigrating.'

Jeanie Hochnall felt more at ease, and placed her arms through the handle loops of the big canvas bag, hoisting it onto her right shoulder.

'I'll get that,' Henderson offered.

'No, no. It's quite all right.'

The bag looked like her - bulky.

'I thought we'd be going to the police station,' she said.

'We can do that later,' Henderson said. 'Anyhow, the tea's nicer here. I can testify to that.'

Henderson had walked it to the bus station. No-one, not even "Mr Henderson's Girls", knew about this meeting. The only person who knew about this meeting was Bill Hoover, and Bill could be trusted. Hoover was a colleague from way back who'd crop up now and then in canteen conversations. Henderson had the vague notion Hoover was working on the West Coast. Now he knew for sure. Bill Hoover was seeing it out in Saltcoats, working as a Community Liaison Officer, when his feet permitted. He'd phoned Henderson direct yesterday and, after a brief chat and a how'd you do, Hoover retold a conversation he had had with a lady that morning.

Earlier on today, and out of uniform, Bill Hoover had picked up Jeanie Hochnall from her old miner's cottage in Hawkhill Drive, Stevenston, and driven her along the coast road to the Sandgate Bus Station in Ayr.

'I think I'll try one of them mochas - I hear them talking about them on the telly.'

Mark Henderson smiled at the beautiful young Polish waitress. 'I'll have the same, two mochas, with the works.'

'What's the works?' Jeanie asked with fear in her voice.

Henderson raised a forefinger to his mouth and hushed the waitress just as she was about to explain. 'Don't worry, you'll be pleasantly surprised.' He leaned forward. 'You're no' a stranger to a sweetie, are you?'

Jeanie Hochnall smiled. 'I'll have the works,' she said.

The waitress smiled back and slipped her notepad inside one of her apron strings with an elegance sadly lacking in her Scottish counterparts, Henderson thought, as he stood up to remove his coat. 'Are you not hot?'

'I'm absolutely melting,' Jeanie admitted.

'Take your coat off then.'

'Is that all right?' she asked nervously.

'Course it is.' Henderson sounded astonished by the question.

'It's just that, my husband bought me it – didn't buy me much but he bought me this – and....'

'Don't you worry, hen, I'll keep an eye on it.' Henderson assured her.

Reluctantly Jeanie Hochnall removed the purple coat. Henderson's sardonic glint of a smile shifted as he caught a whiff of strong body odour. Her perfume was losing the battle. Henderson was shit-scared of that menopausal stuff, when women's boilers, for want of a better phrase, went wonky, turning into erratic heating systems, cold, hot, hot and cold. He didn't understand it, and more importantly, he did not want to understand it.

She folded the coat and placed it beside her, and then hoisted up the big green bag and placed it on top of the coat. It took a few attempts at getting the bag and the coat to sit in harmony.

Jeanie's face lit up, seeing the fresh mocha in front of her, and she started spooning marshmallows, covered in cream and spotted with chocolate shavings, into her mouth.

Henderson was patient, not wanting to rush her. Truth be told, he felt sorry for her already. It looked as if life had been particularly tough on her. Everything about her screamed that fact - her demeanour, and the way she smelled. He felt guilty for even thinking that she smelled, but she did smell. Maybe she was lying about her age. Whatever, it wasn't that important. He just wanted her as relaxed as possible before she told her story.

'So how did you get on with Caroline?'

Jeanie sat bolt upright. 'We cared for her, she was easy to like, she was quiet - well most of the time - but she could be a handful as well.'

'How long did she stay with you?' Henderson asked, retrieving his notebook from his coat pocket.

'She stayed with us a couple of times. She asked to come back.' Jeanie looked toward the ceiling and visibly counted the months Caroline Logan stayed with her. 'The first time was about ten weeks, give or take a day or two - the second time was nearly five months.'

'What dates?'

'Eh?'

'What dates did she stay with you?' Henderson asked, seeming a bit narked.

Jeanie scratched her head. 'She kept running away, kept trying to find her sister. The first time was around October '95, and the next year she moved in at the end of June. I can be more definite on that because we always went our holidays the first fortnight in June.'

'How did you get on with Margaret?'

'We didn't really know her. We visited her twice and met her once.'

Henderson raised an eyebrow.

'She was in a remand home near New Lanark. We took Caroline in the car to see her. She kept asking if we'd go near Maranatha House and she wanted to show us a wee cottage that she stayed at. She pestered the life out of Brian so she could sit in the front. Her wee face was plastered to the window the entire journey.'

'Did she say anything about the cottage?'

'She just said it had its own special picture house in the back garden.'

Henderson scribbled (**Who owned the cottage?**) in his notebook. 'Have you any thoughts on who would want to harm Caroline?'

Jeanie cradled the tall glass cup under her chin. The worry lines on her face were all too evident. 'No.'

'When did your husband pass away?'

'Three years ago.' She sipped from the cup as her breathing became more pronounced.

'How did you feel when you heard about Caroline?'

'Tormented, terrible, I...' she struggled for air now, 'felt guilty, riddled with fucking guilt. Is that what you want to know, Inspector?' Tears started streaming down her face. Thick mascara was everywhere. She wiped at her eyes, making the situation worse.

Henderson rose from his seat and went over to the wall where an imitation Welsh dresser stood. He took some fresh paper napkins from a shelf on the dresser and handed them, one at a time, to Jeanie.

'Is there something you want to tell me, Mrs Hochnall, something that's bothering you? Bill Hoover phoned me after he dropped you off at the bus station. He said he felt you had something - - - - something to unburden, do you have - something to unburden?'

'It's in the bag.'

'What's in the bag?'

She had a wild, manic look in her black, crusted eyes. 'It's in the bag.'

'What's in the bag?' Henderson repeated, still unsure.

'The - remains - Caroline lost the wee one!!!'

Henderson looked at the green canvas bag with wide-awake eyes. Now he could see the outlines of a rectangular shape.

Jeannie rubbed a finger painfully into her left eye. 'I can't open the box. I'm too scared,' she said in a whimper.

Henderson stood up, placed a hand on the table to steady himself as he leaned over and peered inside the bag. A light blue bath towel was wrapped around the box shape. He pulled the towel lightly to the side and it gave way easily to reveal a thick, black, plastic bag with masking tape snaking around it. Henderson tapped his fingers against the shape. It was solid, sounded like wood.

'I couldn't be sure. He was a good man, but I couldn't be sure.' Jeannie Hochnall slumped onto the table

'Did you think the baby was your husband's, Mrs Hochnall?'

'No,' Jeanie Hochnall said with venom smarting in her eyes. 'But I couldn't be sure.'

'Have you any idea who the baby's father is?'

'No. I only buried it. That wee lassie went to the toilet and twenty minutes later she came walking along the hallway with a warm, dead, bloody mess in her hand - - - I put her together again. She begged me not to tell anyone. We washed it. It was too small to tell, but I think it was a wee boy. We wrapped the baby in a christening shawl and placed it in my father's old box. It was the box he kept all the important documents in: birth certificates, marriage certificates, death certificates and insurance policies. We done the best we could. We buried it in my garden, we said prayers. We said an "Our Father", and we said amen.'

'And what did your husband do?' Henderson asked.

'He didn't know; he wasn't there.'

'What do you mean?'

'He was away working. He was always away - lorry driver, continental.'

'Did you tell him? Discuss it with him in any way?'

Any anger in Jeanie Hochnall vanished with that one question, and her chest caved in as black, tainted tears trickled down into the creases in her cheeks. She didn't bother to wipe them away. 'No, no, I did not.'

'What about Caroline?'

'I washed her, I wrapped her in a towel and bathrobe, I medicated her, I held her in my arms for three days. I know I done wrong, but I done some good, and yes Inspector, I would have called a doctor. She didn't want one - I didn't want one, but I would have got one.'

Henderson was taken aback by her outburst, but not with her actions. But still, this one question remained. She had doubts about her husband.

People in the sparsely-filled restaurant were becoming curious. Henderson simply stared out their concerned looks. The concerned looks were mostly female, although a heavy-built chap made a half-arsed attempt to get up and come over. Henderson's wagging finger sat him back down. The big man's distressed wife was only placated when Henderson flashed his warrant card and mouthed, 'Police business.' Henderson turned back around and saw Jeanie rummaging around inside the bag.

'I want you to do DNA tests. I've even got some of his blood.' She pulled out a hairbrush sealed inside a zip-up food bag. 'They get it off the hair, don't they? I need to know. I've not slept since I heard about Caroline dying like that. It was terrible!'

Fucking CSI, thought Henderson as he stared at Exhibit A, now sitting between froth-crusted empty mochas. He felt sorry for this wee woman, scarred by secrets. That was something he'd gleaned from all his years in the force. Women keep secrets. That's the difference between the sexes. They don't need to be asked, they don't go through stupid initiation ceremonies, don't need to get sworn to secrecy. They keep secrets and they live with them.

'I'm gonnae get us that pot of tea,' Henderson said, catching the waitress's eye. He turned his thoughts to the wee *ad hoc* coffin sitting inside that green bag for-life. The irony was not lost on him. The remains of that foetus might not have been fathered by Brian Hochnall. There might be a direct link to Lord Bullock. Henderson began compiling a text message in his head. He switched on his mobile and saw this message from DC Hannah: "M is talking."

'We'll have that cuppa at the station,' Henderson said and helped wee Jeanie Hochnall into her purple coat. *Funny: the coat seemed to suit her now.*

Chapter Thirty

Joe stopped at the bottom of the stairwell, motioning Jim Cassidy to do likewise.

'What is it?'

Joe tensed. 'There's somebody coming in the building.' He saw the second of two men getting out the car and his heart froze, but his guts did not. He recognised one of the men. The man was carrying a small box in his left hand. Actually the box might not be that small; the hand carrying it was massive.

'Jim, go and phone the police right now.'

Cassidy ignored the order, passing Joe at the bottom of the stairs.

'Jim, this is fucking serious. I know this cunt - he'll kill the two of us, no qualms. Phone Henderson; tell him Big Yogi, real name John Hughes, is coming to get Margaret.'

'What are you going to do?'

Joe let the blade slide down his palm and held it in front of him. 'I'll stick this in his fucking heart if I have to. Go, Jim, before they see you.'

Big Yogi's frame was beginning to blot out the light coming through the entrance of 38 Roselea Gardens. Joe moved forward as Cassidy made his way back up the stairs.

Big Yogi stared patiently, letting out an exaggerated yawn. 'Open the door.'

Joe stepped forward, shaking his head, with the knife displayed. 'No way,' he mouthed with all the menace he could muster.

'Whit the fuck are you going to do with that, ya silly fucker?'

'Fuck off, Yogi. I'm asking nice.'

'You don't think I've come here to hurt you, do you?' Yogi looked horrified at that assumption.

'Fuck off, Yogi. Please.'

'I'm no' here to hurt you, I've brought you a present. It's not cheap - he bought you a good one.' Big Yogi held the box up against the door glass.

Joe read - Sony Ericsson T280I.

'You're privileged, we get the shitey T303's and you can't do fuck all with them.'

'What the fuck are you talking about?'

'JJ's bought you a phone. What the fuck do you think I'm talking about? C'mon, open the door. I've not got all day. I'm a busy boy. Do you no' read the papers?'

'What's the real reason you're here? She's got cops watching her. They're holding her fucking hand as we speak - probably called back-up too - so you'd be well advised to be on your toes, big man.'

Big Yogi put the small box down on the doorstep. 'I'm starting to get fucking annoyed now. What's wrong with you?'

'Whitey, I know about Whitey. That's what's up with me – I know.' Joe stood closer to the door.

'Whitey's history.'

'Why does he want to harm her? Why?'

'I've not got a fucking clue what you're talking about.' Big Yogi gestured his younger colleague to start the car up.

'That Whitefield guy. Why was he trying to grab her? I don't know what beef JJ's got with her and I don't care. I'm not going to let anything bad happen to her. Assure him of that, Yogi.'

'I don't know anything about that – JJ's bought you a mobile phone, asked me to deliver it. I can't talk for Whitey, I've got no answers there, but I can ASSURE you that I'm not here to hurt anybody. When you come to your fucking senses, Joe, give him a call.' With that Yogi turned away scratching his arse and said loudly. 'JJ's acting fucking daft these days but he has not got a patch on you – ENJOY!!!'

Big Yogi slowly walked towards the waiting car. Once inside, he rolled down the passenger's window, slowly shook his head and signalled: *phone*.

Joe checked his trousers to really make sure he hadn't shat himself. There was a coughing noise behind him and he spun around. Jim Cassidy was standing beside him.

'Did you phone Henderson?'

'No.'

'Good, Jim. Do you know anything about mobile phones?' Joe gave a heavy sigh.

'A wee bit more than you do.'

Joe opened the door and pulled the package inside with his right foot. 'I think I'll call the Samaritans.'

'Use my landline. It's cheaper.' Jim Cassidy said as he headed back up the stairs.

Joe pressed his ear to Margaret's door. He could hear laughter, loud laughter. He started laughing a little himself. That's what you do when you're terrified, you laugh. He looked at the knife and the pronounced veins on his hand. His pulse was visible. He physically tried to relax, tried willing the blood surging through him to slow down. He tried to appear composed. He failed. His knees buckled as he began to walk.

*   *   *

'Yes,' a woman's voice said curtly.

'This is DCI Henderson calling from Strathclyde Police.'

'Oh.'

'I hope I've got the right number here, I'm trying to contact Lord Bullock - I'm not quite sure if I have his office....'

'I can confirm you have the correct office. I'm Geraldine Fraser, Lord Bullock's PA. But Lord Bullock is not available today.'

'This is a touch delicate, Geraldine. May I call you Geraldine?'

'Perfectly OK, Inspector.'

'Detective Chief Inspector.'

'Sorry,' Geraldine said.

'Geraldine, I'm heading the Caroline Logan murder enquiry in Glasgow and it is imperative that we talk with Lord Bullock as quickly and as discreetly as possible.' Henderson gave an exaggerated sigh and added. 'We would just like to deal with this matter with the minimum of fuss, Geraldine'.

'Would you like me to ask Lord Bullock to come and see you in person?'

Henderson emitted a concerned laugh. 'Geraldine, are you aware of the recent events in Glasgow. We're in the midst of a very brutal gang war. We have a sizeable British press presence, encamped en masse, outside my police station.'

'Could I call you back in a couple of minutes, Inspector?'

'There's no need. We're quite willing to send a couple of officers through to your office, discreetly I assure you. It won't be two big lumps in uniform.'

'Mr Henderson, I'll have to call you back on that, just giv.....'

'If it'll help, I'll send someone down to his cottage in Dumfries.'

'Oh no, he won't see you there – no, no.'

Henderson almost leapt from his chair, and muffled the phone's mouthpiece in case he let out a scream of delight. He released his hand slowly. 'Sorry to rush you, Geraldine. Of course I should let you speak with Lord Bullock first. I'll draw up a formal request and get it to you, quick as. Can you give me your e-mail address, or I could fax - would that be easier?'

171

'What's the best number to get you on?' she asked.

'I'll be on this number for the next wee while. But would you like my mobile number, Geraldine?'

'That won't be necessary, I'll call back soon - twenty minutes max.'

Henderson sat back, smiled and then relished the slow handclap coming from the other side of the desk.

Chief Inspector Anne Swinton rose to her feet. 'I'm impressed, DCI Henderson.'

'I've impressed myself - I knew it was his cottage.'

'It's not hard to guess what went on there.'

'Bullock got her pregnant, I'm sure of that. Jeanie Hochnall's been suspicious about her husband, but I don't think he fits the profile. Anyhow, he's long dead.'

'Persuading Bullock to give a sample could prove problematic.'

'I'll persuade him. If he rings back, which I don't think he will, I'll persuade him. You're welcome to stay and listen in.'

'I'd love to, but there are other "pressing" matters.'

Henderson's face weighed up the pun and gave it the thumbs down. 'I'll keep you posted.'

'Do,' Anne Swinton replied as she left his office.

*   *   *

Henderson looked at his watch: it was exactly twenty three minutes since he'd spoken with Bullock's PA. Hunger was gnawing at him. He opened his door, hoping to catch a junior officer and send them to the canteen for him. His phone rang and the hunger pangs let go.

'Henderson,' Henderson said.

'Sorry, Mr Henderson. It's taken longer than expected getting in touch with Lord Bullock.'

'I'm just glad you rang back, Geraldine. People say they'll call, you take their word and a lot of the time you're left kind of - disappointed.'

'If I say I'll call back, I always do.'

'That's commendable, Geraldine. Your boss is lucky to have you. I hope he appreciates you.'

Geraldine cut in. 'I've managed to speak to Lord Bullock, and he's happy to comply with any request.' She coughed, forcibly clearing her throat. 'There is a however, however. Lord Bullock would like some answers to some questions.'

'Tell him that's my job,' Henderson joked. 'Tell him to call me and I'll happily discuss the matter with him.'

'He has requested that you discuss the matter with me first. He's given me a list.'

'LIST?'

'It's not a big list, Mr Henderson. He just wants the general background on your case. You never said.'

'You never asked, Geraldine, but here goes - recently we've unearthed evidence that the murdered girl suffered a miscarriage several months after it's alleged that she had been in contact with Lord Bullock.'

'Contact?'

'Intimate contact.'

The PA's tone changed immediately. 'This sounds very serious, Inspector.'

'Yes, Geraldine, murder enquiries are very serious.'

'Sorry, Mr Henderson. As I say, Lord Bullock's instructed me to ask several questions.'

'I'll gladly answer any questions you may have, Miss Fraser, but it may be better if I quickly put you in the picture about how my investigation is going and you can tell his Lordship where I'm at, so to speak. You do have a notepad and pen handy?' Again there was hesitation. 'Ready?' Henderson asked cattily.

'Yes,' Geraldine tempered her reply.

'Caroline Logan was eleven years old when she miscarried. Well, we're pretty sure it was her first pregnancy, but we can't be 100% certain. We're more certain that she conceived to someone considerably older than her.....'

'Mr Henderson, Mr Henderson, I don't need that much detail.'

Henderson ignored her. 'We've had a bit of a result. Some devastating evidence has come into our possession. Forensically, it's the equivalent of a treble rollover on the National Lottery.' Henderson gave her plenty opportunity to reply. 'Are you still there Geraldine – Geraldine?'

'Yes,' she said, but her voice lacked its earlier assuredness.

'That's why we want swabs. The good thing is, as far as Lord Bullock is concerned, the sooner we get his swabs, the sooner he's ruled out of this enquiry.'

'That's just the thing, DCI Henderson. Lord Bullock's intimated that he's no recollection of ever meeting Caroline Logan. I could look through his case files to see if he's ever tried the girl.'

'Somebody tried the girl, that's a certainty and the swabs will show who impregnated the child.'

Geraldine Fraser suddenly got very flustered. 'I'll have to get back to you, Mr Henderson. A little bit of a crisis is occurring in the office.'

I bet it is, thought Henderson.

'I'll get back to you before close of work...'

'When do you finish work?' Henderson asked, knowing she'd already put the phone down. He kissed his phone, ecstatic. He sat back, satisfied that he'd engineered a marked change in the dynamics of Geraldine's working relationship with Bullock.

Chapter Thirty One

He stood at her door. He checked his hands, merely out of curiosity. It was apparent the blood was beginning to rush again. He'd phoned her on the mobile. Funny, Jim Cassidy was actually quite a geek when it came to gadgetry. She'd invited him down. Nothing fancy - watch some telly, perhaps a movie. He was OK with that, more than OK, but he did want to talk. Earlier events were still affecting him. He'd tried contacting JJ McGuire, but only got this text in reply: (Busy c u 2mo). Thankfully, Jim Cassidy deciphered.

He tapped his hip pocket and the phone made a frightening, beeping sound. For a split second he thought he'd broken the thing. Then her door opened and he nearly jumped into orbit.

A warm, whimsical smile stretched across her face. 'I've been watching you through the peep-hole. Are you all right?'

'How? - What was I doing?'

'It looked like you were practising saying hello.'

Joe instantly deflated. Any buoyancy he had was gone. 'I'm always nervous, saying hello, I don't know why.'

'You've not really said it yet.'

'Sorry, hello.'

'Hello back.'

'Have you seen the papers today?'

Her face fell. 'My friend was murdered.'

'Whitey – that guy Whitefield was a friend of yours?'

'Who's Whitey?' she whispered, and then she clicked. 'You're thinking about the other guy. No, we didn't know him.' She paused for a moment, then said, 'My friend Connie was murdered. Murdered at his work.'

Joe stood motionless, unsure what to say or do, but simply relieved by her last statement.

'Come in,' she said quietly as fresh tears formed. 'I never knew Whitefield. I would have remembered him.'

Joe entered the living room and saw DC Hannah putting on her coat.

'I'll have to go. I shouldn't be too long, Margaret,' the detective said.

Marian MacCallum cut in, sister-like, saying, 'I'll try not to be in your road - give you a bit of peace to yourselves.'

Joe looked around, stuck for words. He just wanted to sit down with Margaret, ask some questions - hard questions, made even harder with two CID hovering around. He was glad they were here though because, only a few hours ago, he'd realised and accepted he wasn't cut out for the life of a hard man anymore.

DC Hannah pulled the door closed behind her as DC MacCallum made her way to her bedroom, carrying her laptop.

Joe stammered, 'You're welcome to join us.'

'I'll pass.' The detective smiled back at Margaret.

Then they were alone, sitting on the couch. He wanted to ask her so much, but he just did not know which tack to employ. She must have worked for Wagner at some stage, and that meant she was really working for JJ. Maybe he was being prudish, here, but that fact bothered him. He only wanted to do what was best for her. Christ, he was beginning to sound like a prude. Then there was another tester. How would he broach the subject of her Uncle Owny? When he questioned her past, how would he explain away his own? My God she'd only be about five or six years old when that happened.

He turned to speak to her and her mouth was on his. She was straddling him, placing her hands on his cheeks, pulling his face ever further into hers, her tongue tentatively seeking solace inside his head. He didn't know what to do. He tried to stop her, tried to say hold on, wait a minute - but he was lost, lost somewhere beautiful. The taste of her saliva was super-sweet and her aroma highlighted his sense of taste. His arms tightened around her, pulling her downwards onto him. He felt like crying, felt like he should be feeling some sort of pain here. It wasn't guilt, but he was not sure if it was lust or love – but he wanted her now. And it did not matter that a police officer was in the next room. He started fumbling at her clothes and his lips only parted company with hers to gulp in more air as every part of him seemed to be growing. They were both aware of his erection as he fumbled to free it from his trousers. Then she pulled back slightly, as much as he would let her.

'Wait, Joe. Wait.'

Joe's heart felt as if it was going to explode. He sought more fuel for his lungs, but his body knew it needed to exhale. She forcibly pushed him back onto the sofa, her hand stretching and grabbing his two arms.

'Joe, slow down.' She let out a nervous giggle as he tried to engage her lips again. 'Joe, stop. I'll call the police.' Her other hand lifted his head away from her neck, 'Least I know you're interested,' she said.

'I'm interested,' Joe said, finally exhaling. She kissed him again and quickly pushed him back against the sofa. Then, she expertly brushed her groin against his erection, and Joe was at the races again. She stood up on the sofa, skilfully keeping out of his reach. She quickly and nimbly stepped over the small coffee table, and was now looking down on him from the other side of the room.

Joe was lost for words. He didn't really want to speak anyway. He just wanted her.

'I'll ask Marian if it's OK for you to stay.' She seemed a touch timid. 'You do want to stay?'

'I do, I definitely do,' he said, sounding totally exhausted.

Margaret quietly left the room as Joe became aware of the seepage from his erection, now apparent at the entrance to the hip pocket of his Levis. 'Oh God. Can that damage my mobile?' He struggled to muffle that exclamation as he made his way to the bathroom, praying he would not encounter DC MacCallum. Fuck. He felt like a naughty schoolboy, until it dawned on him. Would he need precautions? Christ almighty! Did they still call it that? "Precautions". He was nervous again – shit-scared, to be honest. His head was still mince. He was not sure how to proceed. He was inside the bathroom now, staring at his reflection in the medicine cabinet mirror. He pulled a long length of tissue from the toilet roll, unbuttoned his jeans and began wiping himself clean. He looked at his flaccid penis. 'Please don't let me down,' he said as he began to wash. A whore's bath, as his auld man used to call it. She was a whore. Correction, she'd been a whore. He wasn't taking the moral high ground. He was a lot older than her, but she was a hundred times more experienced than he was. Do most prostitutes not go off sex? A mundane chore, they just go through the motions. Jesus Christ, it'd been twenty years. Shit. They'd had a wee kiss and cuddle and he'd nearly shot his load.

*   *   *

'Don't worry. It happens.'

'I'm not worried,' he lied. 'There was a strong possibility that that was going to happen.' He was surprised by how calm he sounded. She said nothing, just lay there. He continued. 'It's twenty years since I've been with a woman.' He gave a scornful laugh. 'No much change in the meantime.'

'Were you quick on the draw then?' she said with a wry smile.

'Aye - Quick Draw McGraw.'

'I've heard about you.'

'Are you sure about that?'

'Definitely. I've heard that name before.'

'What? Quick Draw McGraw?'

'You're Quick Draw McGraw? Is that your nickname?'

Joe mused more to himself than Margaret. 'No, I was being sarcastic.'

'What were you being sarcastic for?'

'Well, I wasn't really being sarcastic, I was being ......' Joe found it hard to explain what he was being. 'Quick Draw McGraw was a cartoon character. I actually can't remember him too good, but I'm sure he was a horse or he had a horse.'

'Well, you're definitely not a horse.'

'May I continue?' Joe asked.

Margaret stifled a giggle, raised the duvet a touch and had a quick shufty underneath, whispering. 'Maybe you're a wee horse - a Shetland pony. Aye, you're my little pony.'

Joe grimaced for effect and flattened the cover, 'As I was saying before being so rudely interrupted. Quick Draw McGraw was a cartoon character who roamed the Wild West and had a bad habit of fucking things up. His poor horse had the voice of a Negro slave and he was always getting McGraw out of scrapes . ..... I just wish I had a horse that could get me out of my scrapes.' He could hear Margaret let out little bursts of the giggles, he could feel the bed shaking because of that suppressed laughter. He fought hard to control himself from not laughing. 'Aye I could have been Quick Draw McGraw no problem.' He closed his eyes again and lay back. 'I was trying to make light of the wee disaster we both engaged in several minutes ago. Somehow, it seems longer, but that's what I was trying to do. Thing is, I've always been a nervous wreck when it came down to having sex. Sorry - you know - being intimate. I've never been any good. Fuck, I don't think I've ever done it sober - well not until now, and – well, I'd prefer not to count that.'

'Joe – stop talking.' Margaret took his penis in her hand. 'Let's try again, McGraw.'

McGraw responded. She glided on top of him, rubbing his helmet against her pubic mound. Then she inserted him. He reached for her but she pushed him back.

'Just you lie there, McGraw, think of England or something.'

He did as he was told and thought about Robin Hood's Bay in Scarborough. As she rocked gently back and forth like an ebbing tide, her lips hovered for a moment over his. He sucked her expelled air into him.

Each breath he stole from her made him a touch headier than before. He thought of nothing, nothing apart from the next moment her lips would brush against his. Then she kissed him. Again he tried to respond and again she pushed him away, forcibly held his arms off her. She kissed him a second time, and he responded in the same fashion. She pushed him back again. 'Relax, man - please.'

Joe adhered to the last command and she kissed him again. He lay there as she gingerly licked around his mouth. He could feel her tongue drag sometimes on the stubble of today's growth. His facial growth was sparse - normally he shaved more out of embarrassment than need.

Something very strange was happening to Margaret Logan; she was beginning to enjoy sex, and she was realising that she had real feelings for the man underneath her.

Joe's breathing was becoming heavy; he'd lost track of time, maybe that's what's meant to happen, he was sure they....

'Be still – still,' she whispered as her own breathing became heavier. She pulled his face into hers and Joe came.

He lay there with her on top of him. Neither spoke. Each kept their own thoughts, and if they'd shared them, they'd have been astonished by their similarity. She smiled down at him, snaking tender limbs around him. He felt elated and he felt contented and he felt like crying. Then he did exactly that: cried.

She looked him square on and gently kissed him. 'Joe, can I trust you?'

He kind of guessed what was coming. 'Yes, you can.'

'See when I disappeared in Edinburgh?'

'Aye.'

'I – ah l……..'

'Lied about where you went.'

'How'd you know?' she seemed genuinely surprised.

'I'm Quick Draw McGraw,' he said softly.

'I went to see somebody about getting Nicola and Emma back.'

'So who did you see?'

'I think he's a lawyer guy. He's a creepy bastart.'

'So this creepy guy's going to help.'

'No, no, he's like the go-between, the setter-up.'

'The go-between?'

'The go-between with the judge.' She smiled.

'Judge?'

'The judge, who's going to help me.'

179

'How is he going to help? Is he making a judgement – making a decision?' Joe's head juggled scenarios.

'No, nothing like that. He's just going to help.'

'But why is he going to help? Why is he going to help you?' Joe stressed as quietly as he could.

'Because he's a friend, that's why.'

'You're friends with a judge?'

'Aye, in a way. When I knew him, I didn't know he was a judge. Christ, Joe, if I'd known that then, I'd have asked his help a lot quicker than I did.'

'So what was he then?'

'Just Uncle Vanya, Connie's Uncle Vanya.'

'Who's Connie?' Joe said, curbing his anger.

'Cornel Wagner, my friend - the dead guy in the paper - have you forgotten already?'

She was looking upset again. This is hard work, Joe thought.

'Caroline called him Colonel Wanker behind his back, but she did care for him.' She tried smiling through watery eyes and pulled at her face, exposing the underside of her eyelids.

'What weird names your friends have got.'

'Vanya's no' his real name. I found that out when I had a sneaky peek at Marian's laptop and saw a photo of Uncle Vanya outside the Crown Office.'

'That's the Crown Office across the street from the museum – so glad I could be of assistance there, Margaret. Helped you right out, didn't I…......'

'I'm sorry, Joe. I did want to go to the museum, I'm so sorry I had to…....'

'Save it Margaret, just tell me who he is.'

'His real name's Rameses Bullock.'

Joe nearly spat his tonsils out. 'Fucking hell, he was the Lord Advocate - the highest law officer in Scotland.'

'I know that now. But I didn't know it when we stayed with him.'

Joe's stunned expression sought further explanation.

'We stayed with him years ago, when we escaped from Maranatha House.'

'Jesus Christ, how old were you?'

'Caroline was ten, aye she was ten - I'd be thirteen or fourteen.'

'And a High Court judge just happened to put you up.'

Her face fell and she turned away, pulling the bedclothes around her.

Listen,' he said, as she flinched from his consoling hand. 'I'm no' trying to take the moral high ground, you don't have to tell me what happened - I'm just figuring out equations.'

'Equations, Joe. What are you talking about now? I just want them back. Fuck sake, my wee sister's dead. I'm fucking dead, dead inside. Without them, I'm dead inside. Parts of me are cut away, severed, missing. Can you no' understand that? I just want them back. I want Caroline's wee lassie Cheryl back as well. Bullock – Vanya, whatever his name is, can help me. I don't care about what he did to us back then. That's gone. That's back then and I want help now, and then I'll be better, and not feeling - like - like....'

He wrapped his arms around her, overpowered her rejection and pulled her close to him. 'Please don't take this the wrong way, but why would Bullock help the likes of you?'

'You fuckin' know why, Joe.'

'Do you think there's a connection with Wagner's murder and Caroline's?'

She stirred at that, but remained silent.

Fuck sake, a blind cobbler could read this. So why haven't the police figured this out, or have they and they're just fuckin' waiting....

'What's a niggerette?'

He shook his head, stumped.

'Is a niggerette a lady darkie? You don't say things like that now. You're no' allowed to say things like that, these days, are you?'

'I don't know. I've never heard anybody called that.'

'You wouldn't think a lawyer would say words like that. No' even that creepy bastart.'

'What exactly did he say?'

She remembered Brodie's pink, bloated face sweating over hers in the cramped, cloying box closet at the Court of Session. She used the same smarmy tone. 'It would be good to know exactly how many little niggerettes are likely to clamber out from under the woodpile.'

'I think he's making a reference to someone who had the same idea as you, only she was a bit quicker on the draw.'

'What idea's that, Joe?'

'Don't act daft, Margaret.'

'No, say it. Say it, Joe. The word is - blackmail.'

'I'm not going to say it, but if Caroline tried contacting Bullock ....'
Joe saw evidence that she was getting his drift. She looked perplexed, astonished and more hurt than he thought possible.

'We hadn't seen each other in months. Everyone said it was best that we were kept apart until we got into a settled routine. That's what Heather said. She said they all said that.'

'Do you think Bullock killed her or had her killed?'

'I don't believe he would do that,' she said, stunned.

'Bullock's been in the news recently. He's heading an enquiry into the care system.'

'It's a wonder he's no' called me as an expert witness.'

'He wouldn't be too keen for his past to surface now.'

She still seemed puzzled.

'Whitey, the other dead guy in the paper - have you forgotten him already?'

'What about him, I don't know him,' she snapped.

'You sure about that?'

'Course I'm sure.'

'He was the guy who grabbed you in the street that day.'

'But you said his face was covered. That's what you told the cops.'

'I recognised his eyes from the photo in the paper. It's him. I'm certain of that.'

'Well, I don't know him.'

'You should; he worked for JJ McGuire.'

'I still don't know him.'

'Your friend Connie Wagner worked for JJ as well.'

'So?'

'You worked for Wagner.'

'So?'

'If you worked for Wagner - you're working for McGuire, and McGuire is a more dangerous enemy than Bullock. Would McGuire want to kill you or your sister?'

She took in a slow breath, 'I don't think so. We never met him; we just knew most of the money went to him eventually.'

'You don't know something that you are not meant to know?'

'No, Joe.' She slipped from the covers, quickly crossed the room and nimbly retrieved Bullock's number from the dresser. 'I've to phone Bullock on this number at exactly five past five tomorrow. I've tried to phone before but the line's always unavailable.'

'Have you told the police?'

'No, nobody knows. I've only told you.'

'I don't know if that's good or bad. What are you going to say to him?'

'Help me get my children back or I'll tell everybody what you did to me and my sister.'

'Cuts straight to the chase, doesn't it.'

'Well, I'm not going to blurt it out right away.'

'It's OK, I get the gist.

'Joe, I just want them back. That's all I want. I don't want vengeance, I just want them.'

'I know you do. I know.'

'Will you be with me - when I phone - will you be with me? Can you help me say the right words, help me practise?' She pulled at her face again. 'He said I was to be on my own, but will you be with me?'

'Aye, I will.' He ran a gentle hand around her face, tenderly parted her lips and slowly kissed her.

'You're my Prince Charming, Joe,' she said, smiling timidly.

Joe returned in kind and then lay facing her, passive, hushed and seemingly contented, but inside bad thoughts churned. *Why's the police no' figured this out? Can I trust Henderson? He's an old copper. The longer you're about, the more likely it is that you'll be compromised. Even if he's no' bent, when the shite is thrown, they only wipe up after their own.*

He thought about saying a prayer for both of them, but his prayers had been answered. So what was he going to do now, pray for different answers? He made a decision. 'I just need to nip out for a while, Margaret.'

'I thought you were going to stay the night.'

'I'll be back. I just need to go speak with my mum. It's important, but I'll definitely be back.' He leant over and kissed her.

'You're no' going to tell anybody, are you?'

'No, Margaret. I won't tell a living soul.'

He dressed quickly and walked out of her flat, checked the money situation, realised he'd more than enough, and stepped out into the cool night.

He stood at the spot where he'd first met her and first played the hero. There was a wee white Fiesta and a gold Micra, nudged up close and personal, touching front bumper to front bumper. He'd get back to her soon. Now he just wanted to talk to his mother. Let her know, she deserved at least that. *My God, even I deserve that. If I'm going back inside, it might go easier if I'm doing the right, wrong thing !!!*

He stepped from the pavement, flagged an arm and a black cab pulled in. He gave the driver his instructions and settled nervously in the back seat. He hadn't even bothered to put a jacket on and now he could feel the cold, but something else niggled at him.

Will she have visitors? "Family visitors"?

Chapter Thirty Two

He walked into the lounge and saw Jim Cassidy was sitting upright with his legs resting on the sofa.

Cassidy pressed mute on the remote and asked, 'Is everything OK?'

'Watch your programme, don't mind me, Jim.' Joe nodded.

'It's just the usual Saturday night shite. I was even thinking of taking a wee walk down the road and getting a video DV,' he laughed correcting himself. 'I mean a DVD - shows you how often I get a video, sorry, a movie these days.' He laughed again. 'Freda used to love them. That was our Saturday night for years. A chicken curry from The Great Wall and a good picture was her idea of heaven – mine too, if truth be told.'

'Jim, I'm not very good at this.'

'Good at what?'

'You've done a lot for me – I'm grateful. I really am.'

Jim Cassidy switched the TV off.

'Something's happened.' Joe looked to the floor.

'What?'

'Margaret's told me stuff. I'm glad that she's trusted me. That must mean something, eh?'

'What kind of stuff?'

'The bad kind.'

'Do you want a beer?' Cassidy asked.

'No, I just want to talk, ask for help, take advice and do what the sensible people do - get help from their betters.'

'Betters? I'm no' any better than you, Joe.'

'Look, Jim, I need help. There, I've admitted it and you're the one I'm asking. I need help.' Joe slumped into the armchair with his head in his hands. 'She's in real trouble, Jim. I want to do the right thing. I want to do right by her. Do you know what I mean?'

'I think so,' Cassidy said, hedging his bets.

'I'm pretty sure I know why her sister was murdered.'

'Oh…. What happened when you were down there?'

'We cemented our friendship.'

Jim Cassidy merely raised an eyebrow.

Joe half smiled. 'I've said that I'll help her. She's going to make a phone call tomorrow and we'll take things from there. I'll probably be back inside by Monday.'

'Stop, stop right there. Back inside by Monday? What does that mean?'

'I wish Harry was here, he'd know exactly what to do.'

'Harry's dead, Joe,' Jim Cassidy screamed.

'Sorry, Jim - I'm so sorry.'

'Don't be sorry, just tell me what happened when you were with Margaret.'

'Sit down and I'll tell you everything.' Joe took Jim's shoulder shrug as consent. 'I left prison with the half-arsed notion of trying to make amends for the stuff I should've got jailed for. It was a thing Harry used to say to me. When I was down, when things weren't going.....'

'When you were having a wee tantrum?' Cassidy helped out.

'Yes.'

'Don't worry Joe, I heard him say it plenty times. I've not hurt your feelings saying that?'

Joe failed to hide the fact his feelings were hurt. 'When the wee man died, I made a vow to make amends for stuff I'd got away with.'

'You don't look like you've gotten away with it,' Cassidy said

'The guy's name was Owny MacNee, he was Margaret's uncle. We did bad things to him, Jim, and he killed himself. I want to help her, so I can square things with him. You do know that I'm in love with her?'

Yes, I do,' Jim nodded.

'She's in trouble, Jim, big trouble,' Joe said, struggling for breath.

'I'll get you some water.'

'We had sex; made love, whatever you want to call it.'

'What do you want to call it, Joe?' Jim Cassidy asked as he filled a glass at the sink.

'We'll call it making love then, I suppose. If you love somebody, that's what you call it.'

'Correct.' Jim smiled, handing Joe a glass of water.

'I don't know if it's right to involve you, Jim. I mean, you've done a lot for me.'

'I'm already involved. Mark Henderson asked me to keep an eye on her and I've kept the other one on you.'

'You've heard of Lord Bullock?'

'Of course I've heard of him, I'm a prison officer.'

'Bullock helped Margaret and her sister run away from a Care Home. Put them up for a wee while - very nice to them, apparently.'

'Has she told the police this?'

'Not really. She let it slip that she knew him, but that's it.'

'She should be telling them everything. I take it there is an - everything?'

'There's an - everything - all right.' Joe's demeanour was contemplative. 'She doesn't want to talk to the police. She'd rather persuade Lord Bullock that it's in his best interest to help get her children back.'

'I take it "persuades" is a nicer word than blackmail?'

'Do you really need an answer?'

'Take it she wants your help, Joe?'

'Course.'

'And you're going to give it, eh?'

'Course.'

'You probably will be back inside by Monday.'

'She's meant to talk to him tomorrow.'

'What is she going to say?'

'It's an easy speech,' Joe shrugged. 'Help me get my kids back or I'll tell people how you sexually abused me and my wee sister.'

'What age were they?'

'Caroline was ten, Margaret thirteen.'

'You're treading a dangerous path, Joe.'

Joe nodded, saying 'I wish Harry was here, he'd know what to do.'

'What fucking good would Harry be here?'

Joe was surprised and it showed. 'Eh?' he queried.

'You got yourself twenty years trying to emulate McGuire.'

Joe threw Jim Cassidy the dirtiest of looks, but significantly remained silent.

'I know all about it, Joe. Do you think Harry never discussed you with me - I know.'

'Know what?'

'About Duke Street, when you fucked your life up trying to outdo your buddy McGuire.'

'Touchy, Jim-Bob, are you annoyed I've no' been asking your advice?'

'My advice would be a lot better than Harry's.'

'That's a given. He's fucking dead,' Joe scoffed.

'You ruined your life trying to be JJ McGuire. Now you're going to mess up what's left of it trying to be Harry Lawson.'

'I knew I should never have talked to you.'

'Because I'm a screw.'

'Got it in one, Einstein.'

187

'Well I'm not a screw anymore. I wish I was. I'd bang you up in the digger until this nonsense was over with.'

'I owe her, Jim, I feel responsible for her.'

'I know about Big Owny as well.'

'What do you know? You think you know.'

'I know that you stopped it, Joe. Harry told me.'

'I was part of it. We grabbed him from the street.'

'You might have grabbed him. You might have attacked him. But you stopped it.'

'Stopped it too late – fuck, he should have got a good fuckin' kicking, that was all.'

'You stopped the torture. Does McGuire know you called the emergency services?'

Joe looked to his feet, ashamed, as he tried to blank out the memory of Big Owny lying inside that condemned building, beaten to a pulp. 'Of course he doesn't know.'

'You didn't have to do that.'

'Oh yes I did.'

'That proves my point. You're not McGuire. Never were, never will be.'

'I became somebody on that job.'

'So is that why you tried to make your own name in Duke Street?'

'Yes. Jim, I tried to outdo JJ. I failed.'

Jim Cassidy rose to his feet and walked over to Freda's pride and joy. He pulled open the down door, exposing the drinks cabinet inside. He took out the bottle of malt, and said, 'Get some ice.'

'Tell you something nobody knows. McGuire was scared of Owny MacNee. He wasn't just apprehensive or aware of the big man's capabilities, he was scared of him.'

'Were you scared of him?' Cassidy asked.

'Aye, of course I was. Funny thing was I liked him. Met him once and we got on good,' Joe said, returning with the ice-tray.

Jim Cassidy poured two generous glasses of whisky, took the ice from Joe and expertly removed four cubes from the tray. Joe returned the tray to the freezer.

Cassidy handed over the tumbler saying, 'Wedding present, Edinburgh Crystal, had them for forty years and never broke one.'

Joe gripped the heavy glass. He was the same age as the whisky tumblers, although they were bearing up better than him. He looked the whisky square on, and then he drank.

'Were you always scared of McGuire?'

The question jolted Joe. 'Scared?'

'Aye, scared, scared of McGuire. He must have always been a bad bastard?'

'I wasn't that scared, no' really, he always said he liked me.'

Jim Cassidy savoured the malt and asked. 'Did he not like the rest of your pals?'

'Aye, but I was always treated different, and I don't know why.'

'Maybe he saw some qualities in you, Joe. Maybe you were a better person than the others.'

'I think you've been ear-wigging in on too many psychiatric assessments.'

Cassidy laughed out loud. Joe wasn't that far from the truth here. He'd been interested in psychology early in his prison career. Ridicule and derision from fellow officers had made him put psychology on the back burner. Now and then, in the strictest confidence, Cassidy had conversed with prison shrinks, for one reason only - it was interesting.

'What's funny? Am I not that far off the mark there?'

Jim Cassidy laughed again, louder than before. 'Bang on the money, mate, bang on the money.'

'These wee confessionals have a tendency to reveal certain aspects of both parties.'

'I think you paid a lot of attention at your psychological assessments.'

'Necessity is the Mother of Invention.' Joe scratched his head, puzzled. 'Where did that come from?'

'Ah, Joseph, don't try and pull the wool over my eyes. I know you're clever, I've seen the reports.'

'Have you?'

'Of course I've seen them,' Cassidy said, matter of fact. 'Did you always consider yourself to be smarter than JJ McGuire?'

The whisky stalled in Joe's throat and his belly tensed.

'Can you answer the question, please? Did you always think you were smarter than JJ?'

'At school I thought I was, but I was wrong. Came as a severe kick in the balls, I'd myself down as the brains of the operation. Then things changed.' *Fuck it*, Joe thought, *tell somebody*. 'JJ could always fuck my head up. You know McGuire killed his own father when he was thirteen? He followed him home from the pub and hung him from a tree. And then he came and told me, because you've got to tell somebody. They call it

189

patricide, don't they? Christ, I can talk. I destroyed my father, I took the long route. There's not much difference between me and JJ, we both put our fathers in the grave.' Joe looked heavenward and said. 'Wee Harry never had the monopoly on killing members of your own family.'

'You couldn't be more wrong.'

'Pardon?' Joe said.

'Harry didn't kill his family.'

'Sure he did. That's why he kept saying he was innocent, so they'd keep him inside.

'He told me....'

'Told you what,' Joe said, scornfully.

'He told me on his deathbed, told me the real story. Harry's wife killed the two children - then she killed herself.'

'No. Harry drugged them and placed them on the bed, killed Goodwin and fucked-up killing himself.'

'Oh, he killed his boyfriend, but he never killed his wife and he never killed his children.'

'Why would she do that?'

'Who knows? Spite, unsound mind - put yourself in her place. For eight years they'd been playing happy families – then she finds out, all that time, Harry's playing away - no' just that, he's batting for the other side. The only person Harry killed was his blabber-mouth boyfriend.'

'I thought he would have told me. Why didn't he tell me?'

'Why would he tell you? He wouldn't tell anyone. The only reason I know is because I heard him making peace with his past.'

'He would've taken it to the grave.'

'Definitely - that was the least he owed his wife.'

'That's love; oh my God, that is love.'

'I've been shutting the door on love's misguided for most of my life.'

'That include me?'

'Probably, Joe, I don't know. I'm only telling you this because I don't want you spending forty years of your life behind bars.'

'Thirty eight years.'

'Don't nit-pick, you know what I mean.'

'It's just so fucking sad.'

'That's exactly what it is, sad. He took some abuse when he was first jailed, unbelievable abuse.'

'Did he ever fight back?'

190

'What do you think? He was talking to her when he died.' Jim Cassidy stood up awkwardly, 'It was a privilege to be there with him.'

Joe still felt hurt. Why had Harry not trusted him? He'd told the wee man everything. Stuff you do take to the grave. 'What did he say?'

'He said he was sorry.'

'Thanks for trusting me, Jim.'

'I do trust you, Joe.'

Chapter Thirty Three

'I'll get straight to the point, DCI Henderson. Tell you the facts as I know them. The remains of the foetus have been incinerated, as has the bag and the box.' She paused to take a deeper breath. 'The documentation has disappeared and all the computer data has been corrupted.' With that, Anne Swinton sat down.

'I should never have made that call, gloating over the phone like that – so stupid.'

'Mark, that only speeded up the process. I'm certain Bullock would have got the same result at some point.'

'We should have sent it down south.'

'Bullock will have as many friends down there, I suppose.'

Henderson shrugged. 'I'm still going to collect a sample from him. I'll do it personally and I'll question Margaret Logan myself.'

'Even I'm shocked at the levels of corruption through here. We used to make ourselves feel so superior – even had a saying. The "soap dodgers" always make you feel squeaky clean.'

'How do you know I'm squeaky clean? When I made the phone call to Bullock's PA, I could have been tipping the old guy off.'

'Well, it's some act you're putting on.'

'Glasgow's full of actors. It's like Edinburgh's Fringe, only we do it 365 days a year.'

'Without the leaflets.'

'Aye, Ma'am, without the leaflets.'

Henderson walked slowly to his office. As expected, no one spoke to him. He gently pushed the door closed and picked up the phone. He pressed the numbers, sat back and waited. It took a while but she finally answered.

'Hello.'

'Mrs Hochnall, Jeanie, do you mind if I call you Jeanie?'

'Who is this?'

'Sorry, it's DCI Henderson, Mark Henderson, calling from Glasgow. Calling to thank you for your help in this enquiry and calling to thank you personally for your bravery...'

'It's no' bad news, is it, Mr Henderson?'

'No, it certainly is not bad news, Jeanie. I am now able to put your mind at rest. We've concluded our analysis of the hairbrush and your husband's DNA is not a match with the remains of Caroline Logan's baby.' Henderson could hear her crying, so he waited.

'Thank you, oh thank you so much,' she said.

'Jeanie, this is a very complex case. It will be a very long time before this case comes to court. And I'm afraid it will take some considerable time before we can hand your belongings back.'

'It's OK Inspector - I was going ask if the wee one could rest in my father's document box. It seems right, proper. It's for important things and the wee soul's slept there all these years.'

'That's very kind of you. I'll make sure that happens.'

'I feel so bad for doubting him - he was a good man.'

'I'm sure he was - I'm very aware how difficult this must have been for you, Jeanie.'

'Brian was good to her - that was all. Maybe I was jealous. How pathetic is that, Inspector?'

'Please don't do this, Mrs Hochnall, please don't feel guilt. The person responsible for all of this is the man who killed Caroline Logan. You and Mr Hochnall are responsible for giving Caroline some happy times in her short, turbulent life. I would also like to thank you for the care and love you showed that little girl when she miscarried that baby. I have to go now, Jeannie, but I will contact you again. Sadly, I don't know when that will be.'

'Thank you, Mr Henderson. Thank you, Mark.'

*   *   *

In Stevenston, Jeanie Hochnall walked around the darkness of her living room, felt for the table lamp and switched it on. She picked her husband's photo from the top of the television and held it close.

*   *   *

Back in Glasgow, Mark Henderson lay back exhausted, completely done in. Good God, lying is hard work. He wanted a drink, wanted to get fucking hammered. No he wanted to hammer Bullock, pound that face time and again, let him know hurt. But Bullock could never ever comprehend the hurt wee Jeanie Hochnall had owned all these years.

*   *   *

Joe looked at his watch. It was four minutes past five. He nodded once at Margaret.

She fumbled with the mobile, tried to catch it, but it slipped from her hands, bounced off the bed and landed on the floor.

'Fuck. It's not broke, is it?'

'No, they're not that fragile, Joe.'

Joe was quite taken with her fraught, anxious looking face.

'What?' she asked.

'Nothing.'

'So why the look?'

'I'll tell you later,' he said, mimicking her hurt facial expression. 'Make the phone call.'

Margaret cupped the mobile in her left hand, pressed the call button once, and then pressed it once more.

'Well, dial the number,' Joe said.

'I have,' she said looking at him as if he were shit on her shoe.

'Oh,' he winced painfully.

She shushed him, waving her spare arm in mild panic. 'Hello.'

The phone was silent, and then a small cough could be heard.

'Are you there?' Margaret asked.

A low snigger was heard and Margaret's heart sank.

Thomas Brodie spoke in the same robotic tone as he had when he had her pinned inside that cramped cubicle at the Court of Session.

'Did you have the foresight to have a pen and paper ready?' he asked.

'Pardon?'

'I would like you to write. I take it you can write...'

'It's no' you I want to speak to,' she stated.

'You can write. Surely you take down numbers in your profession?'

'I can write and I've got your number.'

'Well, I would like you to take note of the meeting place I've arranged for you and our mutual acquaintance.'

'Have you always got to talk like an arsehole? I want to speak to him.'

Brodie sniggered louder than before.

'Well, tell me where it is,' Margaret hissed.

'The Obelisk on Glasgow Green, tomorrow, quarter past three'

'The Obe...what?' Margaret looked at Joe, but he was no help.

'The Obelisk. It's a prominent erection. You're familiar with prominent erections? Quite close to the old suspension bridge.'

'What are you talking about, you arsehole?' Margaret said in fury. Joe tried to calm her, but she was having none of it. 'Listen, you're just a go-between, a message-boy, with a wee cock, no' big enough to be called an erection, so just tell me where I'm supposed to meet him.'

'Sorry, I was being sarcastic. I'll see if I can be a wee bit more helpful and a wee bit less condescending,' he said in a mock Glasgow accent.

Margaret was about to blow her top again. Joe raised a hushed finger to her mouth

'Not far from the St Andrew's suspension bridge, you'll see a huge four-sided stone statue. It comes to a point and it has a little pyramid on top. You can't miss it; it's bigger than the trees around about it. Vanya will meet you by Copenhagen.'

'By where?' Margaret whined painfully.

'It's the opposite side of Aboukir,' Brodie said drolly, 'meeting his hooker opposite Aboukir.' Brodie laughed delicately at his own joke.

'What are you saying? I never heard that. What did you say?'

Joe touched Margaret's shoulder and mouthed the words, 'I know where it is.'

'It's alright, I know where it is,' she said and then asked, 'Has he mentioned the children?'

'A two-penny fuck wants thru-pence worth!'

She did not ask again, because she knew he'd hung up. Her anger subsided and her thoughts became more positive. At least she was meeting Vanya; she half smiled to herself and turned sombrely to Joe. 'He's gone.'

'Phone him back.'

Margaret pressed a couple of buttons. An operator's voice said that this number was switched off.'

'The phone's switched off.'

'Can you do that?'

'There's a lot you need to learn about mobiles.'

'I'll say,' Joe said, consciously sounding upbeat.

'First thing is they're a pain in the fuckin arse.' Margaret threw the phone away.

Joe pointed through the wall towards the living room and the two police officers. 'What will you tell them?'

'I was hoping you'd help there.'

'You could tell them the score.'

'Is that gonny get my fucking children back ----- is it, Joe? Is it?'

Joe moved away from the bed, alarmed that he might react in kind.

'Sorry,' she said, sounding like she meant it. 'Joe, I just want them back. I know you think he had something to do with her death, but who is gonny believe the likes of us. Seriously, who in their right fucking mind

195

is going to take my word or even your word over his? Jesus Christ, he's a judge. C'mon, who are they going to believe?'

Chapter Thirty Four

On a cold, wet, October morning, a screaming Sun headline shaved the edge off the fear gripping Glasgow. Frank "the Man in the Know" Conroy broke the news that John Joseph McGuire had cancer. Bold red letters spelt out "Terminal" and, underneath, a grainy old black and white photograph managed to make McGuire look even more menacing.

Jim Cassidy nodded at the paper and said, 'Says he's holed up in a secret Swiss clinic.'

'It's bullshit, total bullshit. We know the real story Jim.' Joe said, feeling guilty that he hadn't told his friend about his plans to help Margaret.

*   *   *

She woke early, attempted optimism, but a glance out the window hampered that. It was raining and it was miserable. Glasgow looked like a city that lived inside a big, grey cloud with no beginning and no end. Still, it might clear up, she thought, as she walked into the kitchen and reached for the kettle. The phone rang and she grabbed it quickly, concerned about wakening her guests.

'Hello,' she whispered.

'Hello stranger,' Heather said.

Margaret's bad start to the day nosedived.

'I'm paying you a visit today,' Heather said cheerfully.

'You can't - not today.' Margaret's brain cells scrambled for an excuse.

'And why not?' Heather asked chirpily.

'Eh, questioning. The police need me for questioning. I think they've got some photographs to show me.' Margaret surprised herself with her plausibility. Then she heard movement from the living room and she knew DC MacCallum had risen and was ready for coffee. Panic set in. 'Tomorrow – anytime, in the morning, first thing - I don't mind you being early, Heather.'

'That's a big change,' Heather joked.

Margaret softened her voice as she could hear Marian approaching the kitchen. 'See you tomorrow, then.' She hung up and quietly cradled the phone.

'Who was that?' DC MacCallum asked through a yawn and an exaggerated stretch of the arms.

'Heather. She can't make it today; she was asking if tomorrow was OK.'

'Is it?' Marian MacCallum asked, stifling another yawn.

'Is it what?'

'You've not quite woken up either. Is it OK for Heather to come around tomorrow?'

'Oh, of course it is.'

'Coffee?'

Margaret nodded, smiled and walked into the living room, praying Heather wouldn't ring back. She wanted to speak to Joe, wanted to go over a couple of things - truth was she was terrified of meeting Uncle Vanya today. Last night, her sleep had been disturbed. There were a lot of questions bouncing around inside her head. Questions she could not make any sense of. Maybe they might make sense to him.

*　　　*　　　*

Maurice Golightly put the finishing touches to the breakfast tray - a small porcelain pot of tea, a slice of toast, and a miserly portion of porridge curled in a dessert dish. He'd filled the tiny stainless steel milk jug with semi-skimmed and then poured some full fat milk over the porridge. She insisted he still keep real milk for her porridge. He looked across at his clear cagoule draped across the kitchen door. It put him mind of Casper, the friendly ghost. But don't trust appearances. He smiled to himself. He placed the folded newspaper under his arm, hoisted the tray in both arms and took his mother's breakfast through to her.

He could hear Lorraine Kelly on GMTV. Personally, he preferred the BBC's breakfast news. He'd quickly glossed over today's paper. It was like a stuck record. McGuire was still making the headlines. At least on Radio Scotland there was fresh speculation that the gangster was holed up somewhere in Ireland, orchestrating events from there.

Big Maurice had only one opinion of JJ McGuire. He was a good payer and he was steady.

*　　　*　　　*

Jim Cassidy rushed into the room, fearing God knows what. He found Joe traumatised and standing, watching the phone vibrating and making spasmodic circles on top of the wooden chest of drawers. Seconds earlier, Joe had placed his hand inside his trouser pocket at the exact moment his mobile had gone ballistic. He'd thrown the phone from his pocket as if it was a snapping lobster.

Cassidy looked at him. 'It's a text. Are you not going to answer it?'

'It's broke,' Joe mumbled.

'No, you've just set it on silent.'

'Fuck are you meant to hear it if it's silent?'

'It vibrates.' Cassidy picked the mobile up, pressed "view" and handed the phone to Joe, asking, 'Who's it from?'

'Margaret,' Joe said nervously.

'What does she want?'

Joe read the short message, 'Just saying good morning,' he lied.

Chapter Thirty Five

They'd got off the bus at the stop before the Trongate, crossed Argyle Street, and turned right into the Saltmarket. Things here at least looked a touch familiar. The railway bridge was still the same colour as it was when Joe was sent down. The Empire Bar sitting under the bridge had endured a change of colour. That place was full of memories for both of them. Nearly all of Glasgow's courts were situated within a quarter-mile radius. Margaret had been in all the minor courts and Joe had been in all the major ones. As they walked at a calming pace, Margaret recognised the black tiles covering the grimy facade of the Public Defence Solicitors' Office. It was less than a year since she'd used their services. Across the road were the Victim Support Offices. She'd used them with her sister a few times, too. Margaret pulled at Joe's hand, hurrying the pace, and then she slammed her brakes on.

Joe looked puzzled, thinking she'd recognised someone.

'That's the last place I saw her,' she said, frozen to the spot, with tears running from her eyes.

They were standing outside a building at 194 Saltmarket. The building was old, red brick, and it looked like a Victorian public convenience. It was the city morgue.

'They brought me in the car. I forgot - forgot it was there, Joe. How could I forget that?'

Joe gently wrapped his arms around her. 'Hey, hey, c'mon - you weren't to know, so don't give yourself a hard time here.' He lifted her face up and wiped her tears away with the back of his forefinger. He pressed the wait button on the pedestrian crossing, got the green light and then escorted her across the street and through the McLennan Arch, the gateway to Glasgow Green.

Joe cast a rueful look back at the old High Court of Justiciary, and thought back to that day when he'd walked from that building triumphantly alongside JJ McGuire. Their ears were ringing with cheers and rebukes. There were scuffles breaking out between warring factions and harassed coppers. Reporters and photographers had been clambering over the black, cast iron railings, desperate to get a photograph and a quote on how they'd beaten justice.

Now, the ornate, iron gates to the court were locked. It looked like they'd been locked for a long time. He'd been told that Owny MacNee was allowed to leave court from a different door that day. They sneaked him out the prisoners' entrance on Mart Street - considering the Crown Office's treatment of Owny Macnee, it was the least they could do.

She took his hand, worried by the remorse showing on his face. Joe looked back at her face. For everything that had happened to her, she still had resilience, still had something about her. There was something about today that felt right and he would not even begin to think of the consequences. All that mattered was that she was alright. If things were going to go wrong today, he might get the chance to right those wrongs in twenty years' time. He was frightened, very scared, terrified that he'd make an arse of it. But at least this time he'd be clean and sober.

'It's turned into a nice day,' Margaret beamed.

Joe nodded and smiled as best as he could. Then he looked along the tarmac path towards the Obelisk. That's where she'd meet Bullock. He wondered if he would turn up. They were early, far too early, so they had time to do what lovers do in the park; walk about, kiss and hold hands and maybe think about eating. There was a restaurant at the People's Palace. The restaurant was housed in the Winter Gardens and, way off in the distance, Joe saw the sun glinting off that spectacular glass construction.

*   *   *

'Just bring him the all-day breakfast.'

'It's after one o'clock,' Joe questioned.

'Let the lassie do her job.'

Joe did as suggested, but continued to struggle with the concept of the all-day breakfast. When it came, it was worth waiting for. Margaret had settled for rearranging a bacon and brie panini, whose remnants sat next to her empty coffee mug.

From his seat, Joe could see the meeting place. She would meet Bullock by the Copenhagen side of the Obelisk. It felt a bit like Michael Caine's old movie, "Funeral in Berlin". The Obelisk was called the Nelson Monument. It was impressive. Joe remembered being chased past it in his youth. They'd screamed they were "Cumbie", and screamed lots of death threats. They were fit, well tooled up and very determined. They'd swum across the Clyde trying to catch up with him, but he'd swum faster.

*   *   *

One hour ago at the Obelisk

Margaret read out the inscription on each side of the monument. Pollution and decaying stone-work had made the words hard to make out.

201

'Lord Viscount Nelson. Was that his first name, Viscount?' She scratched her head.

'That'll be his title, Margaret - Lord Viscount. But don't quote me on that.'

'Don't quote you on that? So you don't know?'

'Well, not for certain.'

'Did you not do history at school? You did go to school?'

'Aye, I went to school, no' as much as I should have,' Joe conceded. 'They said he was a great sailor, but they never said his first name.'

'And you didn't think to ask?'

'I was a very polite wee boy - I didn't want to make a fuss.'

'My arse! You just don't know, do you?'

Joe merely nodded and looked at thick, black railings surrounding the monument. There was one word on the opposite side of the monument: "ABOUKIR". Margaret gave Joe a quizzical look.

'I was off school that day,' he said.

'There's not much you do know'

'I'd remember Aboukir. You don't forget a name like that.'

She ran to the next side and saw Trafalgar emblazoned in stone. She couldn't make out the smaller print, but she made out the date, October.

'I know this one. Trafalgar was his most famous victory. Think Trafalgar Square - London.'

'And that was in October,' she said, screwing her eyes, trying to figure out the proper date.

'It says October, so he won his most famous battle in October.'

'Joe, this is October,' Margaret smiled.

'Really,' Joe replied, overly impressed.

'Do you think I'll win my battle?'

The mood turned solemn, and Joe took her in his arms. 'If I have my way, you'll win the war.'

He fought hard to keep his emotions at bay. It was Glasgow Green. Everywhere you looked, there were recollections, some joyous, some agonising; most regretful and tinged with sadness.

Margaret's next question scratched his soul.

'Why are you helping me?'

He wanted to tell her, wanted to explain his part in Owny's suicide. Fuck, this was where he'd drowned himself.

'Why are you helping me, Joe, tell me - that day in the street was different, I was a stranger, so why are you helping me?'

He gently grabbed her shoulders and pulled her to him.

'Because I love you,' he said.

'How can you love me, you don't know me? You don't know the things I've done, where I've been, who I've been with.' She looked around. 'My God, I used to bring punters here. No' that long ago either,' she sobbed.

'So fucking what - big fucking deal,' he said and turned her around, so they stood face to face.

'Don't say that it doesn't bother you, Joe - because I don't believe that.'

'It doesn't bother me, I swear.'

'It will, believe me – I've been here before – first or second argument we have, you'll throw it in my face.'

'I don't know the answer to give here, Margaret.'

'An answer's no' necessary.

She walked briskly past him to the last side of the monument. She looked up, her face beaten and passive, and she read one word.

'COPENHAGEN.'

The word conjured up a memory in Joe. And he thought back to the history teacher's advice to Jim Wallace, weeks after JJ McGuire's sustained assault on him.

'You should've turned a blind eye, like Nelson at Copenhagen.' Wallace had known what the teacher was on about. Joe had thought then the teacher was making a reference to McGuire's threat to scrape Wallace's eyes out.

'So what was Copenhagen?' Margaret asked.

'Sorry,' Joe said, startled at being brought back to the present.

'Copenhagen, Joe. What happened at Copenhagen?' Margaret asked again.

'Copenhagen was Lord Viscount Nelson's horse,' Joe said, raising his arm in mock salute.

'That's a bit silly, a sailor with a horse?' Margaret gave a derisory snigger. 'He wouldn't have it on the ship with him. Fuck, you cannot even get a horse on the QE2.' She looked for confirmation and found Joe stifling laughter. 'What's funny about that? He wouldn't have his horse on the boat with him?'

Joe burst out laughing.

'That's not funny,' Margaret said, as she gave him a dig in the ribs, making him laugh even louder. 'It's not that funny,' she tried to complain, gurned, as sporadic giggles erupted from her.

Then they were holding each other, laughing like they were two lovers in a movie. Just like the movies, they stopped laughing, at the exact same time. He kissed her gently and waited for a response. She half smiled, half turned away, and faced him again. Her face was different now. The passive look was gone and it was replaced by stoicism. He was proud of her, right there and then.

Fuck the past, this is now. Help her right now.

She was crying again. 'When we were in Edinburgh and I,' she hesitated, 'and I…'

'Did a disappearing act?' Joe finished her sentence.

She nodded apologetically. 'Before I met with Vanya's sleazy pal - I had seen this old statue. It was two sisters. They were called Justice and Mercy. They'd been rescued from a garden somewhere. I forget exactly where. I did read it, but I forget. They'd both seen better days.' She smiled that apologetic smile again. 'There were bits missing. They needed a makeover.' She gave a nervous little giggle and Joe took her hands for support. 'Caroline deserves Justice and I deserve Mercy. When I seen that statue, I took it as a sign that I was doing the right thing. Bullock – Vanya, or any other name he uses, is going to get me my children back. Do I deserve that? Getting my kids back is mercy - do I deserve mercy?' Her thinking suddenly changed. 'Are my kids not better off with somebody else? Is Caroline's wee lassie no' better off with somebody dependable bringing her up?'

'You deserve another chance.'

'I've had plenty second chances. This is not the first time they've been taken away.'

'It could be the last time!'

'I'm starting to think like you now, Joe, thinking that he killed Caroline. She probably did try to blackmail him, because he would've been shagging her as well.' She tried to break free from Joe's grasp, but his grip remained firm. 'Have I shocked you, eh?' she asked.

'No, of course not, I'd guessed that anyway. Anyhow, you're not to blame. You were innocent.'

'No' exactly innocent, I'd been with a few men before Bullock - Connie Wagner for a start.'

'Margaret, you don't need to justify your actions to me. D'you know what I was put away for? Murder! Three murders, so I'm not going to look down my nose at you.'

'I thought it was only me – I did it with him so he would leave her alone.'

'Margaret, stop it, stop. You were just a child yourself.'

She looked like she was taking his words in as they started walking towards the People's Palace. He could feel the blade rest uneasy between his belt and the small of his back. If Bullock tried anything - he would OPEN HIM.

Chapter Thirty Six

On the other side of the river, Henderson stood by the Victorian iron bridge on McNeil Street in Hutchison. This place used to be notorious for its sixties' high-rise monstrosities. He'd watched them being demolished in the late eighties. Thousands had gathered on Glasgow Green to see the controlled explosions. He could still remember the genuine grief on the faces of those who'd lived in them as they watched a million memories turned to rubble in an instant.

There were two suspension bridges on this part of the river. He preferred this one, painted blue with gold trimming, to the St Andrew's suspension bridge. He read the plaque boldly riveted to the old black railings by the bridge. Built in 1859, it replaced the busy ferry that took workers from Bridgeton and the Calton across to Hutchesontown.

"Blue is the colour", he whistled to himself as he moved towards the middle of the bridge. All he could do was wait and see who showed up. He'd not told anyone he was here, not even "Mr Henderson's Girls". He wondered how long the Dame Judi tag would last. He'd been called worse, a lot worse. Today, he was taking a leaf out of JJ McGuire's book, going to ground with his whereabouts unknown. He was still kicking himself for being so imbecilic. He couldn't stop muttering the word "imbecile". It kept squirming out of his big, fucking trap. Why did he make that phone call to Bullock? One thing was certain: Bullock had made a few calls - Big Calls. Forensics deserved the bad rep they've been getting lately.

Henderson bit his tongue and grimly looked down into the water. The current wasn't that strong: surprising, given the rain earlier today. He could see the rowers making their way up and down river. He was never a fan of the Boat Race, but he liked seeing the rowing teams practise on the river, loved the darting staccato movement the boats made through the water and then that long glide after the stroke was completed.

Directly under him was a female pair, both wearing shades and looking super-cool. In fact they just looked super. The rowers stared up at him and eventually made eye contact and smiled up at him. He felt like an old pervert caught in the act.

The rowing coach bellowed orders from the embankment with the voice of a posh fog-horn.

'Place it and t-h-e-n----- sq-ue-e-z-e the whole thing - like flat - and aaaaall the way through. OK. Particularly - with this. It's not a fast boat, a pair, so you really get - hold of it and you've - got to --m-o-v-e -- it through, without air, just feel it -- solid pressure on all the time - and then when you get to the finish - just come out. OK, just try that. Don't try to knock the skin off it, just catch - W-H-O-O-O-O-S-H- OK and don't flick the finish, Just W H O O O O SH --- all right.'

Henderson stood six feet from the rowing coach on a huge semi-circular piece of tarmac overhanging the river. The coach was not just advising on technique, or lack of it. He was pointing out the dangers and difficulties ahead, upriver and downstream. It would be great if everyone had a coach like that on life's journey.

Henderson's head spun as he heard a woman screaming wildly behind him.

'Get the fuckin' dug, ya bam.'

She was shouting at her partner, Henderson assumed. He was a rake of a man, wearing a soiled, navy blue tracksuit. He looked as if he was walking on stilts and that the ground underneath him was about to give way. The man was desperately trying to herd a roving Staffie towards the bridge and the city's south side. The dog was having none of it. The man let out an exasperated 'Please, Tyson, please be good.' Henderson changed his thoughts. *You'd need a lot of life coaches for this part of the city.*

Then Henderson spotted George Parsonage, who is unmistakeable with his thick mop of white hair and dressed in orange overalls that would not have looked out of place at Guantanamo Bay. Obviously his big black wellies would.

Some people called him the Riverman and others called him the Ferryman. He worked for the Glasgow Humane Society and one of his tasks was pulling the dead from the river. Today, George Parsonage was teaching a large group of students how to save lives, and he didn't look impressed by their efforts. The grass verge they stood on was supposedly meant to be a stand-in for the banks of a river. The tarmac path the lifebelts were landing on was meant to be the river. Henderson heard the Ferryman say in a dismissive tone, 'Don't think about throwing the rope - just throw the rope.'

That little snippet of information hit a chord with Henderson. He was throwing Margaret Logan a rope today. He looked again at the man in the orange overalls. He'd met him years ago when the Ferryman had pulled parts of Davy Syme from the river. Parsonage had inherited the job from his father. Between them they'd pulled out around 1500 bodies from the Clyde. The vast majority of those were suicides. Henderson remembered that quote from the article he'd read on Parsonage.

"They all struggle. It's survival. It does not matter how determined they are to die, they all show signs of struggle."

The Ferryman had retrieved Owny MacNee's body from the Clyde. Owny had wedged his suicide note between the wooden steps the rowing teams used to carry their boats to the water's edge. He'd sat on those cold, wooden steps for God knows how long before stripping naked and gently sliding himself into the icy waters of the Clyde. The Ferryman had found Owny on the first of January, 1986, forty yards from the Glasgow Humane Society building, at Lifeboat position UN1.

Henderson was looking at that yellow nameplate right now. He put his hands in the pockets of his C&A jacket. He was wearing a flat cap. My God, he looked like "Jack and Victor". He laughed to himself. He was much older than the men who played those pensioners. He looked back at Hutcheson, still amazed by its transition. There was still one blot on the landscape. White smoke billowed from the giant, silver chimney of Ballantyne's Whisky Bond. Fifty years ago, a chimney like that would have blended in no problem, one of hundreds spewing out pollution. Now it stood alone, exposed, like a smoker lighting up in a fancy restaurant.

*   *   *

The cagoule sat folded on the park bench. If he hadn't brought it, he'd have needed it. Still, the weather had changed dramatically once today; it could change again. He liked this place. He'd killed here before. Actually, today would make the hat-trick. He'd brought plenty bread with him and he'd give the waterfowl another feed in about ten minutes or so. He looked around the park, taking in the full splendour of this beautiful, cultivated, open space named the "Lungs of Glasgow". He briefly tormented himself with the notion of crushing the lungs out of an entire city. The fantasy was too big and too exquisite to contemplate. Today he'd settle for crushing out her lungs. That's if things went his way, went to plan. "But things don't always go your way." That was his mother's famous saying. She said it about everything. Every time he threw a lottery ticket in the pedal bin, that phrase would echo around the kitchen.

He flinched as a car horn warned him of its presence. He looked around and saw it was the "parkies" crawling along in a flat-bed Transit. Huge grilles walled the sides of the van, and it was crammed full of autumn leaves. He slowly turned 360 degrees and saw three similar vehicles criss-crossing the Green. All busy collecting the fall. He loved that word. It was American, but it was a better way of describing autumn. "The Fall and the Fallen". He smiled to himself. He'd wait. There was still plenty time. He had all day. He would get her today though, knew it,

208

felt it in his long gnarly bones. He ground his teeth and salivated under taut, drawn lips and sat back on the bench. A few small children had glanced frightened stares at him. He made his mind up. Next time he would stare back.

* * *

'Are you ready?'

'Nearly,' she said.

'I'll no' be far away. Promise.'

Bolstered by that, she stood up and Joe, gentleman that he was, helped her on with her coat. This act seemed to bolster her even more. She slipped her arms into her lime green coat. It had the look of an old-fashioned duffle coat. She looked nice in it. There was no debate there. He'd made references to Paddington Bear. And she'd responded with hints of possessing a hat very similar to the one the wee bear from Peru wore.

She looked cute, that was a given. Joe had a word with himself. He was using that phrase too much, truly bursting the arse out of it.

They walked to the automatic side door of the Winter Gardens. The four old biddies having afternoon tea, recoiled in unison as the dreaded draught blew in. Joe bowed in apology. The biddies smiled in turn.

As they got outside, Joe's stomach began making knots. He stopped dead in his tracks.

'Do you remember your mum's brother, Owen, Big Owny? He killed himself here.' Joe's face looked beaten.

She took his hand and said, 'It's OK, I know.'

'Know what?'

'Know what you and McGuire did.'

Joe looked to the ground. He was speechless. He tried to say sorry, but nothing would come out.

'Inspector Henderson told me you stopped it.'

Joe was confused. 'How would he know that?'

'He just knows. We'd a chat and he told me.'

Joe was even more puzzled now. 'How would he know?'

'He's a policeman. He said my uncle told him you stopped it and that you called the ambulance.'

Joe felt something leave him, felt knots unravel in his gut, felt a load fall from his back and felt tears in his eyes.

* * *

Maurice Golightly leaned against the fence that ran along the Clyde. The noise from the waterfowl was deafening as they squabbled for their share of the food. There were big ducks, wee ducks, brown ducks, white ducks, swans, down-covered cygnets, seagulls and a few pigeons jostling for feeding rights. An old gadgee-boy approached and stood by the fence. He was wearing a donkey jacket, thick grey joggers and cheap trainers. A black tammy covered his head and a good part of his face.

'Hadn't quite pictured you as Saint Francis of Assisi.'

Bread fell from Maurice Golightly's limp hands and he stood slack-jawed, staring at four or five days' growth on the old man's face. He could see a few rogue black hairs mingling amongst silver stubble. It was inconceivable that this was the same man he'd watched dining on Edinburgh's Royal Mile a couple of weeks ago.

'Your own mother wouldn't recognise you.'

'Sadly, she would have,' Bullock said, his eyes misting over as he looked towards the water.

'Where did you get the clothes?'

'From an old woman who was taking this stuff to the Briggait,' Bullock laughed ironically. 'I gave her a two pound coin.' He looked down incredulously at his ensemble.

'You were robbed.'

'I'm well aware of that fact,' Bullock smiled. 'The Briggait's remained delightfully downmarket, one of the few constants in this city.'

Maurice Golightly looked him up and down. 'You'd have no problems getting in the Sally Ann tonight.'

'Will we have any problems?'

Golightly straightened his gait. 'There will be no problems.' He shot a glance at some construction workers' huts near to the Tidal Weir Bridge. 'I take her there - the polis will think a twenty quid fuck and a blow job got well out of hand.' He smiled, relishing his little joke.

'It's all rather exciting.' Bullock smiled and walked away towards the Nelson Monument trying to remember the lyrics to "Wonderful, wonderful Copenhagen".

*   *   *

With the sun in her face, Margaret felt cold. She was nervous, even though Joe was close by, keeping out of sight. She wondered what Vanya would look like now, because he was old when she knew him. Would he be infirm, have trouble walking? He'd be coming here alone. That was the agreement. She clasped the monument's thick railings and looked up at the giant stone needle.

'Hello, Margaret.'

She recognised the voice and spun around and saw an old Jakey staring at her.

As he ambled towards her, she realised there was something familiar about the way he walked, although the way he rolled to the side on each step was more pronounced now.

'What do I call you? I mean – now that I know you're not called Uncle Vanya.'

'There are striking parallels, dear,' Bullock sighed theatrically. 'We share the same melancholy, the same sadness, and regrettably the same frustrated feelings of a wasted life.'

'Really. Would that be yours, mine or my Caroline's?'

'Touché.'

'I thought it was just me you did it with.'

Bullock took on a look of mock surprise and pulled the tammy up exposing his bushy, grey eyebrows.

'I know you were shagging my wee sister. What sentence would you impose on yourself for that crime, Mr Judge?'

Bullock tried to speak, but Margaret stopped him. 'She told me,' she lied, 'you're one devious bastart.'

'I thought we were here to discuss you getting your children back,' Bullock said, very business-like.

'Do you usually go to discussions done up as a tramp?'

Bullock smiled, a touch impressed and a touch aroused.

*   *   *

Less than a hundred yards away, six foot eight Maurice Golightly strained on tiptoe to get a better view of his quarry. Niggled and narked, he gave up for a moment as one of the Parks Transit vans pulled up in front of him. Maurice petulantly made his way around the back of the van. Seconds later he had two bullets in his head and was nestling on the wet floor of the van. The Transit drove off at a crawl in the direction of Bridgeton with Maurice Golightly permanently hushed under the covering that the leaves of the fallen provided. There were a few patches of fresh soil on the path soaking up spilt blood. The park bench was not bare. A pearl white cagoule rested upon it, neatly folded and triangular shaped, like a flag of honour at the end of a funeral ceremony.

*   *   *

Joe was frantic. Where had the big lanky guy feeding the ducks gone? *Shite, I'm meant to be offering protection here.* He returned his gaze to Margaret and the man standing with her. It must be him. He hadn't expected Bullock to turn up in the flowing robes and the curly wig.

211

'Oh fuck,' Joe muttered as he saw two familiar faces approaching Margaret on two different paths. 'Here goes,' he said as he made his way to her.

'It would be a lot easier if you stayed put, Joe.'

Joe began groping for his blade.

'Don't be fuckin' stupid, Joe. I'll hurt you - before I kill you.'

'I'm no' going to let him hurt her.'

'She's no' getting touched, he is.'

'What! The copper?'

'Fuck, how stupid are you, Joe?

*   *   *

'Is it still DI Henderson?'

'No, it's DCI Henderson - - is it still D I C K McGuire?'

'Oh, I was told you were bit of a wit.'

Henderson happily accepted the accolade.

'Wasn't expecting a police presence...' McGuire's eyes, radar, swept the park.

'We're everywhere,' Henderson bluffed.

'No you're not. You're on your Jack and we both know it.'

Henderson shrugged and smiled. 'How big a presence do you have?'

'Adequate.'

'You're looking quite chipper for someone with a terminal illness,' Henderson said, as he began doubting his decision to keep this meeting secret.

'Fuck, you don't believe the papers, Mr Henderson?'

'Frank Conroy, the gangsters' scribe, can't be wrong.'

'He's well wide of the mark this time.'

'So you're OK?'

'I wouldn't go that far.'

'So what's the big mystery?'

'Ah - I'd need legal representation before I could answer that.'

'There's no need. I'm not that interested.'

'Is that the formalities over?' JJ asked.

'Aye'.

'What the fuck are you doing here?'

'I'm the policeman. I ask the questions. What the fuck are you doing here?'

'I'm here to kill that old cunt over there.'

'You're here to do what?' Henderson spat the words out.

'Sorry, Mr Policeman, let me elucidate.' McGuire curtsied. I'm about to kill the former Lord Advocate, Rameses Bullock, known as the Big Bollock by Glasgow's criminal fraternity and those working in the field of law and order.'

'Have you lost the plot?'

'In a way I have. I'm not really in control. There's a good chance an average brief could get me off with this. It's just so ironic.' McGuire laughed.

Henderson was compelled to ask. 'Why – tell me why?'

'Because if I don't, Bullock will get away with it.'

'Hah,' Henderson scoffed up at the heavens.

'Forensics.' McGuire quelled any more protest.

Henderson shouldn't have been surprised. He was, and it showed.

'I see I'm making an impression.'

In response, Henderson could only repeat the question. 'Why you, why him?'

'There's a queue of reasons.'

'Just one will do,' the old copper asked, looking completely baffled.

'Friendship,' McGuire stated.

'Friendship?'

'Let's join them. I'll explain on the way, Detective Chief Inspector.'

*   *   *

Henderson's glance confirmed that Joe had made eye contact; hopefully Henderson would know Big Yogi's presence was not by request. For a split second, Joe thought about making a bolt for the monument. However, a menacing 'Cool it' kept Joe tethered to the spot. He turned and saw Big Yogi's eyes manically scrutinising the entire park, and then looked down at the revolver stuck in the waistband of his trousers.

'What are you looking for?'

'Nothing,' Yogi scowled.

*   *   *

Mark Henderson touched Margaret lightly on the shoulder. She turned and froze, stumped for words, as JJ McGuire forcefully spun Rameses Bullock around.

'This is cosy, eh?' Henderson asked.

Bullock raised his head slightly and spoke in character. 'Sorry – I wasnae bothering the lassie - nae offence.'

'Stop,' McGuire said as he punched Bullock in the mouth.

Henderson raised an eyebrow in rebuke.

Bullock looked at the policeman for help as McGuire fired a kick into his shins.

'Stop the pretence,' Henderson advised.

Bullock fell to his knees, silently, keeping up the charade.

'Leave him,' Margaret screamed

'He paid one of my men to murder your sister,' McGuire said.

'It's simply not true, Margaret,' Bullock broke character, stumbling to his feet.

'Oh it's true. I'll verify it,' Henderson confirmed.

'This is police brutality. How can you condone this, Inspector?'

Henderson smiled. 'Let me enlighten you, Milord, this is just plain brutality.'

McGuire ended the confusion. 'I'm not a policeman. Don't you recognise me? I'm JJ McGuire, Public Enemy Number One.' McGuire spread his arms looking himself over. 'I'm not in disguise, this is my working attire.'

'I can also verify that,' Henderson smirked.

Bullock turned to Margaret, desperately trying to lick moisture back into his dried lips as he gasped for air. 'I don't know anything about your sister.'

McGuire took hold of Margaret Logan and turned her to face him. 'He had Cornel Wagner killed as well. How am I doing, Inspector?'

'Exemplary,' Henderson replied, as he put comforting arms around the shell-shocked girl, who stood open-mouthed.

'Do you think I should've chosen a career in the Police?' McGuire continued.

Henderson could not resist. 'Sorry, but I thought you'd been working with us for years?'

'Are you trying to hurt my feelings again, Inspector?'

'It's DCI Henderson, remember?'

'Let's not crack the same joke again.'

Henderson held Margaret firm as she tried to break from his arms, telling her, 'Look, I'm going to make sure he pays for what he's done to you and your sister.'

'I just wanted him to help me get my children back.'

Henderson continued, 'He had Wagner killed and he was going to have you killed today.'

'Don't be absurd, this is unbelievable,' Bullock plucked bravado from somewhere.

McGuire kicked Bullock's shin again, informing him, 'Big Maurice is on indefinite leave.'

Bullock cringed, tending his injured leg.

'Did you pay up front? Shame, the dead don't do refunds.' McGuire grinned at Henderson as Bullock's face answered the payment question. 'No' his day, is it?'

Bullock began looking in the direction of the Old High Court, hopeful of spotting police.

'I'm afraid it's just little old me,' Henderson said, way ahead of him. 'I've been keeping my own company since the debacle at forensics. I take it the child Caroline was carrying was yours?'

Margaret broke free and took a firm hold of Bullock's donkey jacket, her glare demanding explanation. 'Whose child, whose child are you talking about?'

Henderson explained, 'Caroline had a miscarriage when she stayed with the Hochnalls in Stevenston.'

'No, she would have told me, she would have told me about it.'

'Is it true, your Lordship that you had sex with a ten year old? ' Henderson growled.

'Evidence, where's your evidence?' Bullock's superior look returned, his pompousness strangely heightened by his shabby attire.

'He was having sex with me, I'll swear to that in court.' Margaret said.

'You would swear to anything, wouldn't you?'

'You know what you did to us. I'll tell the newspapers,' Margaret threatened.

Bullock smiled. 'Make your arrest, Mr Henderson.'

'I'm not arresting you. That's futile and I've stopped doing futile. No, your punishment is being decided by a higher power than me.'

'I'm afraid it's going to be death, your honour.' McGuire came in on cue.

Bullock grew in stature. 'Even you are not mad enough to kill a Judge.'

'I'll be the judge of that,' McGuire laughed.

'There's a big difference between depleting the streets of competition, and killing a Lord of the Rolls, Mr McGuire.'

'There are sufficient grounds for my actions.'

'Are you seriously contemplating killing me?'

'I've made my decision.'

'You're not going to stand by and let this thug carry out this threat, Detective Chief Inspector.'

'I'm not here,' Henderson said. 'Nobody knows where I am. Even if I was here, I wouldn't recognise you because your disguise is so --- good.'

'You don't honestly think you'll get away with this.'

'Oh, I won't be getting away with it. But at least I'm up for the trip,' McGuire said.

Bullock was more confused than before. He removed his hat, and beads of sweat were running over the strands of wet grey hair, latticing his bright pink forehead.

McGuire motioned an arm and stood back as a Transit van crawled towards them with Johnny V at the wheel.

'I'm doing this for Joe,' McGuire spoke directly to Margaret. He paused and cast a curious glance at the Clyde. 'I wonder how your life would've turned out if Owny hadn't drowned himself?' Margaret didn't answer, and McGuire turned that question onto Bullock. 'Her Uncle Owny would've played ping pong with your testicles, Uncle Vanya.'

'I know what you did to my uncle,' Margaret said to McGuire.

'I'm no' apologising, hen. That's your boyfriend's department.'

Bullock stupidly tried to slope off. Henderson quickly blocked his path. Johnny V's pistol, pointing out the Transit's window, also got Bullock's attention.

Bullock started sweating as McGuire wrapped an arm around him. 'C'mon, we'll take a wee walk down to the river and feed the ducks.'

Bullock yielded and walked with McGuire. The Transit, DCI Henderson and Margaret Logan followed at the same sedate pace.

*   *   *

Joe saw them slowly move away. It was getting a bit crowded down there. *The only person not there*, he thought, *is fucking me.* He looked to the ground and saw two shadows, his own and the bigger version belonging to Yogi Hughes. He saw Yogi's shadow change shape as the huge legs straightened and tensed up. Joe kicked his heel back with every piece of energy he possessed and stuck his heel into Yogi's right kneecap, using the big man's buckling leg as a launch pad.

Joe ran as fast as he could directly towards Margaret. He did a zig-zag. If a bullet was on its way, hopefully he'd shield her from it. The fact that JJ McGuire was there might make Yogi think twice about shooting.

Margaret held her hands up, gesturing Joe to stay away, as DCI Henderson wrapped his arms around her.

Joe nearly knocked the two of them over as he barged past them and grabbed hold of JJ McGuire and Lord Rameses Bullock.

'Could you not do as you're fucking told, eh Joe?' McGuire smiled and gestured that Big Yogi stay where he was.

Joe took a stronger grip. 'What the fuck are you going to do here? This is wrong, this is so wrong...'

'I'm putting things right, OK?' McGuire stressed.

Joe was dumbstruck and he looked to Margaret and the policeman for explanation.

'JJ's told me everything,' Henderson shrugged.

'I'm going to execute Mr Judge here,' McGuire said.

Bullock let out a derisory snigger.

'You do know my friend's been diagnosed with Alzheimer's?' Joe said, as the colour drained from Bullock and a strange look came over Margaret.

'He's speaking the truth, DCI Henderson. That's why lots of bad things have been happening lately. I spat the dummy out - never could take bad news,' McGuire said, shaking his head apologetically.

'I knew it was you. Just you,' Henderson spoke as if he was annoyed at himself.

'Could you keep a wee eye on Uncle Vanya here while I have a word in private with Joe?'

Henderson nodded.

'It's OK, Joseph, I never really expected you to kill me.' McGuire winked back at Henderson. 'Our own wee private joke.'

*   *   *

Four and a half minutes later they returned, and Joe was crying as he took hold of Margaret. 'We have to go,' he said

'But – but I've got questions.'

'I know the answers. We need to go.' He pulled her close to him and cajoled her to walk towards the river. Then they turned right onto the Clyde walkway and headed for the Broomielaw.

McGuire gave Johnny V the nod, and Bullock was pulled inside the Ford Transit as McGuire and Henderson strolled down to the river. The policeman looked back momentarily and watched the van wobble side to side for a few seconds. The van's movement stopped as the engine revved.

'You should go now. You don't want to fuck up your retirement.'

'How are you going to do it?' Henderson asked, genuinely curious.

'I'll drown the auld cunt. Take the Owny MacNee departure route. Did you know my father killed himself here, Mr Henderson?'

Henderson nodded, as he felt an emotion hover somewhere between sympathy and empathy. 'Have you said your goodbyes?'

'Oh yes,' McGuire said.

'What did you say to Joe?'

'No comment.'

*   *   *

Henderson retraced his steps back to the old suspension bridge, passing those same students still practising their rescue techniques. He stopped halfway across the bridge and looked downriver. He scratched annoyingly at his leg with his right shoe and waited. He saw McGuire carry Bullock like a ventriloquist's dummy to the water's edge. Bullock did not look to be struggling, but McGuire rabbit-punched him anyway; then he looked up at the bridge and they plunged into the river.

*   *   *

Screaming started as sounds of pandemonium came from those rowing on the river. Two pairs turned quickly, yelling instruction at the rowing coach. He in turn started screaming for help from the students, practising with lifebelts in hand. Some of the brighter students were thinking this was a setup. Suddenly, the real thing was thrown their way. The Ferryman ran to his rowing boat, while others ran to the river with rescue ropes trailing like streamers. The rowing coach was directing more boats towards the spot where the men had entered the water. Instructions learned only minutes ago were now forgotten. At least ten lifebelts and ropes were thrown into the Clyde.

Henderson watched from the bridge, relieved that neither man had surfaced, and kept counting the seconds steadily inside his head. Then he saw the man in the distinctive orange overalls row his little boat towards the tangle of ropes and lifebelts, signalling that they pull in their ropes.

Parsonage stood up in his boat, watching and waiting. All was quiet. Henderson stopped counting in his head when he saw the Ferryman lowering a dredging rope into the water.

Chapter Thirty Seven

Soft light beamed into the pastel-coloured room from the high horizontal windows, intensifying the blonde hair of the two little girls who sat quietly reading their pop-up books.

Heather gripped Margaret's hand as she looked to Joe, smiling. 'I think it's preferable that Margaret meets the children alone; there's a possibility I could introduce you later on...'

'No,' Margaret cut in, 'if he's going to be in their lives, then he is going to be in their lives from the very start.' Heather nodded consent as Margaret continued. 'OK, Joe. Are we OK, Joe?

'Aye,' Joe confirmed.

Heather opened the door and the couple walked into the room

'Hello,' Margaret said softly.

The little girls both stood up as a look of hurt appeared on their faces. Emma took her lead from Nicola and they turned away and sat back down with their books again.

Margaret sat onto one of the tiny wooden chairs beside them, as Joe towered awkwardly over them in shafts of sunlight. 'Can I touch your heart, Nicola – I have wanted to feel your heart beating for so long. Can I touch your heart, Emma? Please can I touch your heart?'

Emma's eyes looked up to her mother.

'Don't, Emma, don't,' Nicola said, and Emma turned away again.

Margaret gently placed her hands on their shoulders as they flinched in unison, and then relented. 'Are your hearts beating fast? Oh, mine is beating so fast. I'm so nervous. Oh, let me touch your hearts.' Margaret's arms curled around them and her hands found the centre of their chests. Then she used her head to corral and cradle their heads under her own.

Joe looked and saw three Mona Lisa smiles appear at once. Nicola cried first as they climbed into their mother's arms.

It took a while for the crying to stop, and then Margaret made the introductions. 'This is Joe. He is going to be my husband and he is going to be your Daddy. Joe, this is Nicola and this is Emma.'

Joe stooped and shook both their hands. 'Hello,' he said. When he failed to get a response, he tried again. 'Hello, I'm Joe. It's really nice to meet you.'

They looked at their mother and got a nod of encouragement. 'Hello Joe,' Emma said. Nicola showed a sterner side and merely stared in acknowledgement.

'What will you do when you're our Daddy?' Emma asked as Nicola's eyes rolled backwards.

Joe looked at Margaret, stumped. 'Eh, well I'm not exactly sure what I do. I think I'm meant to take care of you. I take care of your mother and she takes care of me. I know I'm meant to protect you – and – and – tell you the truth, I was actually thinking of buying a book. I think I need help, might have to read up on it.' Joe could see a glazed look take over Margaret's face.

'There might be a book over there with Daddies in it,' Emma said, walking over to the small children's library.

'Pull up a chair, Joe,' Margaret said, pointing to the partner of her small chair. Joe reluctantly obeyed, and there they sat precariously, looking at books together; and then Nicola passed a book to Joe.

*   *   *

Spring

The three little girls, sitting strapped into the back seat of the Nissan Almera, were deep in discussion.

'How can I no' call him Da'?' Cheryl asked.

Nicola and Emma made a joint statement. 'Because he's married to our Mum, Cheryl. You have to call him Uncle Joe - because he's married to your Aunty Margaret,' Nicola added.

'Oh, right,' Cheryl smiled as a penny dropped.

The newly-weds belted themselves in, smiled and faced the children.

'Are we all set for our new life in Leadhills, children?' Joe asked.

Three heads nodded as one.

'Uncle Joe – can we have a dog?'

Joe's eyes sought Margaret's. 'What kind of a dog, Cheryl?' he asked.

'A wee white one like the one we saw yesterday?'

'That was a Westie, a West Highland White Terrier.'

'Aye, one of them.'

'OK, then we'll get one.' Joe opened his window further to let the screams escape and asked, 'Margaret, pass us the paper. They still do the Pets' Page on a Thursday?'

'You're not going to buy a dog now, no' when we're flitting, are you?'

'We'll all move in together.'

The ad specified they were Kennel Club registered. There were four dogs and one bitch, all inoculated and housetrained at nine weeks. They were priced at £375. Joe hoped they'd plump for a dog pup; he was beginning to feel that he needed some male back-up.

'Can you afford it?' Margaret whispered.

'Yes,' Joe answered.

The end